Robert B. Parker's Old Black Magic

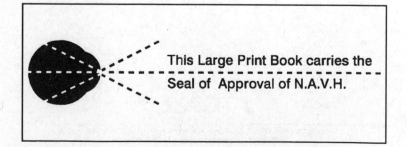

This Large Print Book carries the
Seal of Approval of N.A.V.H.

ROBERT B. PARKER'S OLD BLACK MAGIC

ACE ATKINS

THORNDIKE PRESS
A part of Gale, a Cengage Company

Farmington Hills, Mich • San Francisco • New York • Waterville, Maine
Meriden, Conn • Mason, Ohio • Chicago

GALE
A Cengage Company

LIBRARY OF CONGRESS CIP DATA ON FILE.
CATALOGUING IN PUBLICATION FOR THIS BOOK
IS AVAILABLE FROM THE LIBRARY OF CONGRESS.

ISBN-13: 978-1-4328-5071-5 (hardcover)

Published in 2018 by arrangement with G. P. Putnam's Sons, an imprint of Penguin Publishing Group, a division of Penguin Random House LLC

Printed in the United States of America
1 2 3 4 5 6 7 22 21 20 19 18

For my Plymouth pals,
Bill, Vicki, and Dixie Barke

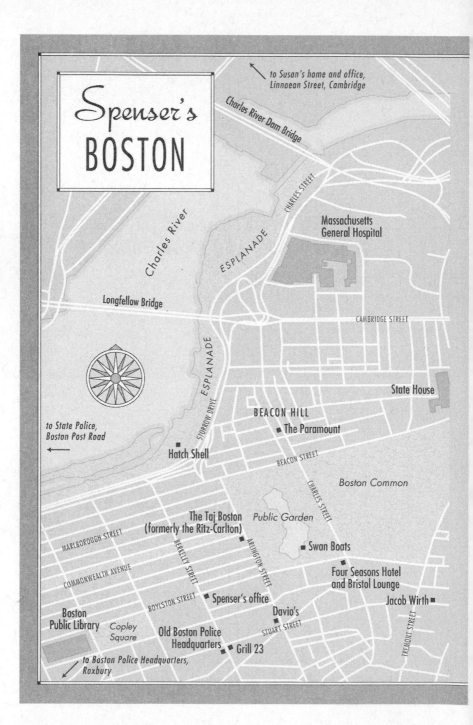

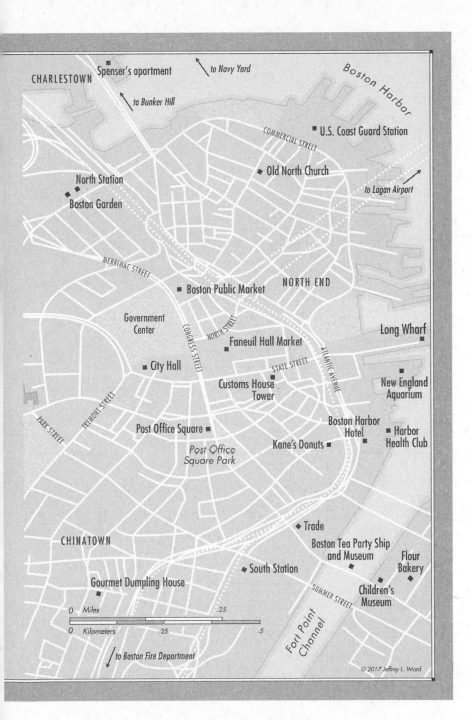

1

"I'm dying, Spenser," the man said.

I nodded, not knowing what else to say. An early-summer rain beaded down my office window, dark gray skies hovering over Berkeley and Boylston as afternoon commuters jockeyed for position out of the city. Their taillights cast a red glow on slick streets. Somewhere a prowl car hit a siren, heading off to another crime. The man sitting before me smiled and nodded, his hands withered and liver-spotted. His name was Locke.

"How long have we known each other?" Locke said.

"A long time."

"But oddly never worked together?"

"Our work as investigators seldom crossed paths," I said. "Different peepholes."

"Recovering stolen art isn't really your thing."

"I've done it," I said. "Once. Or twice."

"You're familiar with the theft at the Winthrop?"

"Of course," I said. "It made all the papers. And TV. Biggest theft in Boston history."

"Biggest art theft ever," he said. "Next year will mark twenty years. I've chased those paintings most of that time, traveling from Dorchester to Denmark with not so much as an inkling of where they ended up. It's beyond frustrating. Maddening, really. And now, well, with things the way they are —"

"One was a Picasso?"

"That was the least valuable of the three," he said. "Picasso, Goya. But the prize of the Winthrop was also stolen, the El Greco. *The Gentleman in Black.* Are you familiar with the painting?"

"Some," I said. "I recall seeing it years ago. When I was young."

"When we were both young," Locke said.

He smiled and reached into his double-breasted suit jacket and pulled out a slick photocopy of a very serious-looking dude with a pointy black beard. The man wore a high-necked lacy shirt and a heavy black cloak. His eyes were very black and humorless.

"He looks like a guy who used to kick field

goals for the Detroit Lions," I said. "Benny Ricardo."

"The subject is reputed to be Juan de Silva y Ribera, third marquis of Montemayor and the warden of the Alcázar of Toledo."

"Oh," I said. "Him."

"El Greco painted him in 1597," he said. "Well before the Pilgrims set foot in America. Long regarded as unimportant by the romantics, El Greco found new appreciation and fame among the impressionists and surrealists. Picasso in particular was a great admirer of El Greco. You see the distorted length of the man's neck, the off-kilter perspective?"

"Some have noted my own perspective is off-kilter," I said. "Although I admit to having more of an affinity for the Dutch Masters."

"I spotted your Vermeer prints when I walked in," he said. "You also have many fans at the Hammond. You helped recover, what was it? *Lady with a Finch.*"

I nodded and offered him something to drink. It was that time of the day when I could bend to either whiskey or coffee. Locke, being a man of the arts, approved of the whiskey. I pulled out a bottle of Bushmills Black gifted to me by Martin Quirk

11

and found two clean coffee mugs left to dry upside down beside the sink.

"Without being trite, that painting you recovered from the Hammond is nothing but a Rembrandt footnote," he said. "This work is something altogether different. A cornerstone of Spanish and art history."

"How much?"

"One can't always put a price on the priceless," he said. "But somewhere in the neighborhood of sixty or seventy million."

Like any serious art connoisseur, I gave a low whistle.

"I wanted to recover the piece myself," he said. "But now? I have to understand the realities of my situation."

"I'm very sorry."

"And I'm sorry to march into your office with such maudlin conversation," Locke said. "But my doctor told me to get my affairs in order, whatever the hell that means. I figured this was the first order, have someone to pass along my files, endless notes, and potential leads. I grew too old for this case two years ago. The Winthrop continues to push, with the anniversary coming up next week and these letters arriving every other week."

"Letters?"

"Yes," Locke said, sipping the whiskey.

"Not really ransom notes. But from someone who claims to have knowledge of the theft."

"Do you think they're real?"

"Perhaps," Locke said. "The letters were very specific about details of the theft. The writer was also aware of an arcane detail of the painting. El Greco himself had written on the back of the canvas in his native Greek."

"Have they asked for money?"

"No," Locke said. "No demands have been made. And no means of communication has been offered. The letters have been addressed to the museum's director, Marjorie Ward Phillips. Have you and Susan ever met Marjorie at a fund-raiser?"

I shook my head and picked up the coffee mug. The mug advertised Kane's Donuts in Saugus, a place I considered to have made many fine works of art.

"Marjorie is a determined, if altogether unpleasant, person," Locke said. "Her staff calls her Large Marj."

"A big personality?"

"How do I put this?" he said. "She has an ass the size of a steer and the disposition of a recently castrated bull."

"Lovely," I said. "Can't wait to meet her."

"Oh, she'll charm you," Locke said, chuckling. "At first. There will be martinis and long talks of art's value to the city of Boston. But don't ever disagree with her. Or challenge her in front of the board. Once that's done, you will be visited by the hatred of a thousand suns."

"If you're trying to talk me into this," I said. "You're failing miserably."

"You must take this case, Spenser," Locke said. "You must. If not, they've threatened to offer the contract to this British investigator. A young man from London who, recent successes aside, has all the earmarks of a four-flusher."

"At the moment, I'm working two separate cases," I said.

"Did I mention the five-million-dollar reward, plus covering your daily rate and all expenses?"

I smiled and turned over my hands, offering my palms. "Perhaps I could find time to meet with Large Marj."

"I know you're joking," he said. "But for God's sake, don't let her ever hear you say that."

"Hatred of a thousand suns?"

"And then some."

Locke smiled, straightening in his chair, and buttoned the top button of his jacket. Both eyes stared at me, one slightly off and one roaming my face with deep sadness and intelligence. His face sagged, his blue eyes drained of much color and life.

"It might be months," he said. "But probably weeks. I have a driver. He's waiting for me downstairs now."

"May I help you out?"

"First," he said. "Will you accept an old man's dying wish?"

"Damn, Locke," I said. "You do go for a hard sell."

"I don't have time to mince words," he said. "I really think they're onto something now. And the last thing the museum needs is an amateur, unfamiliar to Boston, skulking about. This other detective is of the worst sort. He's trying to charm the board into letting him take the case. But they need someone who understands thuggery and violence well beyond red-velvet walls."

"I should add that to my business card."

Locke laughed and reached for the Irish whiskey. He drained it quickly and replaced the mug on my desk.

"Why did you stay on this long if you felt like it was hopeless?"

Locke smiled. "There's something almost mystical about this painting," he said. "Believe me, you'll see. Maybe a way of touching the past. We are all just passing

15

through this world. We'll be gone soon enough. But this painting has remained for more than five hundred years. Perhaps recovering it would have been my shot at immortality?"

I nodded. I refilled our glasses.

"To immortality."

We sat and drank the rest of the whiskey in silence. After a bit, he stood, shook my hand, and without a word walked out the door.

2

"Large Marj?" Susan said.

"Do you know her?"

"I've met Marjorie Ward Phillips from the Winthrop," she said. "But I've never heard her called that horrible name."

Susan and I stood at my kitchen island in my Navy Yard condo as I stirred a fork in my cast-iron skillet simmering with kale, onions, and hickory-smoked bacon. The sprawling brick building had once been a dockside warehouse with big picture windows looking onto the harbor and across to Boston. Pearl snuggled in a ball on the couch as the rain continued in the night. Every few minutes, she'd lift her head and sniff for the bacon scent.

"I understand the nickname is only whispered by museum staff."

"I don't know her all that well," Susan said. "We've met socially. She gives to both Community Servings and Jumpstart. As far as I know, she is both well-liked and re-spected in the art scene. She seems like a perfectly lovely woman."

"Tomorrow morning, I meet with her and the head of the museum board," I said. "A man named Topper."

"Oh, no."

"Yeah," I said. "It's going to be hard not to ask."

"If he's being haunted by the ghosts of Cary Grant and Constance Bennett?"

I saluted her with my Sam Adams.

"What could possibly go wrong?"

"Hard to turn down Locke."

"How bad?"

"The worst," I said. "He said it could be weeks. Months at best."

"God."

I added a bit of sea salt and cracked pepper to the pan. As I worked, Susan walked over to my record player and slipped on a Sarah Vaughan album. In a Dutch oven, I'd already cooked two organic chicken breasts with heirloom tomatoes to serve over white beans. The beans came from a can. Everything else from the Boston Public Market. Living on the east end of town had widened my choices in the city. Besides a few small markets in Beacon Hill, I didn't have many options on Marlborough

Street. Less still after my apartment was destroyed by an arsonist.

I turned off the heat and pulled out two china plates from under the kitchen station. The chicken had cooled a bit, and I placed a breast on each plate along with the cherry tomatoes and white beans. A little sprig of rosemary on top.

"Fancy," Susan said.

"Black-skillet cooking," I said. "Getting back to my Wyoming roots."

"Yee-haw," Susan said.

"Gorgeous Jewish women don't say 'yee-haw.' "

"What do they say?"

"Oy, vey?"

Susan tossed a kitchen towel at me. I ducked.

I set both plates on the table, lit a small candle, and dimmed the lights overhead. Sarah sang about a flower crying for the dew. Susan guarded our food from Pearl while I retrieved another beer and popped the top. When I returned, she was staring out the window at the marina and Boston, the Custom House Tower shining gold and proud from across the harbor.

"I like it."

"The chicken?"

"The view," she said. "The move took

some adjustment. But I like the space. Everything seems so wide open and uncluttered. The city almost looks peaceful from here."

"The drive to Cambridge is about the same," I said. "Maybe better in traffic."

"You were welcome to stay," she said. "We could have made it work."

"Why mess with success?" I said. I drank a little beer.

Susan smiled. We ate for a bit, listening to Sarah and the rain. The lamps positioned around the open space of the condo blossomed with soft gold light. Rain sluiced down the windows, pricks of blue and yellow lights from atop moored ships.

"Why do you think Locke came to you?"

"Besides me being tough, resourceful, and smart as a border collie?"

"Yes," Susan said. "Besides that."

"He said he was concerned the museum might bring someone from outside Boston," I said. "He told me he's more sure than ever that whoever stole those paintings has roots here."

Susan nodded. She forked a bit of chicken with some kale. Her face blossomed with a smile as she lifted a glass to her lips. "And what made you accept?"

"I haven't accepted yet."

"Oh, you will."

I shook my head. I tried the chicken, thinking that perhaps the kale would have worked a little better with some lemon. When in doubt, always add a little lemon.

"How could you pass up working on the mystery of all mysteries?" Susan said.

"There's a five-million-dollar reward."

"Probably for those in possession of the paintings," she said. "Not the Winthrop's hired hand."

"A shamus can dream."

Susan nodded. I slipped some bacon pieces under the table for Pearl. They disappeared within seconds. I raised my hand aboveboard to a disapproving look from Susan.

"And for my next miracle," I said.

"Do you think you can restrain yourself?"

"From feeding Pearl?"

"From smarting off to Topper Whosis, a board surely made of crotchety old flakes, and Large Marj long enough to get those paintings back."

"As I know little to nothing about what I'm stepping into," I said, "I'll have to get back to you on that."

"Just who do you know in the art world?"

"I know a guy at South Station who sells prints of dogs playing poker," I said.

"What about Gino Fish?"

"A man of fine taste," I said. "But in case you haven't heard, he's dead."

"I know," she said. "But this painting disappeared twenty years ago. Right? Wasn't Vinnie working with him back then?"

"Indeed he was."

"Well."

"Vinnie and I haven't been on the best of terms as of late."

"Can't you just hug it out," she said. "Or whatever you mascopaths do."

"Mascopaths?"

"It's my own term for serially overly macho psyches. Overly masculine personalities."

"Would you like me to perform one-armed push-ups before dessert?"

Susan tapped at her cheek. "While you perform, may I use your back as an ottoman?"

I thought about it for a moment and then dropped to my knees. "I wouldn't have it any other way."

3

The Winthrop Museum looked like a big wedge of Spanish wedding cake, lots of tan stucco with a barrel-tile roof and windows protected with intricate wrought-iron cages. A woman named Constance Winthrop had the place built sometime in the early part of the last century. She had so much money, she proclaimed she wanted the Alhambra brought to the Fens. Nearly a hundred years later, I walked up the marble steps before opening hours. A guard led me through an indoor courtyard with a bubbling fountain and lots of statuary. I felt a bit like Ferdinand the Bull being ushered into the ring.

Marjorie Phillips introduced herself from the head of a long oval table. Even though she didn't stand, I could tell she was a sturdy woman. She had a thick, jowly face and a Buster Brown haircut. A reddish and green silk scarf wrapped what I imagined to be a neck thicker than an NFL linebacker's.

I nodded and took off my PawSox road cap, dappled with rain.

"And this is Topper Townsend," she said. "He speaks for the board."

Topper eyed me from behind a rounded pair of black glasses but didn't offer to shake hands. The round glasses made him look as if he'd just mugged Harry Potter off his Nimbus 2000. He was a gaunt man, thin and reedy, as he stood and offered a limp hand. He'd dressed as if he'd been auditioning for page seven of the J. Peterman catalog, with a red plaid shirt and sport green vest. His hair was long and silver, slicked tight against his skull and hanging loosely over his collar.

I took a seat on the opposite side of the table and waited. A pitcher of water sat in the center of the table.

"Would you like some coffee?"

"Cream with two sugars," I said.

"There's a pot by the sink," she said. "I'll warn you. Topper makes disappointing coffee."

Topper gave a practiced droll look like Paul Lynde sucking on a lemon. I walked over and poured a cup and returned to the seat. I noticed a slick black cane with a silver handle resting near his chair.

"I understand you've already met with

24

Locke?" Topper said.

I nodded.

"Poor Locke," he said.

I didn't say anything, stirring my coffee with a plastic spoon. Waiting for them to start discussing details of the paintings and the letters. Topper leaned back and tapped a finger to his lips.

"How much do you charge, Mr. Spenser?" Topper said.

I told him.

"Good Lord," he said. "You must be kidding. That's more than I'd pay my family attorney. And completely unreasonable."

I set down my mug, grabbed my cap, and stood.

"Enough with the bullshit, Topper," Marjorie said. "Let's please get on with this. Sit down, Mr. Spenser."

"Okay," I said. "But I draw the line at begging and rolling over. That costs extra."

"Oh," Topper said. "We've been warned of your dry wit. And that you often find yourself very amusing."

I shrugged, trying to look modest. I flicked off some raindrops that had gathered on my cap.

"What all do you know about what happened here twenty years ago?" Marjorie said.

25

"Only what I read in the papers," I said. "Two men dressed as cops knocked on the door of the museum. A guard let them in through a side door, where he was quickly pistol-whipped and told to call the second man on patrol. Both men were wrapped up in duct tape and handcuffed to pipes in the basement. All surveillance equipment and the tapes were destroyed. The thieves cut the two paintings from the frames, stole a small sketch, and made off clean. Since then, no one has heard a word."

"Until now," she said.

Topper harrumphed. It had been a good long while since I'd heard a harrumph. It was as annoying as it was nostalgic. He took off his round glasses and cleaned them with a white hankie. "The first letter arrived last month," he said. "The others every ten days. Right now we have four and have been told to expect more."

Marjorie didn't react. She exchanged a quick glance with Topper, who sighed heavily and turned to look at the far window, where ivy had grown wild against the glass. Rain tapped against the windows, the trees and gardens of the Fens obscured by the ornate black iron grating.

"Whatever we discuss must stay in this room," she said. "The authorities have warned us about using outside help. But Locke was insistent. More than insistent. He wouldn't let us speak to anyone else."

She opened a legal-sized file and pushed a piece of photocopied paper to me. "The originals are with the FBI," she said.

The first typed letter was quick and to the point. It ran about a half-page, offering to broker the safe return of the El Greco. The author claimed to be only an intermediary for those who had the painting and that the painting was still in good condition and in this country. The last few lines quoted El Greco's words on the back of the canvas. Or what I assumed to be the words. It might have been a recipe for baklava.

"Wouldn't people know about this?" I said. "The Greek wording?"

"The writing was hidden beneath the frame," Topper said. "Only discovered after Miss Winthrop purchased the work in 1921 and had it restored. I've never seen it mentioned in any scholarship of the work. It's mainly known by curators and Spanish art historians."

"But still known."

"Precisely," Topper said. "See? Smoke and mirrors. More lies. More misdirection. This is another waste of time and a great expense to this museum."

I was starting to dislike Topper even more than I thought possible. I stared at him. He swallowed and folded his long bony fingers in front of him.

"Mr. Locke told me you have extensive resources with many unsavory characters in Boston," Marjorie said.

"What can I say?" I said. "I'm a people person."

Topper leaned back, crossing his arms over the hunting vest. Marjorie eyed me, tilting her head slightly to the side, studying me for all the little details. I started to raise my arm and flex my biceps to demonstrate my worth.

"The FBI was convinced the theft was arranged by a foreign collector," she said. "But we don't believe it. Anyone with connections in the art world would find the Dr. No theory to be outlandish and unrealistic."

"Dr. No?" I said, attempting my best Sean Connery. My Scottish accent was a little off. I sounded more like Scrooge McDuck.

"A mega-wealthy criminal who wants to hang priceless art over his gold-plated toilets," Topper said. "Something in a basement to unveil only to his close personal circle. If someone had an El Greco in his possession, the word would've gotten out in the last twenty years. Don't you think?"

28

"I'm not sure," I said. "I don't know many people with gold-plated toilets."

"I believe this was a job committed by locals," she said. "Boston thugs who wouldn't know an El Greco from an El Dorado. I believe it's still close by, stored somewhere in a dank closet or buried deep underground. I can feel it in my bones, Mr. Spenser. Whoever has it has had it for years and hasn't a clue of what to do with it. It's too big, too valuable, and too known for them to sell off."

"Do we have anything stronger to go on?" I said. "Other than your bones?"

"You don't rely on instinct?" Marjorie said. "I've been working in the art world for most of my adult life. *The Gentleman in Black* is a massive loss for the museum and for the art world as a whole. It was the centerpiece of the Winthrop. I am due to retire at the end of this year, and unless I get that painting hung back into that vacant frame, I will consider all I've done for the memory of Miss Winthrop to be in vain."

I nodded and waited. Topper lifted his chin. "I still think his daily rate is unreasonable," he said.

"Oh, put a sock in it, Topper," she said. "I like him. He's tough. Look at that neck, that nose. And he has a good reputation and

29

knows the city. What else do we have? Some candy-ass Brit who spends most of his days eating lunch on the pad of Sotheby's and Christie's?"

"His references are excellent," he said, "but I believe the only way to find that painting would be a time machine. It's long gone, Marjorie. The sooner we all just admit it, we can all move on as a museum and fill the hole in the collection."

"Do you really want us to quit?" she said. "Stop looking. After everything?"

Topper swiveled in the office chair. He reached for the cane and leaned onto it as if contemplating a soft-shoe routine. "I will make my stance known with the board," he said. "It's a waste. A foolhardy scheme at the very best."

I looked at Marjorie and shrugged. She adjusted the scarf and folded her chubby little hands before her. She stared at me while I drank some coffee. She was right. Besides being an ass, Topper made horrible coffee.

"Well?" she said finally. "What do you say, Mr. Spenser? Will you help us find *The Gentleman*?"

"Well," I said. "I often make a habit of tilting at windmills."

4

Vinnie Morris ran, among other ventures, an aging bowling alley in Cambridge, not far from the Frozen Pond Rotary. The building hadn't been updated since the Eisenhower administration and could be described as either run-down or kitschy. Vinnie seemed to relish the Rat Pack feel of the upstairs lounge, with the blond wood paneling and horseshoe-shaped bar. Except for Friday and Saturday nights, the bar was closed, and Vinnie did business near the cash register with several phones, a calculator, and an old-fashioned leather ledger. I didn't ask. He didn't tell.

I walked through the front door and spotted the same beefy guy in the Hawaiian shirt working the front desk. I made a shooting gesture with my thumb and my forefinger and bounded up the curving staircase to the bar.

Vinnie looked to be dressed for the country club. Yellow polo shirt, navy pants, and boat shoes. He had a pair of half-glasses hanging around his neck from a sports band. His salt-and-pepper hair, as always, recently barbered.

He was talking on the phone with someone in a very unpleasant tone.

I helped myself to some more coffee and took a seat at the end of the bar. I was halfway through the B section of *The Globe,* reading a column by Tom Farragher, when Vinnie tossed the cell phone down.

"Do I have to do everything around here?" he said. "Christ. A simple thing. Nothing to it. But no. Christ."

"What was the job?"

Vinnie just smiled, snapped his ledger closed, and walked behind the bar. He reached for a pack of cigarettes and lit up. It had been a while since I'd seen smoking in a bar. I figured if you owned the place, no one would complain.

"When you get to be our age," Vinnie said, "you get tired of being hired help. It's time you ran the show."

"How's the new wife?" I said.

He made a so-so gesture. "She burned all my old tracksuits," he said. "Can you believe it?"

"Yes."

"She likes me to look sharp," he said. "Like I used to back in the day. A younger woman will do that. Make you clean up your freakin' act."

Many framed photographs of professional bowlers hung on a far wall, aged and yellowed with time. I didn't bowl much and couldn't recognize a single one of them. They wore polyester pants and tight sport shirts. Lots of them had mustaches and bad hair. I drank some coffee and turned to watch the cars race along the Concord Expressway. It was midday and they moved fast and free, unencumbered by traffic.

"Okay," Vinnie said. "What do you want?"

"I need to ask you a few questions about your previous employer."

"Broz?"

"The other one."

"Gino?" he said. "In case you hadn't heard, he's dead. Some nutso killed him. Sorry to hear it. But can't say I was surprised. He'd gotten sloppy in his old age."

"And he didn't have you to protect him."

"Exactly."

"I know about the antiques," I said. "But what about art?"

"Sure," Vinnie said. "He sold art, too."

"I'm working for the Winthrop Museum," I said. "Looking for three paintings. One of

33

them called *The Gentleman in Black.*"

"What is it?" he said. "A velvet painting of Johnny Cash?"

"Actually, it's the Juan de Silva y Ribera, third marquis of Montemayor and the warden of the Alcázar of Toledo."

"Oh, sure," he said. "That son of a bitch."

"Know anything about it?"

"I remember someone hit the museum," he said. "But c'mon. That was like freakin' twenty years ago."

"It was exactly twenty years ago."

"And they're just hiring you now?"

"I know," I said. "Incredible."

"Well," Vinnie said, tapping his ash into an empty coffee mug. "I don't know nothing about a man in black or Gino having anything to do with that job. Twenty years ago, I was in the thick of it. I would've known."

"If not Gino," I said, "then who might've pulled a job like that? It was a small crew. Two guys dressed as cops overpowered three guards. Late night. Good Friday."

"And the driver."

"How do you know there was a driver?" I said.

"C'mon," he said. "There's always a driver. Okay, you're looking for a three-man crew. You sure they're from around here?"

"No."

"You know what they look like?"

"No."

"You know who might've ordered the job?"

"No."

"So," Vinnie said. "Let me get this straight. You don't know jack shit."

I shrugged. "I knew you'd understand my situation," I said. "Get to the heart of the matter."

"Did they try and ransom off the painting?"

I shook my head.

"Or use it to knock some time off someone's sentence?"

"Not that I heard."

"You know there was a lot of action going on twenty years ago," he said. "DeMarco's old man was fighting for his territory in the North End. Broz was getting old and weak. Gino was sitting pretty, taking a cut of the action. I don't know. You're talking about a city full of hoods. It would be easier to make you a list of people I know who *wouldn't* pull a job like that."

"I don't think they were pros," I said. "The paintings were damaged. Some of their movements were pretty clumsy."

"They got away with it?" he said. "Didn't they?"

"Sure."

"Then they're pros," he said. "At least now. I don't know, Spenser. I mean, that was a long time ago. Last time I did you a favor, you screwed me."

I nodded. "That wasn't my intention."

"But it came back around," he said. "What do they say? Fool me once. Shame on me?"

"Not exactly," I said. "But I won't fool you. I just need a little direction. Lots of people we knew from back then have gone on to that big penitentiary in the sky."

"Ain't it the truth," Vinnie said. "But where they're headed ain't in the sky."

I smiled. I offered my hand. Vinnie took a moment, nodded, and then set the cigarette at the edge of the mug. He shook his head and then my hand. "Okay, okay," he said. "I'll check around. But no promises."

5

I met Martin Quirk later that day on the
Greenway across from the Boston Harbor
Hotel. A bunch of food trucks had gathered
on the median, circled together like old-
time chuck wagons, selling everything from
gourmet grilled-cheese sandwiches to sushi.
Quirk had double-parked his unmarked
black unit in front of the hotel. You could
do things like that when you were the assistant superintendent of Boston police.

"Thanks for coming."

"You said you'd buy lunch," he said. "I
figured you meant Trade."

"I like Trade," I said. "But I was in the
mood for some Japanese fried chicken."

"What in the fuck is Japanese fried
chicken?"

I pointed to a purple food truck parked
on the crushed gravel. The logo read Moyzilla and featured a friendly Godzilla-like
creature holding a pair of chopsticks.

"Asian comfort food."

"I like Asian," Quirk said. "And I like fried chicken. But not too sure I'll like 'em together."

"Might I recommend some beef noodle soup and spring rolls?"

"You might," Quirk said. "But I have on a nice tie. Soup always gets on the tie."

"And Marty Quirk can't have a spot on his tie."

"Hell, no, Spenser," he said. "Unlike you, I have a reputation to uphold. But I'll get the soup, against my better judgment."

We ordered the food and took a seat at a picnic table. The rain had stopped, but the sun still hadn't shone all day. Warm and gray. The smell of salt off the harbor blew in, with seagulls riding the wind high overhead. Quirk had on a gray suit with a crisp white shirt punctuated with a red tie clipped together with a silver pin. He was a big man, nearly my size, with gray hair and hands like a bricklayer's.

"How's Frank?"

"Getting used to the new captain," he said. "But you know Frank. He doesn't like change. After all these years, still won't pay an extra buck for a decent cigar. I definitely don't miss the smell of those damn things."

"Can we step back and talk for a moment

about the past?" I said. "Some people from the old days."

"What is this?" Quirk said. "*This Is Your Life?* I'm not ready to retire. Not yet."

"I'm trying to get a sense of some of the crews working Boston in the late nineties," I said.

"Something you don't know?" he said. "What is this? A joke?"

"Thieves," I said. "Snatch-and-grab. Bank robbers. Fences. Crews who will do anything for money."

"Pick up the phone book," Quirk said. He nodded toward the Moyzilla truck. "I think our food's ready."

We retrieved the food from the window and sat back down. I ate the chicken with my hands. Deep-fried and boneless, with lots of Sriracha. Throwing caution to the wind, Quirk lifted a plastic spoon and blew on the beef soup.

"Not my line," Quirk said. "Unless they killed someone."

"Who would know?"

"The guys who worked robbery back then," he said. "Bobby Wright ran the squad. But he retired five years ago."

"Can you get me his number?"

"For a bowl of soup?" Quirk said. "Oh, sure, Spenser. Anything for a big spender like you."

"Is it not good?"

Quirk raised the spoon, gave me a hard eye, and then tasted it. He nodded his approval.

"A lot of ghosts from that time," Quirk said. "Too many dead. You remember the shootings in the North End after the Old Man went to the joint and Joe Broz got soft? No one to keep the order. The fucking Italians were turning our nice little town into a goddamn Coppola movie. DeMarco's people in a war with the Morellis. We had one, two stiffs a week."

"And DeMarco came out on top."

"If you can call it that," he said. "And now you got his numbnuts fucking son running his show in Revere."

"I've dealt with him," I said. "A few times."

"Yeah, talk to Bobby," Quirk said. "He'd be a good guy to help. Just what are you looking for?"

"Would you believe a priceless painting?"

"No," he said. "I wouldn't."

"I am currently in the employ of the Winthrop Museum."

Something shifted in Quirk's eye. He shook his head before taking a sip off the spoon, a little broth dropping onto his

40

bright red tie. "Fuck me."

"Well," I said. "You gave it your best shot."

"I keep extras in the trunk," he said. He dabbed a napkin into his bottled water and wiped the stain.

"Remember the heist?"

"Everyone remembers the heist," he said. "But no one got killed that night. So it wasn't my business."

"What about other nights?" I said. "Later."

"You never change, Spenser," Quirk said. "Always sticking your nose in places it doesn't belong."

"Didn't I see you in *The Globe* last week?" I said. "Bill Brett took a picture of you and McGruff the Crime Dog?"

"Christ Almighty," he said. "Eat your fucking fried chicken."

"Always good to see you, Quirk."

He reached for his cell phone and tapped out a message. After, he picked up an eggroll and started to eat. "Texted Wright," he said. "I'll let you know what he says."

"I ran down the same question to Vinnie Morris."

"And what did Vinnie say?"

"He says Gino Fish had nothing to do with those paintings."

"Yep," Quirk said. "That's what a guy like Morris would say. You really trust him?"

"I do."

"I hate to break it to you, but there is no honor system among us and thieves," he said. "That's why they're freakin' thieves. They keep to their own."

Two young women in black sports bras and very tiny running shorts trotted by our table, heading down Atlantic. We both continued to eat, watching as they passed. Their muscular legs and taut abs shone with sweat.

"When did people stop wearing clothes?" he said.

"You have an objection to the current trend in sporting goods?"

"Nope," Quirk said. "I'm a cop. Just making a professional observation."

His cell phone buzzed. He picked it up, chewing, and placed it back on the picnic table. "Okay," he said. "Bobby will meet with you. Five o'clock at Faneuil Hall work? He's got an office close by."

I nodded.

He tapped the phone and then finished his soup. He pushed away the bowl and gave me a hard stare. "How 'bout a friendly warning?"

"Is there any other kind?" I said.

"Keep a wide berth around the department," he said. "You won't find cops like

Frank and me anymore. Those days are over."

"You guys were real sweethearts."

"But we had an understanding."

I shrugged. I ate a little more chicken, the Sriracha sweet and hot at the corners of my mouth.

"Now?" he said. "Folks like Captain Glass? They'd just as soon put a cigarette out in your eye than work with a private cop. They'll do everything they can do to jam you up if you get in their way."

"How would I get in their way on a painting that's been missing for twenty years?"

"Oh," he said. "You'll see."

I didn't move, only looked up as Quirk gathered his trash. "A little hint?"

"And spoil your fun?" he said. "No fucking way."

6

I found Bobby Wright a few hours later at the Quincy Market, sitting outside by the Red Auerbach statue. Like Auerbach, he was smoking a cigar. Both of them puffing away, one lifeless and bronze and the other smallish and black. Wright was dressed in a black polo and khakis with gray running shoes. His shirt had been embroidered with the name Wright Consulting.

"I guess ex-cops can smoke in public."

"You get a freebie smoking by Red."

"Great coach."

"One of the first to integrate the game, man," he said.

I nodded and we shook hands. I took a seat beside him. The cobblestones near the Market were uneven and pockmarked with puddles.

"Winthrop Museum?" Wright said. A halo of smoke around his head. "Quirk told me. I was off that case in less than twenty-four

44

hours. Feds wanted it all to themselves."

"How far did you get within those twenty-four hours?"

"Quick at the scene," he said. "Locked it down. Took pictures and interviewed the guards. I ran some background checks. But like I said, the Feds wanted us out of the way. They flew what they called the Antiquities Unit up from Washington. Assholes. Local guy was okay. I think if he'd had any choice, we would've all worked together."

"Epstein?"

"Yeah," he said. "Epstein. You know him?"

I nodded. Wright smoked the cigar, taking a moment to admire it burning in his hand. He had his legs stretched out in front of him, crossed at the ankles. He flicked a little ash off a neatly clipped mustache as the Market began to fill with tourists for happy hour. A throng of hooting women in pink boas passed us. They wore T-shirts that announced ASHLEY'S OFF THE MARKET.

"Epstein would know a lot more than me," he said. "It's been a damn long time. People get old. Die. Shit changes. I'd maybe go back and interview some of the witnesses. I think some kids from Northeastern saw the men sitting in their car before the heist."

"I've got the original case file coming."

"It's thin," Wright said. "Museum security was a joke. They had a few surveillance cameras and motion sensors. All the thieves had to do was knock on the door and the morons opened up. After they got what they wanted, they stole the tapes and took off without a trace. But you got to ask yourself, why would a guard open up in the middle of the night completely against museum regulations? Who's that stupid?"

"The guard thought they were cops."

"This guy wasn't supposed to open up for anyone," Wright said. "Not even if Miss Winthrop came back from the dead and offered free blow jobs."

"I don't know," I said. "That's a pretty good reason."

Wright laughed. "Say, what's your deal with Quirk?" he said. "The captain, I mean the superintendent, doesn't seem to do favors for anybody. How long have you two known each other?"

"Shortly after the Pleistocene era," I said. "We were investigating the suspicious death of a woolly mammoth."

"Quirk and I both worked out of the old headquarters on Berkeley Street," he said. "Now it's a fucking luxury hotel. Just like Charles Street Jail."

Some classical musicians had set up near

the steps to the Quincy Market. I couldn't see them but heard the classical orchestration of "Rocky Road to Dublin."

"Do you recall the name of the guard you suspected?"

"No," he said. "But you'll see in my report. We spent most of our time with him. The other guy had to go to the hospital. He'd been knocked in the head by one of the thieves. Really nasty wound. These weren't nice people."

"Didn't expect them to be," I said. "What about the Staties? Did they help out?"

"Just to collect evidence," he said. "They took photos of the big mess the thieves left. Fingerprints everywhere. Got some shoe prints. All those busted picture frames. We all thought this was going to turn out to be some kind of ransom situation. Everyone at the museum was waiting by the phone that never rang once."

"Did anything else strike you as weird about the theft?"

"The whole damn thing was weird," Wright said. "The security was terrible. The guards were untrained. I mean, I was shocked it hadn't happened before. Like everyone else, I thought it was pretty much a smash-and-grab and we'd catch the bastards before the end of the week."

"But the Feds went in another direction."

"Damn college guys with tailored suits and fancy-ass ties," he said. "Arrogant as hell. They were looking for Tom Cruise hanging from the rafters, not actual hoods. I tried to talk them into using our resources. But they figured they knew best. Twenty years later, here we are."

"Where would you have gone? Who would you have pulled in to question?"

"Oh, man," Wright said, taking a pull on the cigar. "I knew you were going to ask me that. When I retired, I tried to forget about all those sonsabitches. There are a lot of people in this town who get up in the morning, eat breakfast and get dressed, then head out and look for some shit to steal. It's a profession like any other."

"Butcher, baker, candlestick maker."

"I'll have to think about who did the high-end stuff," Wright said. "I would think whoever robbed the Winthrop would also be into home invasions. I would've started running through my CIs at the time, finding out what they were hearing. See who was in the joint and out. There are a few that come to mind. Guys who like the real fancy stuff. They have buyers in New York. Lots of antique furniture, crystal, rugs."

"You're talking Gino Fish."

"He'd have been high on the list," he said. "But that asshole's dead."

"So I keep hearing."

"What makes me think that Fish wasn't involved is that they left the museum a goddamn mess," he said. "They had free run of the place and left with only three paintings. Two of them weren't even the most valuable in the collection. It's like they had one mission, maybe for the big one, and picked up the rest on the way out."

"Like someone sent them."

"I think they were thugs for hire," he said. "Snatch-and-grab. Real simple."

"And how does that help narrow down the suspects?"

"Ain't nothing but fine and upstanding people in the city of Boston, man," Wright said, grinning. He blew a wide smoke ring that held together for a few seconds and then dissipated.

"Do you know if the evidence ever turned up anything?"

"I doubt it," he said. "I can't say for sure. But I'm sure they weren't so goddamn stupid they didn't wear gloves. They took the videotape. The guards didn't know what hit them."

"You said the guards were suspects?"

"Or just damn stupid," he said. "The guy

I interviewed kept on asking when he could leave. He had to get to some damn comic-book convention. Real weirdo. He was the kind of guy who stayed on the computer in his momma's basement. You know what I'm saying?"

I nodded. I lifted my hand in the Vulcan salute.

"Witnesses?"

"Couple kids who were drunk out of their minds, walking back to their dorms," he said. "They couldn't tell us if it was two or three men. Or really what they looked like. All they recalled is that they were cops."

"Type of car?"

"I don't remember," Wright said. "But check the files and detective notes. I know it wasn't real specific. Something like a dark, late-model sedan. Shit. I mean, what can you do with that?"

"I'm known to make a lot with a little."

"Oh, yeah?" he said. "Where I'm from they call that making chicken shit into chicken salad. Good luck with that."

"Sounds like a terrible recipe."

"You ain't kidding, man."

7

I left a message with Epstein at the FBI office in Miami and walked across Atlantic to Harbor Health Club. I'd been talking and driving since sunup and needed to sweat a bit. Changing out of street clothes, I went straight for a treadmill, stretching my legs and admiring the gentle movements of sailboats on the water. The skies turned a faded blue with pinkish clouds, planes drifting up and down at Logan. A beauteous evening, calm and free.

"You want me to bring you a cocktail?" Henry Cimoli said. "Or do you think you might actually boost up a notch or two?"

"I'm on level seven."

"My grandmother could do that backward."

"Like Ginger Rogers."

"Or a tough Sicilian woman," he said. "How about you get off this crazy thing and work the bag some? I haven't seen Hawk in weeks. Don't want you going AWOL, too."

"Hawk's in South America."

"What the hell is Hawk doing in South America?"

"Whatever it is that Hawk does."

Henry nodded and made a motion like he was turning a key in his mouth and then tossing it over his shoulder. I made it to three miles, getting a decent sweat going, and followed Henry to a row of heavy bags hung from a welded cage. Henry had recently decided to return the gym to its roots. No more Zumba and yoga. Half the gym was boxing and the other half was free weights and Crossfit equipment. He'd stripped the walls back to exposed brick and hung up old boxing photos and faded title cards. *Willie Pep. Rocky Marciano. Marvelous Marvin Hagler.*

"I miss the kid," he said.

"I know."

"Z made you better," he said. "He pressed you to get back in fighting shape."

I wrapped my hands. I didn't disagree.

"He's living the life," he said. "Out there in Los Angeles. You know, he finally got his investigator license?"

"Learned from the best."

"Don't sell yourself short," Henry said. "He learned some from you, too."

Henry was built like one of Santa's elves on steroids. Despite his age, he kept in fine shape with push-ups, sit-ups, and pull-ups. He liked to amaze the young girls by hopping onto the chinning bar and cranking out some reps while singing "The Best Is Yet to Come." He wore white tracksuits. He whistled while he worked.

They thought he was adorable.

"You're slower than fuckin' Christmas, Spenser," he said. "Stick and move. Stick and move. Or have you forgotten how this all works?"

I hit harder. *One. One. One two three. One two three two.*

"You need a regular sparring partner," he said. "Your rhythm is off. A bag ain't a person. You need someone to hit back."

The buzzer sounded. I reached for a water bottle.

"I know plenty who hit back."

"But with skill?" he said. "I doubt it. Back-alley palookas just make you feel tough. If you don't challenge yourself, you'll backslide. And if you backslide in your business, you'll be wearing your ass for a hat."

"Poetic."

"But true."

I pressed on to three more three-minute rounds before Henry worked me out with training gloves. We moved up and back, across wooden floors by high industrial windows. Black fans overhead cooled us down as I shadow-boxed. The knots across my back and in my neck loosened up. I had a nice sweat going, my breathing slow and controlled.

"Not bad for an old guy," Henry said.

"This coming from you?"

"Happens to us all, Spenser," he said. "If I don't ride you, you'll turn to shit. It's all the same. Just harder than before."

"No kidding."

"And lay off the donuts and booze," he said. "That crap'll kill you."

I took a shower, changed back into my clothes, and walked back to the parking deck near Faneuil Hall. I was clean and refreshed, smelling of the cheap aftershave Henry kept in the locker room. Within five minutes, I was back at the Navy Yard.

When I pulled up to park, I noticed a late-model Cadillac idling by the marina. I watched it as I walked to the back of the older-model Toyota Land Cruiser I was driving that year. After grabbing my gym bag, I locked up and crossed the street. The headlights popped on and off. I felt for the gun on my hip as the driver's window rolled down.

Vinnie Morris whistled for me. I took my hand off the .38.

"Christ," he said. "Where the hell have you been? Stopped by your office."

"Ever heard of cell phones?"

"Yeah," he said. "Don't care for 'em."

I adjusted the bag on my shoulder and waited for him to tell me what he'd found out. A brisk wind came up off the harbor, the wind chimes on house boats making delicate tinkling sounds.

"Well," he said. "Got something for you. You know a guy named Devon Murphy?"

I shook my head. Vinnie popped the cigarette lighter in the car and fired up a cigarette.

"Big-time art thief," he said. "He once ripped a fucking Monet off the wall of the MFA and walked out like it was nobody's business."

"Get caught?"

"Nope," he said. "Used it to bargain for reduced time on a bank job in Quincy. I'm telling you, he's got balls. Real piece of work."

"And you think he might have something to do with the Winthrop?"

"Don't know," Vinnie said, blowing out smoke from the side of his mouth. "Don't care. I'm just telling you if you want to

55

know about crooks that are into art, Devon is your guy."

He stretched his hand out of the Cadillac and handed me a little piece of paper.

"He knows me from my time with Gino," he said. "He'd steal anything Gino wanted. Gino would show him some kind of fucking antique in a catalog, and two days later Devon would have it in the back of his truck. He's in Plymouth. And said he'll talk to you. I told him you were stand-up."

"Thanks, Vinnie."

"Like I said, just don't screw me," he said. "I got a reputation to uphold. I called in a favor."

I nodded.

"The fucking Navy Yards?" he said. "This is where we used to take guys for Broz and work them over."

"Now there's a Tedeschi's market," I said. "And a gourmet restaurant down the street."

"Jesus Christ."

"How about a drink at Pier Six?"

Vinnie reached out his hand and ashed the tip of his cigarette. "Some other time," he said. "Let me know how it goes with Devon. If he gives you any shit, I can apply some pressure."

"I'll win his trust with my overwhelming

charisma."

"Well, if that don't work out," he said, "let me know if I can put the screw to his nuts."

I thanked him and walked up to my condo. I turned on a few lamps and fixed myself an old-fashioned with some Bitter-milk mixer and Luxardo cherries. I didn't have an orange but made it work. Lots of ice, a jigger and a half of Wild Turkey.

I sat down at my kitchen table and opened up my laptop. I typed and drank, research-ing what I could on Devon Murphy. It turns out I could adequately drink and research at the same time.

Spenser. Master of multitasking.

8

I met Devon Murphy dark and early the next morning at the Marshland diner off 3A in Plymouth. He was waiting in a corner booth when I arrived, studying the breakfast menu from behind a pair of half-glasses. I recognized him from his mug shots.

"What do you think of biscuits and gravy?" he said.

"I've had the blueberry pancakes," I said. "I had fantasies the whole drive down."

"Vinnie said you're a stand-up guy," Devon said, still studying the menu.

"Sit down too long and you'll develop piles."

"And could be a real smart-ass."

"I prefer a purveyor of truth."

He was a smallish guy with a craggy face and lots of wispy white hair. In his white T-shirt and navy blue windbreaker, he looked a little like an aging Alain Delon. He seemed like the kind of guy who would've enjoyed jumping from rooftop to rooftop before his knees gave out.

"What do you think?" he said.

"About what?"

"Biscuits and gravy," he said. "I can't really decide. That omelet looks good, too."

"Since I'm paying, I'd get the omelet," I said. "Linguica and Vermont cheddar. No competition."

"Done," he said. And tossed down the menu.

A waitress walked over and we both ordered. Within seconds, I had a hot cup of coffee in hand. I mixed in some sugar and leaned back into the seat, taking in the steady rhythm of the restaurant. I liked diners most early in the morning, infused with the smell of bacon and hot coffee. There was always a lot of energy and enthusiasm. Everyone seemed to be laughing, taking their time before starting their day.

"Vinnie said you had some questions."

I nodded.

"About the Winthrop job?"

I nodded again. Damn, I was good at this.

"Just for the record," Murphy said. "I was at Walpole when it happened. If you don't believe me, check the records. You'll see. I was at the end of a four-year stretch."

"And bargained down the time with a

Rembrandt?"

"No," Murphy said. "That was another time. And it was a Monet. For a bank job in Quincy. This was fencing some stolen jewelry from some rich broad on the hill. It was all a misunderstanding. I'd been dating the woman and she gave me a few things to sell. And when I sold them, she tried to make out like I stole from her. She was crazy. The whole thing was nuts 'cause she caught me in bed with her sister."

"That can cause a little animosity."

"A little?" Murphy said. "She wanted to shoot my freakin' dick off."

I nodded again. I drank some coffee. I decided not to take notes, only listen, see where Murphy might lead me.

"Vinnie said you ran in the same circles with art thieves?"

"No," he said. "I was the circle. I was the best damn art thief in New England. Don't believe me? Look it up."

"No one is doubting you, Devon."

"I once stole a fucking suit of armor from some wise guy's beach house in Marblehead," he said. "While he was asleep in front of the fucking television. I remember it like it was yesterday. He was watching Johnny Carson and Burt Reynolds. Carson got Reynolds to shave off half his mustache and

60

they were laughing like crazy about it."

"Have any theories on the Winthrop?"

He shrugged. He drank orange juice from a tiny glass and wiped his mouth with the back of his hand. "Maybe," he said. "Since it was my fucking idea."

"Do tell."

"I'd been wanting to rob that place since I was a teenager," he said. "I once hid under this fancy table and stayed there all night long. The guards were the worst. They maybe made one or two rounds a night. To be there after everyone was gone. Man, now that was a powerful feeling. Better than being a rock star."

"Did you plan it?"

"I planned to rob the place," he said. "But not like they done it. That was an absolute mess. They had all the time in the world and still damaged the art. I'd rather have been arrested than mess up those paintings. Cutting the canvases from the frames. God-damn animals."

"Sound like anyone you might know?"

Murphy looked at me, dead-eyed, and cocked his head. "Hold that thought," he said. "Here comes breakfast."

The waitress slid down the omelet before me and the pancakes before him. Murphy deftly switched them around as soon as she was gone. He seemed to have a very light touch. The plates didn't clatter a bit.

"I have some suspicions."

I cut into the pancakes and waited. I have learned over the years that the best way to elicit information is not to fill the dead air. As Devon Murphy had been around cops since he first boosted a car at thirteen, the method had little or no effect. He just chewed on his omelet, drank the rest of his minuscule orange juice.

"The museum is pretty sure it was a local crew."

"They'd be right."

"And that they didn't know what they were getting into," I said.

"Right again."

"Not knowing where to sell off a priceless painting."

"Whoever they are," he said. "These numbnuts probably couldn't find their asses with both hands and a flashlight. Let alone a solid black-market dealer. That's what turned this whole thing into a freakin' mess."

"And who and why?" I said.

"I can guesstimate a little of the why," he said. "But you're going to have to find out the who on your own. If it's all the same to me, I'd rather not try to start my car in the morning with a gun to the back of my head."

"These people still around?"

"Maybe," he said. "Like I said, I can only speculate. Right or wrong, that may be an unhealthy exercise. The Winthrop is something no one, and I mean no one, likes to talk about. It was so big and caused so many fucking headaches for people. Including Gino Fish, although I bet Vinnie didn't tell you that tidbit."

"No," I said. "He didn't."

"I don't know why he worked for Fish," he said. "He wasn't like Broz. He didn't have class or a code. Fish did for Fish. I worked my ass off for that old queer and got ripped off so many times. He'd give me sometimes twenty, twenty-five percent on something he knew he could sell. That's the way it worked with us. He had a buyer, wrote out a grocery list, and I was the professional shopper. I knew who had things. I knew how to get to those things."

"What did Fish have to do with the paintings?"

"Not the paintings," he said. "Just the Picasso sketch. I know for a freakin' fact that at one time, he had it. I don't know what happened to it. I'm sure he sold it off and doubled his money."

"And you think Vinnie knew?"

"I think Vinnie protected Gino," he said. "He wasn't into the art. He was just out to make sure Gino didn't get ripped off or whacked."

"Must have made you mad someone copied your plan."

"They didn't use my plan," he said. "They used my idea. But you're not going to trick me into talking about who all was involved."

"Are the paintings still around here?" I said.

Murphy looked around the room. Besides a very frail old man working on a massive plate of bacon, no one was in earshot. He looked at me again with his passive blue eyes and nodded.

"Still with the thieves?"

"No," he said. Emphatically. "They've moved on down the line. I'm sure they've switched owners several times with different crews. And collectors. I don't think I could lay my hands on the pieces anymore. A few years ago, I could've taken you right to 'em."

"Where?"

Murphy smiled and ate a bit more. I drizzled some syrup over the pancakes. I polished off half the stack and finished my coffee. The waitress returned, almost by magic, and refilled my cup.

"Okay," I said. "The idea originated with

you, but you were in the pokey at the time of the heist. You suspect the three who pulled off the job but won't tell me names. But regardless of who stole it, they no longer have it in their possession, and it is in the hands of an unknown collector or hood."

"Doesn't have to be one or the other," he said. "Look at Fish. He was both."

"I appreciate your trepidation," I said. "Boston can be an unpleasant little city. But since we're having a nice leisurely breakfast down in ye olde Plymouth, how about just a hint? Some direction to send me on my way with a smile on my face. A spring in my step."

"You talk to the guard yet?"

"Which one?"

"If you're worth your salt," he said. "You'll know the one."

"And that will lead me to?"

"Ask him about the hookers," he said. Murphy grinned big.

"That's how they got him?"

"Yeah," Murphy said. "That part was all my idea. Sex works every freakin' time."

9

Two days later, I found myself in Woonsocket, Rhode Island, drinking a cup of coffee in my Land Cruiser and reading *Arlo & Janis*. Every few minutes, I'd look up from the newspaper and watch the front porch of a two-story white clapboard house clinging to the edge of River Street. Somewhere on the second floor, a guy named Chad Hartman had a one-bedroom apartment. Twenty years ago, he'd been a guard at the Winthrop.

Chad was a white male, twice divorced, currently unemployed except for a comic-book show he occasionally updated on YouTube. They called him SuperChadz online. The night before, I'd watched three minutes of a freeform discussion on a potential Batgirl movie. I decided not to stick around for the next thirty minutes. No one could replace Yvonne Craig.

As my coffee reached the half-empty

mark, my corn muffins from Dunkin' long gone, my cell buzzed.

"I am shocked and amazed," a man said. "Picked up on the first ring. I must be really hitting the big time. What an honor."

"I saw the Miami area code," I said. "I hoped it was Gloria Estefan. Or Madonna."

"Madonna doesn't live here anymore."

"Will the city survive?"

"Just barely," Epstein said. "We're going through a period of mourning."

"For some reason I imagine you now in white linen suits."

"With mesh shirts and Italian loafers without socks?"

"Exactly."

"Oh, yeah," Epstein said. "We have cigarette boats and everything. Every time I start my car, Phil Collins is singing."

"You going too native to recall your time in Boston?"

"Not really," Epstein said. "It was cold. Lots of snow and statues."

"Twenty years ago to the day, you got a call about the Winthrop Museum," I said. "Ring any bells?"

"Aha," he said. "Indeed it does."

"Four days ago, the museum hired me to finish what you started."

"A little late on the trail."

"Colder than my morning coffee," I said. "I hoped you might warm things up for me."

"My superiors might frown upon me talking with a Boston snoop."

"What do you have to lose?" I said. "The museum wants my help. You're long off the case, chasing dope runners and assassins in bikinis."

"You grasp my situation down here so clearly," he said. "How can I not help?"

"How far did you guys get?"

"I assume this isn't an official conversation?"

"Is it ever?"

"Okay," Epstein said. "Not so far. We had two guys from D.C. help out the local office. They were supposedly art theft experts. But really they were two pompous dipshits who'd taken some seminars in France. They didn't know nothing about nothing. How to conduct interviews, build a suspect list, follow the trail."

"And what did you do?"

"The best we could," he said. "But we were ill-equipped for this kind of thing. We kept on waiting for a call or letter about ransom. That's where we excelled. But we never heard a word. We had a ton of cranks and followed every lead. Crazy stuff. I even worked with some medium who told me she was in direct contact with Constance Winthrop. She said Miss Winthrop saw the paintings in a red room with a very bad man. The man was Russian or something. Hell if I remember."

"But nothing solid?"

"I liked a couple guys who had connection to Old Man DeMarco," he said. "Remember him? Real nice guy if he didn't shoot you over a plate of spaghetti."

"Now the son is in charge."

"Apple fall far from the tree?"

"Maybe a few inches."

"You want me to check in with the Boston office?"

"I do."

"And perhaps review the file?" he said. "And pass on any pertinent information that probably still is highly confidential?"

"Gee," I said. "You really get me."

"One big thing, Spenser," he said. "Did anyone at the museum tell you that the big one, the guy in black, might be a fake?"

"No," I said. "In fact, they did not."

"That's only a rumor," he said. "But worth you knowing. And one we took seriously. I know at one time our people were thinking this may have been an insurance-fraud case. They were having the painting appraised and found out it was old but not painted by the guy they thought."

"El Greco."

"Didn't he play for the Pirates?"

"That's Bobby Del Greco."

"Wonder if they're related," Epstein said.

"Probably not."

The front door to the two-story apartments opened and a fortyish man with a thin frame and a potbelly walked down the cracked concrete steps. He had short black hair, a short black goatee, and was wearing a black T-shirt with the Bat symbol. Sometimes my job is too easy.

I thanked Epstein and hung up. I got out of my car and approached the man, who was trying to get into a decades-old Mitsubishi compact with a busted windshield.

"SuperChadz?" I said.

He stared at me, keys hanging loose from his hand.

"I'm your biggest fan."

10

"What do you want?" Chad said.

"My name is Spenser," I said. "I'm down from Boston. Working for the Winthrop Museum."

"Oh, no," he said. "No way. I'm done with all that."

"Not today," I said.

"I don't have to talk to you," he said. "I don't have to talk to anyone no more. Not about that. No more reporters. No more cops. Just leave me the hell alone."

"Don't make me get tough," I said. "If you don't give me answers, I might give SuperChadz channel the thumbs-down."

"Are you making fun of me?" Chad said. He stared at me through a pair of oblong prescription glasses with a reddish tint.

"Just a little," I said. I smiled. "How about we just take a walk? Or let me buy you lunch? I only had two corn muffins in my car. That was hours ago."

"I already ate a tunafish sandwich and some Cheetos."

"Then a walk along the river will do you some good," I said. "You fill me in on a few details, and I'll be out of your way. You don't and I'll meet you here every day until you decide to talk. I have what some might say is an obsessive personality."

Several old houses cut into apartments stacked against one another at the bend of River Street. They were wooden and brick buildings that probably used to house all the Canucks who'd come to the town to find work. The sidewalk continued past a garage and a fish-and-chips place to the historic district. Nearby, someone had moored a decaying fishing boat in their yard.

"I told the cops everything I know," he said. "Jesus Christ, man. I don't even remember much about that night. Why don't you talk to the cops?"

"I have talked to the cops," I said. "A few, in fact. And they feel like you were holding back. Like perhaps you knew some of the robbers?"

"Bullshit," he said.

"Come on," I said. "Give me a few minutes and then you can get back to simonizing the Batmobile."

"I have another job," he said. "At the Dollar Store. I'm going to be late."

"How much do you make an hour?"

He told me. It wasn't much. I handed him a twenty and said I'd give him a dollar a minute. I pulled off my PawSox cap and artfully curved the bill, sliding it back in position on my head. I was a true artist when it came to breaking in ball caps.

"Before that night," I said. "Did anyone strange approach you about access to the museum?"

Chad shook his head. He crossed his arms over his protruding belly as we walked.

"Anyone reach out to you?" I said. "Try to be your friend that you never met?"

He gave me an odd look. But he was an odd guy.

"I didn't know these guys," he said. "Hell. One of them punched me in the stomach. The other one beat the crap out of my friend, Tony. It was only his second night on the job. I got him the work and he never forgave me."

"Can you walk me through it?"

"I don't remember anything," he said. "They wrapped me up in duct tape and threw me and Tony into the basement. The next thing I knew the cops were there and cutting me free. I didn't see anything. I didn't hear anything."

We followed the winding sidewalk for a quarter-mile to a walkway that spanned over a dam. I thought about holding him upside down over the falls, but it wasn't guaranteed to work. I tried for a more subtle approach, asking the most obvious question.

"Why'd you open the door?"

"Because they said they were cops."

"Did they look like cops?"

"It was hard to tell," he said. "It's not like now. The cameras were black-and-white, real fuzzy. But they had on uniforms."

"Did you think to call for confirmation?"

"I fucked up," Chad said. "Okay? Is that what you want me to say? It's a long way from Boston just to get an apology. I'm sorry. I'm sorry those paintings are still missing. I know it was a big deal. But damn, I was only a kid. Why won't they just leave me the hell alone?"

"Any other reason you might've opened that door?"

He looked at me and then turned his head. "No way."

"Are you sure?"

"Like I said, they told me they were cops," he said. "They were dressed like cops."

"I know what you told me," I said. "And the real cops. But it's been a long time. Maybe you left out a few little details?"

We continued walking out onto the dam itself and into the deep roaring sound of the river breaking over the falls. I had to repeat my question as we stopped and looked over the guardrails.

"Like what?"

"Like maybe a late-night visitor?" I said. "Maybe a woman you just met?"

Chad stood against the railing and felt at his stubby little goatee. I still had my hands in my jeans pockets, wide-stanced and sure-footed, in case he made a run for it. Given his lack of physical fitness, I didn't think he'd get far.

"Who told you about the girl?" he said. "Nobody ever asked me about the girl."

"Who was the girl, Chad?"

His mouth still hung open a bit. I waited. Upriver, the shops at the old mill had just opened for business and a yellow school bus pulled up near the history center. Children in matching blue shirts wandered out into the parking lot, backpacks over their shoulders, giddy with the happiness of being free of school.

"No one," he said. He looked at me through his rose-colored glasses, his weak chin trembling.

"She must've been someone."

"I got to get to work, man," he said. "Are

you trying to get me tossed in freakin' jail?"

"It's been twenty years," I said. "Statute of limitations ran out this morning. Even if you helped rip those paintings off those walls and danced them out to the 'Toreador Song,' nothing can be done."

"You sure?" he said. He took a long swallow.

"Cross my heart."

Chad leaned against the bridge railing. The river frothed and churned down by the dam and around the scattered boulders. I followed the flow down past the shops and along the other old mills built along the path, now empty. A lot of Woonsocket felt empty, a relic of better times.

"I met her at a bar," he said. "She came over to the museum a few times. She thought my job was pretty cool. You know, having the run of the place every night, wandering around all those creepy old rooms. Damn, she was hot."

"Prettier than most girls you've known?"

He nodded, his Batman T-shirt fluttering in the warm wind. He took a deep breath, but when he started to speak, he couldn't seem to find the words.

"How many times?"

"Three," he said. "Maybe four. I don't remember. It was pretty wild stuff. She did

76

things to me that I never even thought about. She did this one trick with her tongue —"

I held up my hand. "I get the idea, Chad," I said. "What was her name?"

"Charity," he said. "She said her name was Charity."

I didn't have an answer to that, just let the word hang and allowed him to continue.

"She wouldn't return my calls," he said. "Later. You know? I figured when she saw me on the news and stuff, she thought I was bad luck. Like some kind of loser for letting those guys in and losing those famous paintings."

"Did it ever occur to you that she may have set you up?"

Chad started to speak, but again couldn't seem to find the words. He opened his mouth wide, and then, not formulating anything sensible, just as quickly closed it. The water kept on churning and breaking over the falls. A morning breeze swaying tree branches along the river.

"Where did you meet her?"

He told me about a bar at Northeastern that used to be right off campus. He said he used to hang out there a lot, sometimes getting a beer or two in uniform before going on for the night.

"You won't be able to find her," he said. "Charity probably wasn't even her real name."

"Really?" I said. "I'm shocked."

"I met her through the bartender," he said. "He was a really nice guy."

"And what was his name?"

"Crazy Eddie."

"Last name?"

"I don't know," he said. "He ran the place and told me the girl was a regular. A sure thing. We got to talking one night. Turned out she was really into comics and superheroes. She had a major crush on Superman."

"I know," I said. "Same thing happens to me."

"You won't find her."

"I found you," I said.

"That was easy," he said. "I wasn't hiding. Not anymore."

I handed Chad my card and told him I'd be in touch.

11

A big box containing Locke's personal files was waiting at my office when I got back to Boston. I'd bought a steak sub at Al's and opened it up on my desk as I made coffee. It was hard to investigate on an empty stomach. Perhaps damn near impossible. My new coffeemaker spit out the coffee faster than Usain Bolt in the hundred-meter, and soon I was back to the good ol' days of twenty years ago. I recalled it wasn't a good year for the Sox. They didn't win as many as they lost and Wally the Green Monster arrived at Fenway.

I tried to put the image out of my mind and opened the file.

The knock on the back door of the Winthrop came at shortly after midnight that Good Friday morning. It being Good Friday didn't seem to have any special significance other than probably a lot of cops had to work the scene and miss Mass. Wright and

79

his detectives had interviewed the guards Chad and Tony, Marjorie Ward Phillips, and two kids who attended the nearby city college. There was also a canvassing for potential witnesses in the area, who hadn't seen or heard a thing. The college kids said they'd seen cops outside the Winthrop shortly before midnight. "We were drunk and didn't want trouble," one of the kids said. "I didn't really get a good look."

They were the only ones to see the robbers' faces, besides Chad. Everyone agreed they were white males. The drunk kids couldn't decide if there were two or three people in the car. They saw only a man behind the wheel and another man in the passenger seat. I chewed and tried not to splatter marinara on the pages.

After I polished off half the sub, I stood up to stretch. I opened the blinds in my turret and looked across Berkeley Street. A trendy new womenswear shop had opened on the ground floor, replacing Shreve, Crump, & Low. I watched a comely young woman in a navy romper and no shoes strip two mannequins and start to redress one. The young woman was very pretty. The mannequins very naked.

I felt somewhat dirty and returned to my desk.

I read and reread Chad's interview.

In the first report, Bobby Wright had interviewed him personally. He didn't go easy on SuperChadz. He tried to trip him up several times, knowing Chad was already rattled and had no sleep. I flipped through the pages but found Wright didn't get far.

There were sketches of the two men. As with many police sketches, they could be about anybody if you squinted hard enough and made some minor adjustment. One man was tall and sallow-faced, with a mustache. The other was short and kind of chubby. I was pretty sure I was looking for the Laurel and Hardy of crime.

Another fine mess. I set aside the sketches.

I stacked the two narratives, as told by the guards, in front of me. I commenced eating the second half of the steak pizzaiola sub. Melted cheese and homemade marinara on fresh bread. I was making up for lost time. Despite my best efforts, some marinara leaked onto the narrative.

After reading the Boston Police files front to back and side to side, I returned to the window. One of the mannequins was covered up now in a very short red dress. It had been arranged to look as if it was casually talking on a cell phone. The young woman, fitting a miniskirt on the other,

looked up and saw me standing in the turret.

With my coffee in my right hand, I waved
with my left. She smiled and waved back.
Making friends and not influencing people.

I sat down, leaned back into my chair, and
set my feet at the edge of the desk. I had
some ideas about tracking down the girl
who'd stolen Chad's heart along with the
priceless paintings. I wondered whether to
bring up the validity of the paintings with
Large Marj and Topper, or whether it mattered. The painting was missing. They'd
hired me to get it back.

I was stuck on the North End war at the
time, and how that might be obscuring the
tracks of the thieves, when the phone rang.

"Spenser," a woman said. "I need you."

"Many women do," I said. "But my heart,
and other parts, belong to another."

"Damn you, it's Marjorie Phillips," she
said. "Where are you?"

"In my office, eating a sub and watching
performance art down on Berkeley Street,"
I said. "Some very interesting nudes making
social commentary."

"How long will it take you to get to the
museum?"

"Fifteen minutes," I said. "What's the
rush?"

"Another letter arrived this afternoon," she said. "It's wonderful. So exciting."

"What's so exciting about it?"

"The chase," she said. "We're on. They want to meet."

"Okay."

"And they have offered proof of the paintings," she said. "For half a million, they will return the Picasso. Can you believe it? If they can produce the Picasso, surely *The Gentleman in Black* is still with us."

"Perhaps we might slow down and plan our next steps."

"Goddamn you," she said. "Don't you think I know what I'm doing? That's why I need you to the Winthrop right this very second."

"When do they want to meet?"

"Tomorrow," she said. "In the Common. And I must absolutely go alone."

"Of course," I said. "But you won't."

"I won't."

"I'm headed your way."

12

It was almost closing time at the Winthrop. Marjorie Phillips was upstairs in the Red Room, staring at the big gold frame that once contained *The Gentleman in Black*. I had an odd feeling coming up the steps, seeing Marjorie standing there, arms akimbo and looking at the blank space. The moment seemed too private for me to intrude.

I started to take a step back and wait for her in the office. But she stopped me.

Without looking behind her, she said, "Join me, Spenser."

I walked along the terrazzo floor, the colorful little stones buffed to a high shine. Every sound was magnified, the room lit only by the golden afternoon sun.

"This is my favorite time of day," she said. "I prefer to see the works in natural light."

I didn't say anything, only removed my hat. My father told me that only a rube would wear a hat in a museum. Or a church. "What are we looking at?"

"Can't you imagine it?" she said. "How full the room is with *The Gentleman* back at his post, watching you in all his bold glory and grandeur?"

"Sure," I said. "Why not?"

Her eyes had yet to leave the empty space. A trapezoidal pane of sunlight shone across the floor. Dust motes played in the light. Marjorie breathed heavy and made agreeing sounds deep in her throat. She wore black today, a dress down to her ankles, with a lot of bangly bracelets and earrings that resembled bird swings.

In her crossed arms, she held a letter in a basic white envelope. Without a word, she handed it to me.

"What about the FBI?"

"They are useless."

"Fingerprints," I said. "Sometimes people get sloppy."

"Not him," she said. "He's careful."

"How do you know it's a him?"

"Just a feeling," she said. "But a very strong one."

I shook the letter loose from the carefully torn end of the envelope. Like the others, it was neatly typed on a word processor in glorious eighteen-point Times New Roman.

The letter insisted on a Saturday meeting at ten a.m.

> Frog Pond. $500K wire transfer for Msr. Picasso with information on others. This is an act of civility. Don't disappoint me or all is lost.

"Chatty bastard."

"We have the money," she said. "And I have the authority. The old board gave it to me years ago."

"Does Topper know?"

"There's a lot Topper doesn't know," she said. "Or need to know."

"No arguments there."

"I don't want this sloppy," she said. "We get sloppy and we will lose the precious link. By the way, Topper doesn't care for you a bit."

"Sad to hear," I said. "We had so much in common."

"He's a pompous ass," she said. "But he not only speaks for the board, he *is* the board. Whatever Topper says goes. He stacks friends and family in all the other positions. It's been that way for the last fifteen years. Every so often he'll go behind my back and make business decisions that he has no right to make. Or no authority."

"Just what does he do for a living?"

"Lives off an inheritance," she said. "Just as his father before him, and so on. So very Brahmin that you don't inquire."

"I noted the silver-handled cane."

"It's a family heirloom," she said. "Never goes anywhere without it."

"You think he'd try to stop you from paying the ransom?" I said. "If he knew about it?"

"Well, he wants you gone," she said. "And has already hired another investigator. The British so-called investigator. Expect a phone call from Topper tomorrow afternoon."

"But in the meantime?"

"In the meantime, we have a lot to do," she said. She turned and looked at me in profile. I nodded. "I don't want the FBI to know. I don't want the board to know. I don't want the police or any of your associates to understand what's going on. You are going to help me, Spenser. It's going to be just me and you tomorrow."

"And a half a mil on deck."

"Don't worry about the money," she said. "That's the least of our concern. You accompany me to the Common. Once I can verify the painting, I will wire the money into their account."

"You've gotten it all figured out."

"Would you rather not be involved tomorrow?" she said. "I can do this alone and you can sit around and discuss new terms with Topper."

"I'd rather have a colonoscopy with a garden hose."

She walked forward, hitting a velvet rope a few feet from where many paintings hung from a large wall with red wallpaper. Some of the frames were as large as dinner tables and others as small as a paperback book. All seemed Spanish in origin. Portraits of people and dogs, devils and saints. I watched as Marjorie unhooked the rope, stepped forward, and reached out to the gilded frame. In the faintest of sunlight, I saw the torn edge of a piece of ancient canvas. As she felt the texture in her fingers, she closed her eyes.

"If this person actually makes contact," I said. "What do you want me to do?"

"If they bring the Picasso?"

"Yes."

"Nothing."

"And if they don't?"

Marjorie reached back from the empty frame and faced me with all her largesse. She looked down at my running shoes and up to my bare head. She nodded slowly, an

88

idea already burrowing in her mind. "I want you to snatch up the son of a bitch and shake loose whatever he knows."

I tilted my head and nodded back.

"Do you have a problem with that, Mr. Spenser?"

"Not at all," I said. "I'm actually quite adept at such matters."

"And we keep this just between us?"

I nodded. We turned from the wall of art and walked toward the marble staircase. We headed back down toward her office, our feet making big echoing thumps in the airy, empty museum.

13

The Top Hat wasn't far from the Winthrop on Huntington, within spitting distance of the Northeastern campus. Inside, the bar was dim and as cold as a Baskin-Robbins. An old jukebox sat in a far corner playing "Mack the Knife" as a bartender served a shot of what looked to be antifreeze to an old gent in Boston Sewer Department coveralls. In a far back corner, two college-aged girls played pool. A ball ricocheted off the bumper and flew onto the floor.

I picked it up and handed it back to the girls before sitting at the bar and ordering a Sam Adams. It had been a long day and I deserved a reward.

The bartender was a young guy, too young to have been around twenty years ago. He was a little chubby, with one of those Hitler Youth haircuts and a long brown beard. Basic black T-shirt, jeans, and a chain hooked to his wallet.

"We don't serve Sam Adams," he said.

This was a first for me.

"Allagash?"

"Only PBR and shots."

"Retro," I said.

"It's a dive bar," he said. "That's what we do."

At some point, the Top Hat had been a dive bar. Now it just played the part of one, catering to college kids and hipsters. Three guys at a nearby table drank beer and played a game of Jenga. They were appropriately tattooed and bespectacled. One of the girls playing pool wore a floppy black fedora and a vintage Iron Maiden shirt. Her friend had on a man's white undershirt, cutoff jeans, and knee-length black socks.

"How long has this place been here?"

"Nineteen fifty-two," he said. He set down a PBR. I recalled when it used to be a decent beer made in Milwaukee. Now the brand was owned by a Russian holding company capitalizing on nostalgia.

"Who owns it now?"

"Todd and Terry."

"And who are Todd and Terry?" I said.

"Todd's a graphic designer and Terry is in a band," he said. "Their parents bought it for them."

"Must be nice."

"Yeah," he said. "They didn't want to change anything. The college tried to buy this whole block last year, but they wouldn't sell. Too much history here."

"You don't say."

The living history next to me in the Sewer Department coveralls was blurry-eyed drunk, bald, and red-faced, with unkempt white whiskers on his face and objectionable breath. Three empty plastic cups sat before him, arranged in a sad pyramid.

"You must come here often," I said.

He shook his head and didn't answer. He only pointed to the bartender for another shot of Prestone.

"That's Otto," the bartender said. "He came with the place. He's here every day at four. On the dot. We kept the original jukebox and we kept Otto. Everyone just loves him."

Otto picked up an empty cup and showed it to the bartender. I looked around the room, noting the standard Christmas lights hanging from the ceiling, the mirrors advertising liquor, and several old movie posters for gangster films. *Godfather, Goodfellas, Scarface,* and *Married to the Mob.*

"What's up with all the Mob stuff?" I said.

"This place used to be a Mob bar," the bartender said. "I heard the original owner got whacked a long time ago."

"You know who?"

"That was before I was even born."

"Of course it was."

I turned to Otto. "Do you know?" I said.

Otto looked at me, trying to focus on my face. He stifled a belch and turned up the fresh shot. The two girls that had been playing pool wandered up to the bar. The girl in the floppy hat had brown hair with purple highlights at the ends. The other girl's basic men's tank top highlighted a left arm covered in sleeve tattoos. Lots of flowers and dragons.

"Hello," I said.

"Don't I know you?" said the girl in the floppy hat.

"I doubt it."

"You're a professor," she said. "Right?"

"I'm the dean," I said.

"Of what school?"

I smiled. "School of hard knocks."

"Is that what happened to your nose?"

I put a finger to my most disfigured attribute and winked at her. The girls giggled. Spenser. Ol' friend of the world.

The bartender snapped open a couple more PBRs. The tattooed girl wandered off to the juke box, selecting Frank Sinatra singing "My Way." The bar was dim and cool and not a bad place to spend a weekday afternoon. I figured its having been a Mob bar might, or might not, be true. But it would be worth looking through property records. Maybe making some calls to some friends in the bar business.

The side door snapped open, letting in a lot of bright light. A thin man with slick black hair walked up to the bar. He wore a summer-weight navy suit and a starched white shirt open at the collar. I could smell his aftershave even before he sat down.

He asked for a pint. He was given a tin can of PBR.

"Nice view," he said. His accent reminded me of Dick Van Dyke dancing with a broom. He watched the girl in the cutoff jeans lean over the table to make a corner shot. Her shorts were very short.

"Man can't even get a decent pint in Boston," he said. "What's wrong with this picture?"

He kept a very short beard, black stubble. He had dark skin and eyes, a dimpled chin, and a yellow pocket square in his coat.

"My name is Marston," he said. He offered his hand.

"Alfred P. Doolittle," I said.

"No," he said. "You're not. You're Spenser. You can't fool me."

"With a little bit of luck."

"Figured it'd happen sooner or later," Marston said, tilting the beer. "We'd bump into each other. Me and you working the same case. Least for now."

"Just stopped in for a drink," I said. "Might play a little bit of Jenga."

"No such thing," he said. "You got the same little morsel from Mr. Chad Hartman. The poor chap was hustled."

I drank some beer. "Are you following me?"

"All is fair," he said. "In this high-stakes game."

One of the kids at the small table piled one too many pieces on the Jenga tower and the whole thing collapsed. There was a lot of hooting laughter and another round of beers being bought. The problem with hipsters is that they were so damn agreeable.

"What do you think?" Marston said. He took out the pocket square and wiped at the wet bar before setting down an elbow.

"I think we're both wasting our time," I said. "The only thing original about this bar is the sign outside. Twenty years is a long time, friend."

"But it was worth you checking out."

I stared at him. "All leads are."

"I've heard all about you, Spenser," he said. "But this is a bit out of your league. This is an international case worth millions of dollars. I don't think you quite have it in you, old boy."

"Call me 'old boy' again," I said. "And you'll learn what league I'm in."

"Oh, my," he said. "Oh, my. A tough. Wow. We have an authentic Boston toughie on our hands. What fun. Well, I wouldn't waste too much of your time chasing down dead ends. I stopped in as a courtesy. The Winthrop board has decided to go with someone much more experienced. You'll be notified tomorrow."

"I'll be waiting by the phone," I said.

"Call it professional courtesy," he said.

He smiled, laid down a twenty, and left the beer before heading out. The bartender and I watched him go. The doorway grew bright for a moment and then turned dark.

"What an asshole," the bartender said. He stroked his long beard.

I lifted the can of PBR and toasted him. I pushed the twenty Marston left toward him and told him to get Otto another round. Otto straightened up, quickly finding some dignity, and thanked me. He seemed to be awake from his regular afternoon stupor.

"How long you been coming here, Otto?" I said.

"Forever," he said. "And a day."

"You remember a guy named Eddie?" I said. "The bartender?"

"Crazy Eddie Ciccone?" he said. "Sure, sure. He was a real gent. Treated me regular and everything. He left a long time ago. You and him friends?"

"No," I said. "But we're about to be."

"Sure miss Eddie," he said. "Good times."

"Thanks, Otto," I said, patting his back. "Never doubted you for a minute."

14

That night I met Locke for dinner at Legal Seafood at the Long Wharf.

He was waiting for me at a corner booth overlooking the harbor. I ordered a real beer, an Allagash White, and Locke had a vodka gimlet made with fresh lime juice and garnished with a cucumber. He looked as if he'd aged ten years from earlier in the week. He coughed several times into his fist until the drink arrived.

"Paul Marston," Locke said. "He's a real prick."

"He followed me to Woonsocket," I said. "I should've been more careful."

"Marston's a tricky little snake," he said. "He's tried to cheat me before. Bribed my sources. Gotten trusted confidantes to work with him instead. He's better at manipulating people than actually doing the legwork."

"Either way," I said. "Looks like Topper wants me gone."

"But," he said. He coughed a bit more. "You have Marjorie Ward Phillips on your side. She's decided she likes you and can use you. Don't underestimate that detail."

Outside the plate-glass windows, tourists milled about the aquarium and IMAX theater, the Duck Boats unloading from their final voyage of the day. Tall lamps flickered on as the sky darkened along the waterfront.

"What can she do against the board?" I said. I sipped the beer, washing away the taste of the Top Hat.

"They're scared to death of her," he said. He played with the little stirrer in his cocktail. "You have yet to meet the real Large Marj. Just you wait. The only reason she hasn't challenged Topper and the board is because she's fixated on something. What have you found out so far?"

"I have a name of a man who might've influenced one of the guards to open up that night."

"I knew it," Locke said. He smiled wide, blue eyes shining. "I just knew they had someone on the inside."

"He owned a crummy bar years ago," I said. "But he has a common name. At least for Boston. I plan to chase him down after tomorrow morning."

"What is tomorrow morning?" Locke said. He raised his white eyebrows.

"Can you keep a secret?" I said.

"Did I not mention I am a dying man?" he said. "Who could you trust more?"

"Large Marj got another letter," I said. "They've promised the return of the Picasso sketch for five hundred grand. She secured money from a donor and is ready to wire it to an account of their choosing. And I'm going along to make sure they play fair."

"Alone?"

"Just me and Marj," I said. "The Dynamic Duo."

The waiter brought me a large plate of the seafood cioppino, a rich tomato broth with mussels, clams, scallops, and a lobster claw. Locke had the salmon salad, picking at the meal in bites too small for Susan Silverman.

"If the letters are real," I said, "the original crime may be irrelevant. The museum only wants the paintings back."

"True," he said. "But if you know the source, you might find out where and with whom they ended up."

"Can I tell you what a pleasure it is to dine with someone who speaks proper English?"

Locke smiled. His hands shook as he cut

100

into the salmon with a fork and took a small bite. I ordered another round of drinks. What the hell. I was on the Winthrop tab.

"If the contact is less than forthcoming, Marj wants me to shake the truth out of him."

"Are you prepared to do so?"

I smiled. I cracked open the lobster claw and forked out the meat.

"What if it's a con?" he said.

"Then it's back to plan B," I said. "I find the guy who owned the Top Hat bar and move up the food chain. And try to watch my tail next time for annoying little Brits."

"There was a time, maybe ten, twelve years ago when I thought I had *The Gentleman,*" he said. "I was almost sure of it. I'd flown to Paris to meet with some reputable people who deal in disreputable objects. I was prepared, and approved, to pay up to five million for the return of the El Greco. They offered photos and even paint chips that appeared to be of the period."

I sipped some of the broth. The bartender brought me a fresh beer.

"What can I say," Locke said. "There is no fool like an old fool. I'd been set up. Thankfully, I had not brought the money as instructed. It was a group from Marseille and they were convinced I had the authority to make a call and transfer the funds."

"What happened?"

"Didn't you wonder what happened to my eye?"

"I figured it had something to do with your illness."

Locke shook his head, taking a few more bites of food. The bright lights of Boston shone down onto the harbor in slick green, yellow, and red. "It was a very long night in the Saint-Germain."

I nodded. I picked up the beer and swirled what was left in the bottom of the glass.

"Be careful," he said. "Trust no one. And underestimate no one. Can you be sure that Marston doesn't follow you tomorrow?" he said. "He has a knack for really screwing the pooch."

"I will take many precautions," I said.

"Good."

"Spenser," he said. "I may be unreachable in the coming weeks. I wanted to let you know I will be entering a special program with Boston General."

I told him I was very sorry. He shrugged and drummed his fingers on the table. "Well," he said. "So there is that."

"I'll find the painting," I said. "And return it to the Winthrop."

"Even when Large Marj, Topper, and the

lot of 'em turn against you?"

"Especially then."

Locke laughed and softly banged on the table with the flat of his hand. He smiled broadly. We finished dinner with another cocktail and I helped him out onto the brick turnaround at the Long Wharf. He needed to balance on my arm as we made our way out.

A black car pulled up and a man in a black suit opened the door for Locke. I took a deep breath and shook his hand. His hand felt as hollow as a bird's.

"Well, then," he said. "Good luck."

I helped him into the car and waved as he left. The black car turned onto Atlantic and drove slowly away, streetlights flickering all the way.

15

I walked the Common at daybreak, a faint bluish-gray sky overhead, performing some early reconnaissance work with Pearl. In four hours, Marjorie Phillips would arrive at the garage under the park prepared to transfer half a million dollars. She did not want to involve the cops, the Feds, or any friends I might have. If Hawk were in town, I could've asked him to watch my backside while I watched Marjorie's. But since Hawk was somewhere in Brazil performing the samba with a comely brunette, I was on my own.

I might've asked Vinnie. But given our tenuous relationship, it didn't quite merit his involvement. Not yet. Instead, I scouted the edge of the Frog Pond. A big fountain spewed up water from the center as light came alive in the clubhouse. In a few hours, children would be frolicking and splashing.

Several paths led away from the pond to

Beacon, Tremont, or Boylston. A car could be waiting for someone on Charles Street, which split the Common from the Public Garden. Or they might try and run back down into the garage. *The world's a city of straying streets.*

Perhaps I should change into faster shoes.

"I have a bad feeling about this," I said to Pearl. Pearl wasn't listening. She was fixated on an obese squirrel helping itself to a bounty of spilled popcorn.

She tugged at the leash, paws scraping at the asphalt. The Common spread out wide in green, undulating hills.

I ushered her to the path heading toward Park Street. A homeless man occupied one bench, snoozing in a green sleeping bag, an empty bottle of Aristocrat vodka below him. A man in modern black workout gear zoomed past us, an iPhone in his left hand, looking to break a personal record. A gaggle of bicyclists soon followed, sending me and Pearl to the grass. We continued on.

I didn't spot any art thieves. Not that I would know what an art thief would look like. We wouldn't know even if the person showed and took a seat next to Marjorie. Marjorie said she would inspect the sketch and could tell whether or not it was a fake. If the person double-crossed her, I would stop them. If they ran, I would chase. If they put up a fight, I would subdue them. What could be easier.

Unless the art enthusiast brought friends. Or was armed. Or had sent an intermediary who did not have the Picasso. I would just have to do what I did best. Improvise.

"If you were trying to escape," I said, looking down at Pearl. "Which way would you go?"

Pearl looked up at me, tongue hanging loose from her mouth. She didn't seem the least bit concerned. I bent down and scratched her head. A lot of new gray was forming around her eyes and muzzle. Given the gray at my temples, I wasn't one to judge.

We continued to walk toward Park and then doubled back on the opposite side of the Frog Pond. The café was open now, and I walked in and bought a cup of coffee. I had walked these steps thousands of times, but I wanted to see it fresh, refamiliarize the routes out of the Common. My speed wasn't what it used to be. But like any good defensive back, I knew how to work angles.

I was nearly back at the entrance to the parking garage when my cell rang.

"What the fuck did you do?" Marjorie Ward Phillips said.

"Good morning, Miss Phillips," I said. "What a lovely day."

"Did you meet with Paul Marston without my consent?"

"I did not."

"That's not what I heard," she said. "Topper called me this morning."

"Then you heard wrong," I said. "He followed me to a bar yesterday."

"Drinking on the job?"

"Yes," I said. "But it was Pabst Blue Ribbon. I didn't really enjoy it."

"You are to report to me if anything like that arises," she said. "How do you know he's not going to follow us this morning?"

"I will take precautions."

"Why didn't you take precautions yesterday?"

"I usually don't work for a client who pits sleuth against sleuth."

"Perhaps you should be more careful."

"Perhaps."

"My nerves, Spenser," she said. "God, I couldn't sleep. I'm so jumpy."

"Deep breaths," I said. "And a cold compress."

"You have told no one?" she said. "If you have told someone, I will make sure you never work in this town again."

"I doubt it," I said. "But no. I didn't tell

anyone."

"And our plan is the same."

"I think our plan stinks," I said.

"Excuse me?"

"We have no idea who we are dealing with," I said. "Or how they intend to rip you off. I still have friends with the Boston Police. They can have plainclothes officers watching the entire park."

"I won't have it," she said. "The deal was offered. You agreed to it."

"I was wrong," I said. "Let me make a call."

"You do and I'll have your balls roasted over a spit."

I took a breath and shook my head. "Lady," I said. "I have made a promise to a very good and honorable man. I have been warned about you. But hadn't known your full potential until now. If you want to play it this way, then fine. But when it all turns to goose crap, don't jab your little finger in my chest. I don't like any of it."

"We stick to the plan."

"I watch," I said. "You give me the signal and I'll stop them."

"Good."

I waited for an apology. None came. Marjorie Ward Phillips didn't seem to be the type to say she's sorry. "Well, you better be goddamn ready," she said. And hung up.

I sat down and finished my coffee, watching several people setting up yoga mats on a flat spot of lawn near the ball fields. The instructor spoke of being present on this wonderful day. I reached down with my free hand and patted Pearl's head.

"Gratitude is the fairest blossom which springs from the soul," I said to Pearl.

Pearl lifted her head and licked my hand.

16

"You'll be fine," I said. "Remember the signal."

"I touch my left ear," Marjorie said.

"That's right," I said. "And the cavalry comes charging."

"You said it would only be you."

"My strength is the strength of ten."

"Oh, yes," Marjorie said. "Of course. You've said that. And where will you be?"

"Just across the wading pool," I said. "At the café. We get out of the car, walk up to the Common, and both take our places. If you are satisfied with the goods, make the transfer. If you have trouble, give me the signal."

"Please don't call a Picasso 'the goods,' " Marjorie said. "It cheapens the work a great deal."

"How about 'the stuff that dreams are made of'?"

"You do an absolutely terrible Bogart,"

she said. "And I'm in no mood for joking."

"This may be a setup."

"It may very well be," she said. "Or it could be the first steps. The Picasso could be the proof we need. We get the sketch and the Goya and *The Gentleman* will follow."

We left her Mercedes in the underground garage and walked separately, me twenty paces behind her, up to the Common. Marjorie was easy to tail. She was a very large woman in an ill-advised tight red dress and with a bright green scarf around her neck. I could've tailed her from Newton.

I bought a bottled water at the café and sat under an umbrella.

The Common was leafy and green, boundless and restless, unseasonably warm that morning. Kids frolicked and played in the spray pool, splashing and laughing. I remembered taking Susan here to ice-skate many moons ago. During the winter, they froze the pond over and rented skates and sold hot chocolate from the café.

That morning, I'd nearly sweated through my black T-shirt. I'd worn a lightweight windbreaker covering the .40-caliber Smith & Wesson in a shoulder holster with an extra magazine in the pocket. I carried about thirty rounds. If those didn't work, I'd grab a water pistol from one of the kids.

At ten minutes past the hour, I didn't think anyone would show. I didn't trust a thief who wasn't punctual. As I stood, tossing the bottle in the trash, I spotted a young man in a black hat and sunglasses. He had on a black Adidas T-shirt and pegged workout pants. He was tallish and walked with purpose and carried a large leather satchel. I noted that his tennis shoes appeared to be new and gleaming white.

Across the pond, Marjorie sat on the bench clutching her purse in her lap. The way she held herself reminded me of Jonathan Winters doing Maude Frickert. If she had on some metal specs and a little doily collar, she'd be a ringer. Her makeup had started to run outside the perfect temperature of the Winthrop.

The man in the Adidas tee seemed to take no notice of me. Or his surroundings. When he passed Marjorie, he stopped and asked her a question. Perhaps just a friendly tourist seeking direction to Old Burying Grounds? Marjorie nodded and stood. He pointed over at the café where I waited. She looked confused for a moment but nodded. They both headed my way.

I returned to my seat and took out my phone to look occupied. I made sure the windbreaker covered the holster.

Marjorie and the mystery man took a seat under a large umbrella. The young guy sat close and opened up the satchel. He pulled out what appeared to be 8×10 photographs. Marjorie wasn't pleased, throwing up her hands in disgust. Her large face turned a bright red.

"That wasn't the deal," she said. Her voice rose to the occasion. And carried.

The man replied something. He pointed to her phone.

"I certainly will not," she said. "Where is it?"

He mouthed the word, *close*. I stood up. She looked up at me but did not make the signal. The young guy glanced back to me and then to Marjorie. He knew something was up and looked poised to move. *Feet don't fail me now.*

"I will not be fucked with," she said. "And you will not get a penny."

He leaned in and tapped at the photographs. Marjorie picked them up and tossed them in his face. I waited for her to touch her ear. But she only turned to me and stared, openmouthed with anger and confusion, her body deflated like a large balloon.

Of course, he spotted me. Everyone at the Lily Pad Café could see we were together.

The man snatched the photos, tucked

them into his satchel, and began to walk away. Marjorie stood and reached for his arm, but he jerked free and ran toward Park Street.

"Well," she said. Her voice boomed. "What the hell are we paying you for?"

I ran after him, parting a sea of suburban moms holding goggles and sunscreen. I passed slow joggers and nearly toppled a street performer playing an electric guitar and a kazoo. The guy nearly made it to Park but then broke quick at the Brewer Fountain, running toward the T station.

The guy darted into the doors of the T station. I was right behind him, running down the steps, seeing him turn toward the outbound Green Line. Lucky for me, the outbound train hadn't arrived. He tried to mill about in a gathering on the platform, but I spotted him. He spotted me and took off again for the exit.

The station was big and cavernous, with a lot of old tile work. Tall fans rotated over the platform to keep the air moving. The young guy disappeared again into a stairwell. I turned and ran up the steps. He was halfway up to Park Street when I caught him by the back of his T-shirt and yanked him down to the steps.

The satchel fell to the floor. His hat fell

off as he covered his face with his hands.

"It's just a job, man," he said. "Just a job. Cool out."

I reached for the satchel, unlatched it, and pulled out a large manila envelope. When opened, it was completely empty.

"Who sent you?"

"I don't know."

"Why'd you run?"

"I don't want trouble," he said. "No job is worth this."

"Where's the sketch?"

He shook his head, reached into his jacket, and tossed me a small ticket. I scooped it up off the ground. A claim ticket to a hotel baggage check. "I don't want trouble," he said. "I met this guy in a club. He paid me fifty bucks. Here. Take it. Fucking take it."

I grabbed the ticket and placed it in my pocket as two MBTA cops ran down the steps and told me to raise my hands and step back.

"I'm a licensed investigator," I said. "You'll find my license and permit in my back pocket."

"Goody for you," one of the cops said. "That's your fucking problem, Mannix. Mine is keeping order down here. Now put up your fucking hands and step back, sir."

17

"Assault and battery," Rita Fiore said. "Attempted robbery. Wow. I didn't know times had gotten so tough, Spenser. I'll make sure the business office speeds along the check."

"Trying to cover my bases," I said. "Make a few bucks."

"Always happy to find an excuse to escape afternoon meetings at Cone, Oaks," she said. "Would you like to hear about a class-action lawsuit against a Fortune 500 company? It involves an exciting accusation of employee misclassification."

"I'm good," I said. "Perhaps later."

Rita and I followed a guard down to out processing. My bond had been paid. Now it was time to collect my running shoes and other personal belongings. They took my shoes so I wouldn't hang myself with the laces. I stood there in stocking feet to get them returned. I asked about the other man who was brought in with me.

The woman didn't reply. She stood over a long table and shuffled out my watch, wallet, and keys. I placed the wallet and keys in my pockets and slipped on the watch. The lights were bright and fluorescent, the floors scuffed linoleum. The jail had the lovely scent of urine and Lysol. "Where's my gun?"

The guard shook her head. "Your weapon was impounded," she said. "You can discuss it at your court appearance."

"Can they do that?"

"Unfortunately," Rita said. "Yes. But I'll get your pistol back for you. In the meantime, get that slingshot out of your desk."

I shook my head and found a chair. I slipped on my Asics. It felt civil again to be wearing footwear. There was little dignity standing around in your athletic socks.

"Come on," Rita said. "I'll give you a ride home."

"Service with a smile?"

"Don't worry," she said. "I'll bill you."

"No, you won't."

"No," Rita said. "I probably won't. I just can't wait to hear the whole story."

We walked out through a variety of locked doors, being passed from guard to guard, until we were in the main lobby of the Suffolk County Jail. We walked out together into the fading light on Nashua Street. I could see the Charles River, smell the brackish water under the early-evening sky. In the distance, I spotted the weird suspension of the Zakim Bridge. If I wanted to, I could've walked back to the Navy Yard.

"How about I buy you a drink?" I said.

"What would Susan say?"

"Susan knows you've moved on," I said. "You only have eyes for Sixkill."

There was a lot of wind off the harbor, blowing Rita's wild, very red hair across her eyes. She smiled and tucked the hair behind her ears.

"What can I say," Rita said. "He's younger. I need more stamina."

"And on another coast," I said.

"Oh, what the hell," she said. She pressed the door lock on her key chain. A black BMW's lights flickered. "It's nearly four-thirty. My day is shot anyway. Where are we drinking? The Taj? The Elliott?"

"The Four Seasons," I said.

"Are we celebrating your release?"

"I'm not exactly sure," I said. I reached into my pocket and pulled out the checked baggage ticket. I played with it in my fingers like a card sharp.

"A clue?"

"Or a dead end," I said. "What I think

was there is probably there no more."

"And what was there?"

"A very early sketch by Pablo Picasso."

Rita snorted and climbed behind the wheel. I crawled into the passenger seat, the car obviously not made for men of my size and shape. A garden gnome would have been completely comfortable riding shotgun. We zoomed away from the jail.

"Will you ever give me a straight answer?"

I told her about taking the job with the Winthrop, the recent letters to Marjorie Ward Phillips, and the little meet in the Boston Common.

"Holy shit," she said. "Who was the mystery man?"

"Don't know," I said. "He claimed he was just a courier. But he was holding this in exchange for the museum releasing the funds."

"You think the Four Seasons concierge has the Picasso?"

"At best, they will," I said. "At the worst, we can have a cocktail. And I can wash the bad taste of being arrested out of my mouth."

"Oh, it's good for you," she said. "It builds character. But why did you call me? Why didn't you call Belson? Or Quirk? They might've untangled the whole mess easier than a high-priced lawyer in tight pants."

"Are they really that tight?"

"Wouldn't you like to find out."

"Quirk said the department was done with favors," I said. "And the new head of Homicide isn't my biggest fan."

"And I am?"

"Who better?"

Rita worked the gear shift like Mario Andretti as we headed down Storrow and back toward the Boston Common.

18

We took Storrow past the Hatch Shell and cut over to Arlington, by my old apartment on Marlborough, and edged the Public Garden. Rita braked to a fast stop at the Four Seasons entrance on Boylston and left her car idling, waiting for the attendant to open her door. "From the shithouse to the penthouse," she said. "Just like you, Spenser."

"How are we feeling today?"

"Double martini," she said. "Ketel One. Straight up with extra olives. The word *vermouth* only whispered into the glass."

"Order me a beer," I said. "I'll be with you."

"And miss out on finding a Picasso?" she said. "Fat fucking chance, buster."

We walked into the lobby and over to the concierge station. The Four Seasons, as one might expect, was a fancy place. White marble, brass, oil paintings. The staff was attentive and mannered, even to a jailbird like me.

I handed the ticket to a bellman and we waited.

"Have you called the Winthrop?" Rita said.

"Nope."

"Don't you think they would've sent their attorney to bail you out?"

"Nope," I said.

"And why not?"

"It was a secret mission," I said. "Only known to me and the museum director. The board has already hired a new investigator. A real British dandy named Paul Marston. You'd like him. He smells like the fragrance aisle at Kmart."

After a long moment, the bellhop returned and handed me back the ticket. "My apologies, sir," he said. "That item has already been retrieved."

I looked at Rita. And then shrugged.

"Is Tommy O'Shea still your house dick?" I said.

"Sir?"

"Does Mr. O'Shea still run security around here?" I said.

The bellhop nodded and asked if I'd like to see him. I said very much. I looked at Rita. "Tell him he can find us at the bar," I said. "This lovely lady deserves a drink."

I offered my right arm to Rita and we made our way from the lobby into the cool coziness of the Bristol Bar. Many men noticed the fit of Rita's pants as we passed.

"You're taking this whole thing awfully well."

"Win some," I said. "Lose some."

"Really?" she said. "You must know something you're not telling me."

"Extra vermouth," I said. "Right."

She ignored me and we found a place at the edge of the bar. I knew the bartender and we made small talk for a bit. I introduced Rita and he expertly made a martini as cold as an aircraft wing. It looked so good, I forwent a beer and asked to have what Rita ordered.

We clinked glasses.

"I'm going to frame your mug shot," she said. "Put it right on my desk next to my picture of my poodle."

"You have a poodle?"

"The things you don't know about me," she said. "It breaks my heart."

I'd finished my martini and asked for a tall ice water when O'Shea walked up and took a seat next to me. He was a big guy with a lot of unkempt brown hair, packed like a sausage into the skin of his black suit.

He looked like he could use some sleep and a shave.

Sandwiched by the Four Seasons house dick on one side and Boston's toughest legal eagle on the other, I felt safe enough to order another round.

We shook hands. I introduced Rita.

I lay down the ticket stub.

"Sorry about this," O'Shea said. "We've searched everywhere for it. Can you tell me what it looked like?"

I held my hands about a foot apart. "Probably a package about yay big."

"Probably?"

"A gift left by a friend."

"Is it very valuable?"

"To some," I said. "I noticed two security cameras in the vicinity of the concierge station. The item was probably retrieved between ten a.m. this morning and noon."

"And you would like me to roll the tape?" O'Shea said.

"Pushy bastard, isn't he?" Rita said. She put down her empty drink. "Why do we deal with him?"

"The world is round," O'Shea said. "What can I say? I owe him one."

"Or two," I said. "But who's counting?"

I downed my drink in record time and we followed O'Shea to the security office in a room behind the front desk. A smallish guy in glasses and a blue knit shirt and khakis sat at a computer keyboard. O'Shea told him where, when, and what we were looking for. With some deft strokes of the keyboard, we looked over his shoulder at a large monitor. I saw two concierges appear on the screen. A man and a woman. The man was showing a middle-aged woman a map, marking locations. Soon a man in a business suit appeared and there was talking, but the door behind the stand didn't open. The counter read 10:08. We watched a variety of people come and go. Directions, advice, and a few large pieces of luggage came and went from the left luggage room. When the marker hit 10:35, a tall, thin man arrived at the desk. We couldn't hear what was being said. But he presented a room key and identification. The woman at the desk looked at the ID and handed it back to the man. She nodded to the male concierge and he disappeared into the back room.

"Looks like he's a guest," O'Shea said.

The security guy at the desk fast-forwarded the footage and the bellhop reappeared with a small package, about yay big, as I'd surmised. The man reached into his pocket, handed him some cash, took the package, and headed out of the camera's frame.

"Hmm," I said. "Back it up."

The guy backed it up to the arrival of the man. Rita stood next to me and craned her neck in to study the man's face. "Handsome man," she said. "Well dressed. I bet that suit cost a few thousand bucks."

I asked for the image to be frozen. And then if we could zoom in and take a closer look at his handsome face. The guy at the keyboard did as I asked in about two seconds. I leaned in to the desk. I studied the man. Rita was right. The guy had style. He wore a light blue linen jacket over a pink button-down and crisp white pants. I couldn't see the shoes, but I'm sure they were equally impressive.

He had styled blond hair and delicate features. The same slim build, narrow shoulders, and lean frame. He was clean-shaven, with perfect hair.

"Let me call the concierge on duty," he said. "Maybe he'll know the guest."

"Not necessary," I said.

"You know him?" Rita said.

"Yep," I said. "We go back a long way. He doesn't look like he's aged a bit."

"And," Rita said. "Are you going to enlighten us?"

126

"His name is Alan Garner," I said. "He used to be the personal secretary to Gino Fish. Alan was the gatekeeper to him. Some said they were more than friends. He worked the front desk at Gino's operation."

"You know where to find him?" O'Shea said.

"That won't be hard," I said. "I can't wait. I'm absolutely giddy with questions."

19

Late that night, Marjorie Ward Phillips left me a curt message on my voicemail. The board wished to see me early the next morning at the Winthrop. I was advised not to be tardy, as important business needed to be addressed. There was no mention of the Picasso sketch, the botched exchange in the Common, or my subsequent arrest.

I listened to the message, deleted it, and went to bed. Early the next morning, Pearl and I went for a long walk through Charlestown and down along the Navy Yard marina. I ate eggs scrambled with locally sourced sausage, took a shower and shaved, and drove to the Winthrop.

It was raining that morning as it had been on my first visit. The meeting was in the second-floor boardroom. This time, the room was filled with Marjorie, Topper, and, as I'd guessed, many of Topper's friends. They were all older white men. Many of them indistinguishable from the next.

When I entered, Marjorie asked me to sit. This time someone brought me coffee. It was even worse than I recalled. Topper sat at the head of the table. He again presented his outdoorsy look with a casual green plaid shirt, khaki cargo pants, and hiking boots. He held his cane in his hand as he directed the board to please take their seats. His white hair, damp and lifeless, hung limp to his shoulders. His eyes were magnified in his big circular glasses as he took a seat and theatrically shuffled papers.

Since I had walked into the room, Marjorie would not make eye contact. She sat with her chubby arms under her bosoms. Her face locked in a sour look.

"Mr. Spenser, we understand you were arrested yesterday," he said. "The Winthrop will not tolerate that type of behavior. Nor can we stand a barrage of bad press at this moment. Your role was made clear at our last meeting. Whatever you were doing in the Boston Common yesterday was of your own design and of your own volition."

"No," I said. "It wasn't. Perhaps Miss Phillips would like to explain."

Marjorie tightened her sour expression. She shuffled in her seat and worked to look even farther in the opposite direction. Had she been an owl, she might have been able to rotate her thick neck in a complete circle.

"Miss Phillips has discussed how you involved her in this ill-conceived plan," he said. "Your first payment will be your last. We will not pay for any of your services moving forward. If you have something to say, say it now. But our decision is final."

"Gee," I said. "This is the perfect place for a Spanish Inquisition. Perhaps you'd like to tie my arms behind my back and tie me to the ceiling."

"If that's all you wish to say," Topper said. He lifted his chin and pursed his purple lips. "Then we are finished. It's a rainy day. Please watch the slick steps as you leave."

"No," I said. "That's not all I wish to say. Sit down, gentlemen. And Miss Phillips. If you want to fire me, fire me. But I've had enough secrets. I was asked by Marjorie Phillips to accompany her to the Common. She was the one who hired me and she asked me to provide security at an exchange for the stolen Picasso print."

"At which you failed miserably," Phillips said. She grumbled as she spoke, like a cornered cat over a morsel of food.

"No," I said. "The go-between didn't bring the sketch. You demanded to see it before transferring the money. Instead of giving me the signal things had gone astray, you gave away my position. When you told me to stop the man, I did. That's what landed me in the clink."

"You were the one who spooked him," she said. "You don't know how to keep your place, Mr. Spenser. You were told to sit and wait. I had the situation firmly in hand. We nearly lost the sketch forever, along with any contact with those who have the Goya and El Greco."

"A creative take on events," I said. "Good luck moving forward."

Topper licked his lips. He played with the cane at his side, stroking the silver handle. He tilted his head and smiled at me, nodding. "Oh, we don't need luck," he said. "We only needed the right man for the job."

He reached in front of him and tilted upward an oblong sketch, about as large as a legal piece of paper. It was a sketch of muted blues, whites, and browns. The Picasso sketch.

"Our curators verified the authenticity this morning," he said. "No thanks to you, it will be hanging back on the museum walls by the end of the week. With great promise that *The Gentleman in Black* will follow."

I shook my head and stood. Many gray heads with saggy necks watched me. No one

131

spoke. Marjorie Ward Phillips continued to place her gaze directly on Topper. "A check is waiting for you at the front desk," he said. "Do not expect us to validate any further expenses."

To punctuate his comments, he rapped his cane against the board desk. The rain continued to sluice down the great bank of windows behind him. The iron bars locking us all into the small, tight-aired room.

"I'll grab a Winthrop T-shirt on the way out," I said.

Marjorie turned to see if I was leaving. I caught her gaze and nodded in her direction. I grabbed my ball cap and left the room. I got the check, walked down the marble steps, and found Paul Marston standing at the landing. He was eating a green apple.

"Tough break, Spenser."

"When did the second call come in?"

"About noon," he said. "I took the call, made the arrangements, and voilà."

"And who was it?"

He shook his head.

"Because you have no idea."

"I am not at liberty to discuss the details," he said, smiling. He took another bite of the apple and chewed. He was wearing a blue plaid suit with a light blue shirt and a yellow tie. A bright yellow flower adorned his lapel. He looked a lot like a Depression-era carnival barker.

"Can you shoot water out of that flower?"

"Funny, Spenser."

Even at a safe distance, the smell of his aftershave made my eyes water. "You won't get back the painting," I said. "You just paid double the value of that sketch is all. It wasn't a lead. It was a shakedown."

"Maybe," he said. "At least I didn't get arrested."

"See you around," I said.

"Give it a few days," he said. "I'll be back in London within the week. And *The Gentleman in Black* will be hanging right and proud back on the wall."

"Not if I get it first."

He pushed off the stairs and laughed. "Haven't you heard, sport?" he said. "You've been terminated."

"That puts the reward in play, doesn't it?" I said.

He placed the apple core on the marble railing and walked toward me. For a moment, I wondered just how far I could toss a dandy Brit. But I worried I'd be thwarted by his ominous stench.

"Stay away, Spenser," he said. "Any reward rightly belongs to me."

"You couldn't find your way around Boston on a Duck Boat."

"And what the hell is a Duck Boat?"

"Exactly," I said. "The only thing you know about this case is from tailing me."

"No one cares where this all started," he said. "Only where it ends."

"True," I said. "But if you don't want to go back to London in a steamer trunk, you better stop following me."

"You'll never know."

"Maybe lighten the aftershave," I said. "Just a little dab will do. I can smell you a mile away, Marston."

He snuffled some kind of retort and I walked back into the rain, directions to Alan Garner's apartment already loaded onto my phone.

20

Alan Garner lived off Shawmut Street in the South End in a very stylish-looking row house swallowed in ivy. The building was red brick, with windows and a front door painted a funereal black. Flower boxes bloomed with impatiens and ivy. Rain tapped at the hood of my car and I hit the windshield wipers to clean my view.

I'd had a long time to admire Garner's house, as I'd been sitting across from it for nearly four hours. A zippy little green Mercedes coupe, registered in his name, was parked within a few steps of the stoop. As I waited for Garner, I listened to Ron Della Chiesa's "Strictly Sinatra" and "Music American" on WPLM. Despite the Frank-heavy name, Ron had selected Tony Bennett's "Are You Havin' Any Fun?"

I checked in with Susan to let her know an early dinner was doubtful.

"Another woman?" she said.

"If you must know," I said. "Rita Fiore bailed me out of jail yesterday."

"That tramp."

"I know," I said. "The nerve."

I ran down yesterday's events.

"Why didn't you call me?"

"You were out with colleagues late," I said. "And I was up early to meet with the museum board."

"Did they offer you a raise?"

"Actually, they fired me."

"But you're still on the job?"

"Yep," I said. "You know me. Ol' Spenser. Loyal as faithful hound."

"You're loyal," she said. "But not to those dusty old relics at the Winthrop."

"True."

"Did you speak to Locke?"

"No," I said. "He has more pressing matters than my relationship to the board. Or Large Marj."

"Call tomorrow," she said. "Let's go for a run. We can talk, clear our bodies and minds."

"I'd prefer our bodies."

"Rain or shine, buster."

I asked her to describe what she was wearing at the moment, but Susan hung up too soon. Conjuring different mental images of Susan naked, I watched the front door of

136

the row house. And much to my amazement, Alan Garner magically appeared more than an hour later. He wore a khaki-colored suit and a pink shirt, and carried a bright blue umbrella.

As he drove off in the Mercedes, I started the car and followed. Garner turned up on Dedham, crossing over Tremont to Dartmouth, heading toward Copley Square. Tony was now singing "On the Sunny Side of the Street" as it rained like hell in the South End.

Can't you hear that pitter-patter. I tapped out the rhythm on the steering wheel as I tailed Garner three cars behind. I kept an eye on the distinctive shape of the taillights. I checked my rearview many times to make sure no pesky Brits tailed me.

Garner didn't seem to be in a hurry, slow off a stoplight by Copley Place, moving on toward the square and past the public library, where the front doors and windows were golden and warm. He continued over Boylston and finally turned into a public lot on Newbury Street.

I kept driving a block over and illegally parked on Comm Ave. If I got a ticket, I'd mail it to Topper Townsend.

I grabbed an umbrella and doubled right back to the parking lot. I nearly missed

Garner, walking west on Newbury toward Mass Ave. Besides the bar at the Ritz in Paris, Newbury Street happened to be Susan Silverman's very favorite place on earth. When she entered any of the many boutiques, salespeople would genuflect in her presence. Sometimes the streetlamps dimmed upon her arrival. Luckily, no such signs alerted Garner to my presence. Just a big, middle-aged man in a ball cap. Nothing to see here. Situation normal.

Garner walked past the brick row houses. Shoe shops, tanning salons, nail parlors, and Ben & Jerry's occupying the storefronts or down in the old cellars.

At Exeter, he crossed over Newbury to a brownstone, mounting the steps. A hand-painted sign in the window identified it as *Haut de Gamme.* I'd stayed awake long enough in French class to know that meant very fancy stuff. Subtle.

I waited five minutes, standing next to a fire call box. I watched as Garner passed by the window. A woman took his raincoat and umbrella, and he disappeared from view. I figured he'd be settled in by now and not expecting me.

When I walked in, Garner was straightening the sleeves of his khaki suit jacket.

"I'm looking for some early Thomas

Kinkade," I said. "Something from his rare Christmas period."

Garner stared at me. Sensing a problem, a woman in a short black dress looked to him. And back at me. She still held his umbrella in hand, coat draped over her forearm. "I'm sorry," she said. "We only deal in —"

Garner leveled a hard look. "He is well aware."

"There's a poster shop down the street," she said. "At the comic-book store."

I nodded, watching Garner. He didn't have a fleck of rain on his suit. His blondish hair had been combed straight back, big and bold. Garner was a slim man, clean-shaven, with dark tanned skin and bright green eyes. He was tall and unathletic, his shoulders more hunched than I recalled. A few lines around his eyes and mouth. The skin under his jaw had grown soft. But vanity didn't let the clothes and style go. He'd kept that.

"How about a Picasso, then?" I said.

"Sir," she said. "We don't deal in prints. We sell only originals. Many of the museums sell prints of popular paintings."

Garner tapped his index finger on his chin. He continued to stare.

"Oh, no," I said. "I'd like an original. Maybe just an etching. About yay big."

I mimicked a box with my hands. I was

getting pretty good at it.

"Sir," the woman said. "We do not have any Picassos. Not at the moment. We do have a wonderful collection of New England landscapes. Most are surprisingly affordable at under twenty."

"Twenty bucks?" I said. "That's a bargain. I'd been prepared to pay half a million."

"I'm sorry," the woman said. "I'm confused."

"Alan?" I said.

Garner nodded, making a cradle of his chin with his thumb and index finger. "That work has already been sold."

I pulled out my cell phone. "Glad to inform the police," I said. "I'm sure they'd like to hear all the details. Paperwork and all that."

The woman's face drained of color. She put a hand to my elbow and told me I'd have to leave. She didn't have much success in budging me. I had a distinct weight advantage.

"I understand time has run out," he said, smiling. "On any complaints."

"Maybe," I said. "But I'm sure *The Globe* would love to print the whole story. From the Common to the Winthrop. And all parties involved. Especially the exclusive Haut de Gamme."

This time Garner's face drained of color. He looked at me, up and down, before nodding. "May I interest you in a cup of coffee?" he said.

"Read my mind."

"But Mr. Garner," the woman said.

"Cream," he said. "Two sugars. Mr. Spenser and I are old friends. We have so much to catch up on."

21

"So," I said. "How's life? How you been?"

"How in the world did you find me?" Garner said. We were seated at a small antique table with two high-backed chairs. He crossed his legs and picked up a china cup. Steam rose from the edge, rain falling outside the window that looked onto Newbury Street.

"I can't divulge trade secrets."

"My association with the gallery isn't widely known," he said. "I'm just a consultant to the owners."

"Ah," I said. "A consultant."

"Spenser," Garner said. He set the cup back on the saucer. "What the fuck do you want?"

"The El Greco," I said. *The Gentleman in Black.*"

Something flickered in his eyes. He pursed his lips and tilted his head. "And what makes you think I would know what you're talking about?"

"Because you ransomed off the Picasso," I said. "I figured this art would be a package deal."

"That's where you're wrong," he said. "And for the sake of argument, why do you think I had any connection to some Picasso? I mean, really. That's a bit outrageous."

I smiled and shook my head. It was good to see Alan again. Brought back so many unpleasant memories of Gino Fish. I watched the rain out on Newbury, all the colorful umbrellas bobbing along the sidewalk. Somewhere out there I could imagine Catherine Deneuve and Nino Castelnuovo dancing.

"I heard some rumors about a Picasso being returned to the Winthrop," he said. "But I have absolutely nothing to do with that. If you even attempt to tie my name, or that of this gallery, to that business, I'll have my lawyers crawling all over you."

"Yikes," I said. "Lawyers. Plural."

"I have made many mistakes in my life," Alan said. "My association with Gino Fish was one of them."

"A big one."

"Yes," he said. "But I was a young man then."

"And now?"

"I am a legitimate art dealer," he said. "Take a look around. This is one of the finest galleries in Boston. Don't you smell it?"

"What's that?"

"Wealth."

"I can smell the bullshit."

He rolled his eyes and sipped at his coffee, his leg rocking back and forth over his knee. I looked around. Lots of oil on canvas, tasteful dim lights. Antiques and Oriental rugs.

"Very high-end," I said. "Did I tell you I took French in high school? B-plus."

"Well, if that is all," he said. "I have some very important calls to make."

Satisfied, he stood and welcomed me to do the same. I kept on drinking the coffee. I liked the coffee. I liked the view of Newbury Street in the rain. I liked the feeling of watching Alan Garner squirm, not knowing what I know. But knowing I knew something.

"You should have sent someone to pick up the sketch at the Four Seasons," I said. "Going back was sloppy."

Alan's self-satisfied grin crumpled. He straightened his tie and swallowed. His assistant peeked around a corner and he fanned his hand to send her away.

"I don't mind the rain," I said. "In fact, I

kind of like it."

"Who told you?"

"No one told me," I said. "You showed your face on their security cameras."

"Shit," Alan said.

"As they say in the old movies," I said, smiling, "the jig is up."

"Do you have any idea how much Gino disliked you?" he said. "You gave him physical hives when you appeared. You got under his thick old skin like no one else."

"Gee," I said. "That means a lot."

Garner sat back down. He reached into his jacket pocket and pulled out a silver cigarette case. He pulled out a thin little smoke and set fire to it. He tilted his head back and spewed smoke out of his mouth in a very theatrical way. I couldn't help but think of Clifton Webb in *Laura*. So charming and so damn guilty.

"Did Fish have the art when he died?" I said.

He shook his head. "Will you really go to the police?"

"Faster than you can say Jackie Robinson."

"I believe it's Jack Robinson."

I shook my head. "Never heard of him."

"This has nothing to do with Mr. Fish," Garner said. He tapped the ash off his thin little cigarette. "This is my business. And my business alone. I went out from under his wretched little shadow some time ago. If you happened to pay attention to what goes on in the art scene."

"I'm more into the hoodlum arts," I said. "And a fancy front on Newbury Street can't change that."

"What exactly is it that you want?" he said. "The deal was made. Money exchanged and the item returned."

"I want them all," I said. "Everything."

"I'm afraid I don't represent the other items," he said.

"And I'm sorry if I don't believe you."

"The museum's other representative offered me quite a sum of money," he said. "Don't you think I'd agree to that arrangement if those paintings were in my possession? Do you think I could just hang a Goya and an El Greco in my window and make a sale? I know you're very new to this, Spenser, but wealthy people don't buy hot paintings. Who would want to place their position at risk by owning stolen art? And in this case, two pieces of very famous stolen art."

"But you could find it."

"You think far too much of me."

"You learned from one of the craftiest,

most devious, backstabbing fences ever to set foot in Boston. I have faith in you, Alan."

"Is that a compliment?"

"Sure," I said. "Why not? Take it."

"Are you, or are you not, working for the museum?"

"Just like always," I said. "I work for myself. Times don't change."

"I can't have the gallery's name connected to this," he said. "The owners took great steps at —"

I held up a hand. "I get it," I said. "Confidential."

"Let me ask you something," Garner said. "Just for the sake of argument. Would I share in the reward?"

"If you led to the recovery of the art?" I said. "And the art was still in good condition?"

Garner nodded. He'd finished the cigarette and started a new one. I took great enjoyment at his jittery fingers fumbling to light the end. Always come armed with the facts and everything will fall right in line.

"This is, as they say, some very hot stuff."

"How'd you come by the Picasso?"

Garner laughed, spilling smoke out of his nose. He waved the smoke away with his hand and shook his head. "The lineage of the art isn't important," he said. "Even

Sotheby's doesn't name their sellers. It could damage the name of some very important families."

"Or in your case, some VIHs."

"Excuse me."

"Very important hoods," I said.

"That's not terribly original, Spenser," he said. "Surely you can do better."

I shrugged. I finished up the coffee. This time I stood and left Garner staring pensively out the window. The chair was a deep red, with dark wood arms shaped like the heads of eagles. He had his legs crossed at the knee and ashed the cigarette in his hand.

"I may be able to locate El Greco," he said. *The Gentleman.*

"Now we're talking."

"And if I did?"

"I'll see what I can do about the reward."

"And the other man?" he said. "The Brit. What do I say if he finds me, too?"

"He won't."

"How can you be so sure?"

"Because he's not me," I said.

"Oh," Garner said. "Thank God."

"Gotta thank someone," I said. I left a card and walked back to the front door. I winked at the receptionist. She did her dead level best not to smile.

I admired her restraint.

22

It took only three phone calls to locate the right Crazy Eddie Ciccone.

But it took four more to arrange a meeting with him at Cedar Junction, the max prison formerly known as Walpole. He was serving time for armed robbery and possession with intent. I figured he'd welcome a visit, as he was not two years into a twelve-year stretch. A greeting from the outside world might really brighten his day.

"Who the fuck are you?" he said.

We sat across from each other on uncomfortable stainless-steel seats, thick plexiglass between us, speaking on a telephone. He was a big guy with a fat stomach and thick arms. He had a big head and a wide nose and a dimpled chin. His hair was black and close-cropped, silver on the sides. Something or someone had placed a nasty gash over what had been his right eyebrow. His lip was busted and his eyes bloodshot.

"You're missed at the Top Hat lounge," I said. "Very fondly remembered at happy hour."

"Come on," he said. "What the hell is this? I ain't got time for this shit."

"You got a lot of time, Eddie," I said. "Or are you too busy crafting newer and better license plates?"

"I don't press no plates," he said. "Do your homework. I work in the fucking laundry."

"You in a rush to get back?"

"Whattya want?"

"You know a guy named Chad Hartman?"

"Nope," he said. "Never heard of him."

"Oh, sure you do," I said. "Think back twenty years. When you were young, free, and running with the DeMarco crew. He was a security guard at the Winthrop Museum. Protecting pieces of priceless art from bad people."

He folded his meaty arms over his chest and leaned back. He gave me a hard eye from behind the glass. They were dark, nearly black, but it was hard to scare someone from behind three inches of plexi. Only a gorilla at the Franklin Zoo had instilled fear at that distance. His name was Kit, a three-hundred-fifty-pound silverback.

"You set Chad up with a fine, upstanding

girl," I said. "Called herself Charity. I'm betting she went to parochial school. Our Sister of Absolute Mercy."

"Come on," he said. "What is this, a gag?"

"Charity had talent," I said. "Chad said she could tie a constrictor knot with her tongue."

"Funny," he said. "Okay, I'll bite. Who sent you?"

"I came on my own volition."

"What's that mean?"

"It means you and me need to talk."

Crazy Eddie touched the wound over his eye, contemplating who I was and exactly what I wanted. He didn't look like a guy who did a lot of quick processing.

"I need some direction," I said. "You're just the man to help."

"Yeah?" he said. "In case you ain't too fucking smart, the guards monitor these things. They hang on every word like it's *Days of Our Lives*."

I leveled my gaze at Crazy Eddie to let him know I was serious. He stared back and started to pick at a tooth with his little finger. His big black eyes round and protruding like a cod's.

"I'm looking for a friend," I said. "I believe you can help me find him."

He didn't say anything, only stared. He

had that raspy, uneven breathing of a guy way out of shape. He scratched at his neck and leaned back from the glass, peering again over his shoulder at the guard by the locked door.

"Just like you," I said. "He had a nickname."

"Yeah?"

"They called him *The Gentleman in Black.*"

"Never heard of him."

I explained the black coat, the frilly white collar, and the severe black beard. "Ever heard of Benny Ricardo?"

"Nope."

"Placekicker for the Lions," I said. "Looks just like him."

"I don't know no Benny Ricardo," Eddie said. "And I don't know that man in black. I ain't got time for this shit. I got shit to do."

"Twenty years is a long time," I said. "Statutes of limitations run out. Parole board could be gracious to those who might offer assistance."

"Parole board, gracious to me?" he said. "Yeah, right. Last time we met, they wouldn't even look me in the eye. Someone said 'denied' before my ass was even in the seat."

"Back when you ran with DeMarco's crew," I said, "you took care of the Top Hat lounge, among other businesses, for the Old Man."

"You heard wrong," he said. "I run my own business. I don't know no one named DeMarco. Who's that?"

"You help me, and I can help you," I said. "What do you have to lose?"

"I don't know you," he said. "I don't know nothing about you. Guard said your name is Spenser."

I modestly explained my background. And the great work I'd done in the city of Boston.

"Private cop?" he said. "Nope. No, thank you. A cop is a cop. All you guys get off on screwing guys just trying to make a living. Feed their damn kids. All I was doing was running a warehouse in Revere and got popped for someone else's cargo. I'm safer behind these walls."

"We keep the wall between us as we go."

"No shit," he said.

"Actually, it's to each the boulders that have fallen to each."

"Whattaya, nuts?"

"Maybe."

"Stay away from me, Spenser," he said. "I don't need this crap. Not now. Not ever.

I'm just doing my time, keeping my head down. Making sure my wife is still around by the time I get out and that my kids still know my face."

"Maybe you should duck more," I said. "And keep your chin down."

He touched his lip, eye twitching. Ciccone looked over his shoulder and then back at me. He leaned in close to the glass, as if it afforded privacy. He leveled his eyes at me and shook his head. The guard behind him was intently studying his cell phone.

"The Gentleman in Black," I said. "Where'd he end up?"

"Don't ask me about that," he said. "Ever again. That's a long time ago. Too much blood."

"For whom?"

"Wouldn't you like to know."

"That's why I'm here."

"Enough," he said. "Just because I'm doing time in Walpole doesn't mean I'm untouchable. Those people are still around. I don't want no trouble. Unnerstand? This is some old, toxic shit and you ain't gonna trick me into playing no bullshit games."

Crazy Eddie slammed down the phone and motioned for the guard to return him to washing dirty linen. He mouthed the words "Fuck off."

Maybe he wasn't so crazy after all. I didn't like it, but Eddie wasn't a man easily bent.

23

"Just what would you do with five million dollars?" Susan said.

"You mean what would we do?"

"Of course," she said. "I didn't mean to be presumptuous."

"I'm not sure," I said. "I'd have to take it up with my mistress. The mistress, of course, comes after the snazzy sports car."

"I am your mistress," Susan said. "Perhaps I would trade you in for a younger man."

"On my money?"

"Share and share alike."

It was the next day and, as promised, we'd taken a nice run along the Cambridge side of the Charles. We followed the trail past the boathouses, MIT, and ultimately across the river to the science museum. On the way back, we slowed to a nice walk, catching our wind, our sweat drying in the midday sun. Charles Eliot's sycamores stood tall and green, lined up in an endless row along Memorial Drive.

"Maybe I'd quit being a snoop," I said.

"Impossible," she said. "They'll have to carry you out of your office feet first."

"True," I said. "And you? You wouldn't have to work. You could focus more on charity work. Fund-raising."

"And leave my patients?"

"Yep."

"Never," she said. "Shrinking is not unlike snooping. We are both naturally curious people."

Susan wore black yoga pants and a blue sports tank. That morning, she'd worn her hair up in a bun, and small black curls flitted down the nape of her neck. Her tan skin shone with sweat.

"If I get the paintings back, the Winthrop may offer some reward," I said. "But not all."

"You don't trust them?"

"Not as far as I could throw Large Marj."

"Careful," Susan said. "You might hurt your back."

The path we followed was straight and well worn. We passed by young couples with fancy strollers made for jogging. Old people sat on benches. Closer to the river, some college-age kids played with a dog. We didn't bring Pearl on runs anymore. She'd gotten to the age that she just preferred a short afternoon stroll on Linnaean Street.

"I may regret saying this," I said. "But in a way, I trust Alan Garner."

"Because you trusted Gino?"

"I didn't trust Gino," I said. "But I do trust Vinnie. And according to Vinnie, these paintings were never in Gino's possession."

"And then there were two."

"Both Quirk and Crazy Eddie hinted people were killed for them."

"Would that surprise you?"

"Not in the least," I said. "I've known people killed over spilled beer."

"Won't Quirk tell you?" she said. "Or Belson?"

"Quirk wants me to find out for myself," I said. "It's a fun little game he plays. I'd never ask. But if I did, he'd say he wants to keep me sharp."

"And now you have to work both ends of time," Susan said. "The original thieves. And those who might hold them now."

"The reward money makes it easier," I said. "And tougher. With the story about the Picasso in *The Globe,* every nut in Boston will be digging through their uncle's basement."

"Maybe they'll find something."

"My bet's on Garner," I said. "I think

158

we'll strike a deal."

"And this guy following you?"

"Chasing his tail," I said. "If Crazy Eddie Ciccone won't talk to me, he's sure as hell not talking to a guy who pins fresh flowers on his suit jacket and smells like French nail varnish."

"Because you have a common touch."

"If Ciccone decides to deal, he'll check me out," I said. "I do have a reputation in certain circles. People know I'll do what I say, and I've spent a large part of my career enforcing that. Both good and bad. Even Jackie DeMarco would have to vouch for that."

Susan pointed down the concrete path toward the Harvard Bridge. The river was choked with canoes and small sailboats. Geese fluttered their wings along the banks down by the boathouse.

"How about a race?" she said. "The winner buys lunch at the Russell House Tavern."

"Deviled eggs and Bloody Marys?"

"What else."

"And the winner perhaps also can decide on post-meal activities?"

"Like lying down and taking a long nap."

"We have gotten sweaty this morning," I said. "We both could use a shower."

"At what point do you think your libido will catch up with your age?"

"I hope never," I said. "Any complaints?"

"None whatsoever."

"The race is from here to the Weeks Bridge?" I said.

Susan gave me a grin worthy of the devil himself. "Do you think you can handle it?"

"Just watch me," I said.

And without a warning, I started the long dash down the footpath. I didn't look back once.

24

Two days later, a well-dressed older gent rapped on my office door. The door was slightly open, and I invited him in. I'd spent the last few hours reviewing Locke's files and needed a break. The man introduced himself as Dominic J. Nuccio, attorney at law.

Nuccio wore a slightly rumpled blue suit, a red tie, and a white dress shirt with gold cuff links. His face was gaunt, and he had a lot of stiff salt-and-pepper hair that seemed to be a wig. A gold watch on his wrist seemed only slightly smaller than a dinner plate. His hands were worn and liver-spotted. I knew his name and reputation. Most called him The Shark.

"What can I do for you?" I said.

"Do you mind if we shut the door?"

"No one's listening," I said. "There's a girl in the furniture showroom, but she's usually listening to punk bands on her

161

headphones. And for some reason, completely inattentive to my business."

"Still," he said.

I got up, stretched, and closed the door. It was a bright and beautiful summer day downtown. The a/c rumbled from the window. I had been hoping to get a phone call from Garner. If I didn't by three, I planned to walk down Newbury and visit his gallery. Try and put a bit of a shadow on the high end.

"I'm not at liberty to discuss all the details," he said.

"But you represent an individual who might know the whereabouts of the Winthrop paintings?"

He looked genuinely surprised. I leaned back in my chair and placed my hands behind my head. That morning I wasn't dressed for court, in Levi's and a faded Sox T-shirt. My holster and ball cap hung on a nearby coat rack. Nuccio's toupee looked odd on his skeletal head, more hat than hair.

"I knew your name," he said. "And I had you checked out. People say you're a straight shooter."

"Only to those I've shot."

The Shark smiled. I'd seen Nuccio's face in the paper many times, representing many fine citizens against murder, racketeering,

162

and drug charges. Sometime back, I recalled he'd self-published a book called *Boston, the Mob & Me.* For some reason, that wasn't on his business card.

"What's Crazy Eddie want?"

"I'm here for someone who knows about that painting," he said. "And would very much like to reunite the work with the museum."

"That's awfully nice of them," I said. I looked at my watch. I placed my hands flat on my desk. "Come on. Let's go. No time like the present."

Nuccio smiled at me. It looked like it pained him a great deal. "They do have some concerns," he said. "And requests."

"Immunity," I said. "The five-million reward."

"Of course," he said. "They can't gain possession of the works easily. They expect to be compensated for their time and genuine philanthropic effort."

"I don't speak for the museum," I said. "But I'm certainly listening."

"My client doesn't trust the museum," he said. "They know they'll go straight to the authorities. Getting involved in some kind of federal sting would be very embarrassing to my client's current business."

"In case you didn't see the story," I said.

"The statute of limitations has run out."

"You and I both know how that goes," he said. "They'll punish my client for something else entirely. The Feds like to win any way possible. Most of the time by cheating the system."

"They may be a little angry," I said. "Twenty years without a clue until a few days ago. Even that didn't go as smoothly as some think."

"My client wasn't involved with that Picasso," he said. "The who and why of that piece doesn't involve my client. This involves the one by the old Spanish master, that guy in black."

"The Gentleman in Black," I said.

Nuccio shuffled in his seat. I didn't offer him coffee or whiskey. I wanted him to get to the point. Perhaps he'd been sent by Crazy Eddie or perhaps by Alan Garner, although Garner didn't need a third party at this stage. He'd make arrangements and offer details on what he wanted. The Mob attorney in my office seemed to represent a true unknown entity. As he spoke, the sunlight caught the crystal face of his watch. He could probably land a spaceship with that thing.

"What's the deal?" I said.

"A guarantee of the full reward," he said.

"And no prosecution. We will want that in writing. Handshake agreements don't hold like ink."

"The reward was for the return of all three," I said. "You're only talking about one."

"The most valuable," he said. "Yeah, I do read *The Globe.* Those other pieces are chicken scratch. Everyone wants the Big Guy. Am I right? Or am I right?"

I wasn't sure this wasn't a trick question. Nuccio took off his glasses, blew his hot breath on the lenses, and cleaned them with a white handkerchief.

"They won't offer a dime," I said. "Without proof of life."

"For a painting?" he said. "How's that life? It's not a living, breathing thing."

"I know, it doesn't make much sense," I said. "But that's what they call it anyway. They need absolute evidence that they have the painting, and that the painting remains in good shape. That makes quite a bit of difference when it comes to the reward money. Nobody knows what it looks like now. Maybe it's been stuffed in the trunk of an Oldsmobile Cutlass for twenty years. That would make a big difference."

"I assure you that the painting is in fine shape."

"I'm sure you're good to your word," I said. "But I'm naturally cautious."

Nuccio smiled. "Who's this other guy?" he said. "The one with the picture in the paper. Whosis Marston? Is he your partner or something?"

"Far from it."

"Then what's his deal?"

"I'm an independent contractor," I said. "I can promise to independently make your case to the museum board. But I won't even pick up the phone unless I can vouch for what your client can offer."

Nuccio raised his eyebrows and straightened his tie. "My client wants proper credit where credit is due," he said. "There's a lot of flies buzzing around the goodies. He's the only one who deserves to make everything right here. And be compensated for his effort."

"I heard there was a lot of blood," I said. "To control these paintings. Is that how your client ended up with the Big Guy?"

Nuccio's mouth twitched, eyes roving over me from behind the glasses.

"I don't know anything of how or where the painting changed hands," he said. "All I know is that my client can get it and wants to do the right thing."

"He must be quite a guy," I said. "Pillar

of society."

"Five mil for a work worth more than ten times that?" he said. "Yeah, I'd say my client is definitely stepping up and doing the right thing."

"Proof of life," I said.

He nodded. "Yeah, yeah, yeah," he said. "All that stuff."

"And I'll see what I can do about a guarantee."

"It's quite magnificent."

"Have you seen it lately?"

"No," he said. "But I remember seeing it as a kid. It always scared the bejeezus out of me. That guy looked as if he could see and knew all."

"And now?"

"Let me see what I can do," he said. "Everyone's nervous. Don't call me. I'll call you."

Nuccio shook my hand and walked out. He left my door wide open, and when I walked over to close it, the girl Lila from down the hall poked her head out.

"You think he's lying?" she said. Her hair was a bright blue today.

"Only when his mouth was moving."

25

I didn't mind being paranoid. As I liked staying alive, paranoia could be a great friend.

When I left my office and crossed Berkeley Street, I immediately checked around for Paul Marston or anyone else who might want to do me harm, either on foot or in a nearby car. It was still light outside, but the city had thinned of commuters, who had been replaced with the night crowd. The well-heeled and the well-dressed headed out for dinner and drinks. Several cafés had their doors open, with standing fans blowing across their patios. Wine bottles were uncorked; cocktails clinked.

I had big plans to order a pizza and stay in with Susan tonight. As I walked, an uneasy feeling creeped across my upper back. I slowed my pace and pretended to peer into the window of the big Nike store on Boylston. Hot damn. Twenty percent off basketball shoes.

I glanced behind me. I didn't see Marston, but I did notice an older guy in a dark ball cap and a navy windbreaker. He had on mirrored sunglasses and walked with a steady gait, not slowing a bit as he passed by my back. I dismissed him and continued walking toward my SUV.

I retrieved my trusty Land Cruiser from the garage and headed back onto Boylston toward the Common.

At a stoplight at Arlington, I glanced back and spotted the same scruffy guy in a dark sedan. Or at least I thought it was the same guy. The setting sun made it tough to see the figure behind the wheel. But I noted the same dark ball cap and mirrored sunglasses.

This scruffy guy wasn't too bad. As the traffic pushed off, he followed close but not too close. I followed the Common and turned north on Tremont. He turned north on Tremont, too. But as downtown was that way, lots of people turned in that direction. I cut up onto Congress toward Government Center. The sedan was close behind me. Given the look of the car, the man could very well be a cop. Or a federal agent. Or a meat inspector for the USDA wanting the secrets of how I tenderized my chicken.

I always said it took a tough man to make

a tender chicken.

Instead of heading north on Washington to the Charlestown Bridge and home, I turned south on New Chardon, passing Haymarket Square, Hanover Street, and Rowes Wharf, speeding along the Greenway. I had to hand it to the guy following me, he did it with skill and precision. Little effort, no jerky movements. If I hadn't been at a high level of paranoid, I might not have even seen him slide in and out of traffic, slow down, and pick up as I braked and sped up.

At Seaport Boulevard, I caught a red light.

When it turned green, I didn't move. Boston drivers, not being the most patient, expressed their dissatisfaction by honking. A few yelled some colloquial expressions. I peered in my side mirror, catching the sedan two cars back. As the light flashed yellow, I slid into the intersection and turned on red.

I raced over the bridge into the Seaport and, a few blocks over, whipped into a parking lot. It was one of those pay-as-you-go places, and I circled around the parked cars and came back out, nose to the road.

A half-minute later, the silver sedan flew past.

I waited about thirty seconds. And then I pulled out to follow the scruffy guy.

He wasn't expecting me. I followed him in and out of the roads around the Seaport. Even with the wide, empty streets and long passages along the docks, it took him a few minutes to spot me.

I couldn't say for sure. But I'm pretty damn sure he smacked his palm against his forehead.

It took a few minutes before he begged off. On Congress, right around the Westin and the Convention Center, he mashed his accelerator and tried to leave me toddling behind. I tailed him up and around to an on-ramp for 93. In the setting sun, in and around traffic, I chased the scruffy man all the way to Quincy.

Somewhere over the Neponset River, I lost him.

I was good. But not perfect.

I had the car's make and model, but I couldn't get a tag number. Maybe it was something. Or nothing. Perhaps he just caught a glance of himself in the rearview and decided to race home and clean up.

I found the nearest off-ramp, got off, and then headed back toward Charlestown.

Over the Charlestown Bridge, the modern buildings at MIT showed gold and silver, the river a coppery color as it twirled and swirled beneath me. I turned on Chelsea and dipped down into the Navy Yards. I had just picked up the phone to call Susan when I spotted yet another sedan turning out fast behind me.

And then another. At that moment, I knew there was a conspiracy against me eating pizza.

I drove faster along First Avenue and then took a hard turn up Seventh Street. As I cut up and over, a minivan pulled out from a side street and nearly T-boned my Toyota.

I braked suddenly, and the sedan came up hard and fast by the driver's door. I pulled the .38 revolver from under the windbreaker in my passenger seat and aimed out my open window.

The sedan's window dropped down. The sedan was a Cadillac. The man in the passenger seat was Vinnie Morris.

"Spenser?" he said. "What the fuck? You're driving like a nutso. You know they got family shit around here. Christ."

"Good to see you, Vinnie."

"What the hell's the matter with you?"

"Just taking precautions."

"Yeah?" he said. "Well, goody for you. Do you have a minute?"

"For you, Vinnie?" I said. "Always."

"Good," Vinnie said. " 'Cause me and you need to talk."

26

"Some people are gunning for you, ace," Vinnie said.

"No kidding."

"You see 'em?"

"I've seen one," I said. "He needed a shave."

We were upstairs in my condo. Vinnie had left his people parked down the street. His driver was the guy with the big stomach and the doo-wop hairdo who liked Hawaiian shirts. He wore a red one today, with green parrots and yellow flowers. He looked kind of like Magnum PI after he'd said to hell with the clean living and exercising.

"Older guy," I said. "Scruffy gray beard. Drove a silver sedan. Maybe a Chevy."

"Yeah," Vinnie said. "That guy. We call him Scruff. Everyone knows him. He hangs out with the Joker and Two-Face, all those fucking guys."

I looked at him. Vinnie cracked a smile.

"Want a beer?" I said. I walked to the refrigerator and opened the door.

"Got something with more kick?" he said. "Been a helluva day."

I reached up into the cabinet and found a half-empty bottle of Wild Turkey 101. I got out a nice crystal glass and added a few cubes of ice. I poured a couple fingers and handed him the glass.

"Now we're talking," he said. "Come to Papa."

Vinnie wandered around the condo with the bourbon, craning his neck around, checking out the empty brick walls and the big plate-glass window looking out onto the marina and harbor.

"Nice digs," he said. "Lots of space. You can afford living like this? As a freakin' snoop?"

"Sure," I said. "Amazing what you can earn with honest work."

"You call what you do honest?"

"Relatively speaking."

I cracked open an Ipswich Ale and took a seat on the barstool. He continued to wander around my place, walking close to the glass, looking down at his guys, and then circling back.

"How's Susan?"

"Good."

"And the dog?"

"With Susan," I said. "I was trying to bring them a pizza when I got rerouted."

"Didn't mean to scare you or nothing," he said. "Like I said. We need to talk."

He set his glass on the marble bar, condensation forming around the edges. He'd taken only a few sips, the whiskey and water a lovely caramel color. Vinnie leaned against the counter, nodding with his private thoughts. He wore a plaid cotton shirt with small pink-and-purple designs. A known shooter — and alleged boss — could pull off a shirt like that. His pants were a light gray, and he wore dark brown loafers with tiny tassels. Everything looked clean, crisp, and new.

"Who's looking for me?" I said.

"Who else," he said. "DeMarco's people."

I nodded. "Jackie himself?" I said. "Or the hired help?"

"Don't know," he said. "But some inquiries were made and I thought you'd better know. To, you know, watch your fucking ass."

"Duly noted."

"You talk to Devon Murphy?"

I nodded.

"And?"

"And he said the whole job was his idea."

"I fucking knew it," he said. "That shifty little bastard would've been the only one crazy enough to try and pull off a job at the Winthrop. I think he's robbed about every museum in New England."

"Problem is he was at Walpole at the time."

"Shit."

"Yep," I said. "He acted like he knew who did it. But he wouldn't tell me."

"So it was a bust?"

"Not exactly," I said. "He said he'd planned to bribe one of the museum guards that night with a woman of questionable character. I found said guard and the guard admitted he'd met a nice girl named Charity. Then the guard was nice enough to pass on a lead to a certain guy at a certain bar."

Vinnie took a long swallow of the bourbon. I uncorked the bottle and poured him another. He didn't interrupt my generosity until the glass was half full again.

"So you fucking got it?" he said. "Or one of those paintings. Right? I seen it in the papers."

"That didn't have anything to do with my investigation," I said. "A local antiques broker contacted the museum."

"Who?"

"Alan Garner."

"Fucking Alan Garner?" he said. "This just gets richer and richer. Alan Garner. Gino's little squeeze. Gino must've talked in his sleep."

I sipped my beer. Outside the windows, the sky had turned a pinkish black in the twilight, the lights of Boston flickering on across the water. I checked my watch. Susan would be expecting her pizza just about now. Susan didn't eat much but liked her food delivered on time.

"I promise you," Vinnie said. "Gino never mentioned that score."

"I know."

"That must've been something Garner did later," he said. "You know. On his own."

"I agree."

"So who's this fucking guy with a fucking bar that the guard at the museum told you about?"

"Ever heard of Crazy Eddie Ciccone?"

Vinnie was in mid-sip and choked out a little bit of bourbon, some landing on his immaculate shirt. He flicked away the drops with his fingers and shook his head. "Don't pour me any more liquor," he said. "Okay? Cut me off."

"I pulled his record," I said.

"And?"

"Bad dude," I said. "Professional wheelman. Armed robbery. Manslaughter. Ran some coke up from Florida."

"A lot of coke," he said. "Crazy Eddie. A fucking avalanche of coke."

"For whom?"

"You really need to ask?" he said, bringing the glass to his lips.

"No," I said. "But since you're here."

"Ciccone ran in DeMarco's old man's crew," he said. "When the Old Man had his garage in Revere. They did all their business out of there, and Ciccone was one of his main guys. Did the pickups. Mainly hustled all that coke back then. There was a reason they called him crazy. He couldn't fucking shut up. Yammering and yammering away."

"Cocaine, the wonder drug."

"You want to talk to him?"

"I tried," I said. "Went to Walpole and he gave me the cold shoulder."

"Of course he did," Vinnie said. "He'd rather cut off his schmeckle than talk family business."

"That's loyal."

"You bet," he said. "But that's what stirred up Jackie. Anything about the Old Man or any of his old man's people and he goes bullshit on it. Don't make it a thing unless you have to. Okay? I'd rather not have to step into a big flaming pile of crapola if I don't have to."

I nodded. Vinnie set his empty drink on the bar.

"Everyone's just real jumpy about this on account of what happened to Benny Barboza."

"And who is Barboza?" I said. "What happened to him?"

"Benny and Eddie ran in DeMarco's crew," Vinnie said. "Sometime in the late nineties, Benny got whacked. He was missing for a few weeks until some kids playing in a park noted the smell coming from the trunk of a car. It was a mess. Lots of blood. Gore. Surprised you don't remember it from the papers."

"Because of the heist?"

Vinnie picked up the drink, downed the rest, and set it back on the bar. He turned to leave.

"That's up to you, ace," he said. "All I know is that Benny got killed in a very unseemly fashion."

27

I made it to Susan's. We ate. We drank a bottle of cheap red wine. At some point, I don't recall, she forced herself on me and committed unspeakable acts. The next morning, I changed into a pair of fresh jeans and a stylish pocket T-shirt and drove to Kane's and then down to Roxbury and BPD headquarters. After a short wait, Quirk agreed to see me.

"If I'd known you'd brought donuts I would have let you in sooner."

I cracked open the box from Kane's on his desk, picked a cinnamon sugar, and took a seat. He used his advanced investigative technique to look over the rest and grabbed a coconut. He extracted it with a napkin, as if culling evidence from a crime scene.

"Be careful," I said. "The coconut sprinkles might go flying."

"I'll take my chances," Quirk said. "You've shown up early, by your standards. You're shaved, clean as a ten-dollar pistol, and whistling shit from *Babes in Arms.* Either you hit the lottery or got lucky last night."

"I got lucky last night," I said. "Susan got me drunk on a cheap bottle of Chianti."

"Is that all it takes?"

"Usually much less."

As Quirk took a bite of the donut, a few shaved sprinkles fell across his desk like snow. He carefully set the donut on his day planner and reached for his coffee. The mug read *World's Greatest Grandfather.* I had no doubt.

"And?" Quirk said.

"And what?"

"You didn't come flitting around head-quarters to deliver donuts like the freakin' donut fairy," he said. "Whattya want?"

"Benny Barboza."

Quirk smiled. He picked up the donut and had a few more bites. Without a word, he stood and walked to his door. The office was glass, but the door was solid. It shut with a tight click and he sat back down and folded his extra-large hands in front of him. He continued to smile. His white hair had been buzzed short, making his features seem even more granitelike.

"This was the blood you warned me about."

He nodded. "You want some coffee?" he said.

"Already drank a pot," I said. "Benny ran with Old Man DeMarco's crew in Revere. At the same time as the trouble with the Morellis over the coke."

"Wow," Quirk said. "Look who showed up for class. Gold fucking star, Spenser. Really. After all this time, you still astound me."

"And you think Benny Barboza was tied in with the Winthrop job?"

Quirk shrugged, finished the donut, and neatly folded the napkin before tossing it in the trash. He dusted what remained off his hands and picked up his coffee mug. He didn't answer, only sipped his coffee. Someone appeared at the glass wall behind me and he held up his index finger to give him a minute. Quirk's finger loomed as large as a stop sign.

"Why didn't you just tell me when we had lunch?" I said.

"Wouldn't be professional just to tell you everything," he said. "Would it? Besides, I like to keep you on your toes, Spenser. I just was curious how long it would take for you to circle on back to the Barboza murder."

"And how'd I do?" I said.

"Slower than molasses."

To console myself, I finished the donut. Quirk stared at me for a moment and, without breaking the gaze, yanked open a desk drawer, extracted a file, and tossed it onto the donut box. "I've had this waiting for a week," he said.

I picked it up and opened it. Photocopies of the Barboza murder case file.

"Barboza was a creep," Quirk said. "A suspect in a half-dozen killings for the Old Man. We couldn't get him on any of them. They called him Benny the Blade because all the folks he sliced and diced. If you ask me, he got what was coming to him. Justice was served."

"Boston justice."

"It's still justice," Quirk said. "Don't think for a minute that it doesn't mean something to the victims' families."

"Who probably weren't nice people themselves."

Quirk shrugged. He picked up the mug extolling his virtues as a grandfather and leaned back into his chair. A few more framed photographs had joined the ever-present glass cube of family on his desk. I'd heard he had a grandson who'd just joined the department as a rookie patrol officer. What Boston needed was more Quirks. If they could clone him, crime would be at an all-time low.

"When Frank and I worked this thing, we didn't give a flying fuck about some missing painting," he said. "Sure, we cared if he had it and it was a motive. But we worked Homicide, not Robbery. It was just a foot-note. A damn asterisk in the file. We turned the information over to Bobby Wright, who in turn turned it over to the Feds."

"Wright never mentioned Barboza."

"Why would he?" Quirk said, smiling. "You didn't freakin' ask him. Did you?"

"Okay," I said. "Do you think he was part of the crew who stole the painting?"

"Yep."

"And do you think he was killed because of the painting?"

"I have no idea," he said. "In case you're wondering about the depth of our friend-ship, that's officially an open case. I hear from Barboza's sister every year on the an-niversary of the murder and she reams me out a new a-hole."

"Does she think it's about the Winthrop?"

"I don't know, Spenser," Quirk said. "Why don't you ask her about your goddamn missing painting? And by the way, I do have official police work to do beyond just meet-ing with lousy Boston snoops who bring me donuts."

"Great donuts," I said. "Right?"

He shrugged and nodded.

"As we both know, knowing and proving are two very different things."

Quirk nodded again.

"Who killed Barboza?"

"We liked the Morellis," he said. "Jimmy Morelli called it and it got done. They were battling it out for a mountain of cocaine bigger than the Matterhorn back then. Not to disappoint your current theories, but I don't think Barboza's death had a damn thing to do with the Winthrop. He was just caught in the crossfire of a war in the North End. When it gets down to it, it's all about money, power, or sex."

"To be clear, was there any evidence of the Winthrop job during your investigation?"

"Only talk," he said. "It's in the files."

"Did the name Crazy Eddie Ciccone come up?"

"Of course it did," he said. "That guy had been a pain in our nuts for years. But like I said, read the freakin' files. Old Man De-Marco, Benny Barboza, Crazy Eddie Ciccone . . . all of those assholes worked out of that garage in Revere."

"You think Jimmy Morelli knows anything?"

Quirk laughed and shook his head. "Why don't you just go ask him," he said. "That son of a bitch is tougher to open up than a green walnut."

"I heard he's retired."

"Ain't it a kick," he said. "The hoods get to slow down and live the easy life, while the crime dogs like us are still busting our hump. Doesn't seem fair, does it?"

I stood up and offered my hand. Shaking hands with Marty Quirk might break a few knuckles.

"Heard the commissioner is retiring at the end of the year."

"No kidding," Quirk said. "Interesting news."

I smiled and tapped my finger on the Kane's donut box. "Any chance of me escaping BPD headquarters with this box under my arm?"

"None whatsoever," he said. "You wouldn't make it five feet."

"Benny was a good man," Tracy Barboza said. "A wonderful man. A caring brother. A loving husband and great father. He was only married to a couple of their mothers, but that didn't stop him from taking responsibility. He took care of 'em all up until the day he died."

We sat across from each other at a round green picnic table outside Kelly's Roast Beef on Revere Beach. It was an overcast day, warm and muggy and smelling heavily of the sea. From where we sat, you could see the waves lapping against the shore. People had set up blankets and umbrellas along the beach, drinking beer and lazing about in portable chairs. Many had brought dogs. I had great admiration for dog people.

It was nearly two o'clock by the time she could meet with me. I decided to double down on lunch with the surf and turf, a lobster roll and roast beef sandwich. Tracy

Barboza said she wasn't that hungry and ordered onion rings and a Diet Coke.

"What they did to him wasn't right," she said. "Nobody deserves that."

Tracy Barboza was a stocky, middle-aged woman with bleached blond hair braided on each side of her head like a German beer maid. Her face was long and a bit flabby, with a healthy portion of eye makeup on her lids and lashes. She wore sunglasses on top of her head and an extra-large T-shirt reading *Reclaim Revere* dropping long over a pair of shorts.

On the phone, she'd told me she did volunteer work for a local group planting gardens in blighted neighborhoods.

"I've seen the file."

"You seen the pictures?"

I nodded. No longer as interested in the final portion of the rare roast beef.

"You seen what they done to my Benny?"

"I'm sorry."

"Wasn't right," she said. "You want to shoot somebody, shoot somebody. *Boom. Done. Dead.* But this? Did you see they cut his throat and knifed him twenty-seven times? By the time they found my brother in the trunk of his own Cadillac, he looked like a side of beef. Cops knew who did it

188

but were too scared to do anything about it."

I wanted to assure her that Quirk and Belson were afraid of no one. But instead I filled my mouth with the lobster roll and let her continue talking. The wind blew hard and fast off the shore, nearly taking our paper plates with it. I liked it at the beach. For a long while, Henry Cimoli had a condo right down the street.

"Do you know Eddie Ciccone?"

"Crazy Eddie?" she said. "Sure. Sure. Everyone knows Crazy Eddie. I went out with him a few times in high school. I'm telling you, he was all hands. Nice Catholic girl like me with an older guy like Eddie? I wouldn't have even thought about him, hadn't been his friendship with my brother. Eddie and Benny. They were friends, thick as thieves. Never saw anyone cry as much in my life as Eddie at the funeral. Be honest, I didn't think he would make it. Don't ask me what happened to him, because I don't know."

"He's in Walpole."

"Figures," Barboza said. "The trouble they got into. Christ."

"I tried to talk to him," I said.

"And he wouldn't."

"Nope."

"That's Eddie," he said. "Loyal even past death."

She helped herself to a few more onion rings and then pushed the rest away in an act of restraint. I handed her a couple napkins and she wiped the grease from her hands.

"Both of them worked for Mr. DeMarco?"

"Sure, sure," she said. She wiped her brow with the napkin. "Sorry. It's been a hell of a day. Putting in a tomato garden over where the dog track used to be and working like a bastard all freaking morning. We got two people coming from the mayor's office tomorrow and we want things looking nice, you know? Used to be a junk lot, filled with all kind of shit. Amazing what you can get to grow if you just break up the ground and stick in some plants."

"Who else did your brother work with?"

"Mike Marino," she said. "All those guys who hung out at Mr. DeMarco's garage. Mikey Mike. He was a real piece of work, too. Midget short, but funny. God rest his soul. You know he got the cancer a few years ago? I just heard he died last year. Back when we were kids he used to cruise the beach in a convertible Olds Cutlass. Cherry red. Even with the top down, everything smelled like Old Spice and fucking ciga-

190

rettes. My brother. His friends. God."

"Crazy Eddie, Benny, and Mikey Mike," I said. "Interesting guys."

"You ain't kidding," she said. "I know people call them a crew. Or the Mafia or whatever. But they just did business. Okay? That doesn't mean anything. Maybe some of that business wasn't completely legit. But what is? Benny and his pals had a real time of it back then. I miss them a lot."

"Speaking of not completely legit," I said. "Did Benny ever talk to you about art?"

"Art?" she said, sort of laughing. "Benny? You got to be kidding. Whattya mean?"

"Paintings," I said. "Maybe a big one, life size, of a scary-looking Spanish guy with a pointy beard. Apparently had a thing for black."

Tracy played with the rubber band that wrapped one of her pigtails. "No," she said. "Why?"

"Your brother may have been involved with the Winthrop heist," I said. "About a year before he died."

"The Winthrop?" she said. "Are you kidding me? They have a five-million-dollar reward to find those paintings. Jesus."

I nodded. Across the street, a white Jeep Cherokee pulled to the curb by a green-roofed shade shelter. I could see the bulky

191

outline of a man behind the wheel but didn't think much of it. I went back to Tracy and the rest of my lobster roll.

"If Benny had those paintings, could I get a cut?" she said.

"If you can find it, I don't see why not."

"Why do you think Benny had something to do with the robbery?"

"I wish I could tell you everything," I said. "But I can't."

"You think maybe this painting was the reason someone killed him?"

"Maybe," I said. "Right now I can't say for sure. I need to know more."

The Jeep hadn't moved. The man still stayed behind the wheel. Maybe he was waiting for his kids at the beach. Maybe he was meeting friends. Maybe he was some kind of weirdo who liked to watch people in bathing suits. Or maybe it was someone watching me. The man had on sunglasses and some kind of woven cap. He turned toward Kelly's and then quickly turned back.

"Afterward, did anyone go through your brother's things?" I said.

"Sure," she said. "I did. And so did our mother. We gave his clothes and most of his crap to Goodwill. But I think Eddie came over and got his CDs."

"Did Eddie go through his things, too?"

"I don't remember," she said. "That was a long time ago. I just remember Mr. De-Marco being really good to us, especially my mother. He took care of everything. The back rent, Benny's car, the funeral. We didn't have to pay for nothing, and then every month until my mother died, he sent her money. Can you believe that? She didn't have to worry about a thing. Mr. DeMarco was like that. A real class act. Wish I could say the same for his son. Jackie is another freakin' animal."

I did not disagree. "Did you keep anything of Benny's?"

"Some," she said. "Yeah, sure. But you'd think I'd remember some big weird painting."

"Maybe," I said. "Depends on how it was stored."

"Holy shit," she said. "We got to check. Like now."

"Where's Benny's stuff?"

"Benny left behind so much crap," she said. "He rented a place up by Point of Pines yacht club. Took me two weeks to clean it all out."

I looked back to the Jeep. I didn't mind being followed, but I hated to be insulted. The driver had a pair of binoculars, watching us talk at the little table. I started to wave and let him know he'd been spotted. Instead, I stood up and turned in that direction.

"Hold that thought," I said. "I'll be right back."

I jogged across Beach Boulevard, coming up behind the Jeep, and walked up on the driver's-side door. I knocked hard on the glass.

Paul Marston looked up from his seat. He shook his head, placing the binoculars on the seat beside him. Slowly, he let down the driver's window. I could see the hat more clearly now, a tweedy little British hat most often preferred by cabbies or newsboys. He looked ridiculous.

"The hat gave you away," I said. "The last man to wear a hat like that in Revere was run out of town on a greased rail."

"Is that some kind of threat?"

"You didn't follow me here," I said. "Unless you're much better than you look."

"You wouldn't know," he said. "Only reason you see me now is I wanted to talk."

I leaned in to the Jeep. "Then talk."

"Who's the woman?"

"My hairstylist," I said. "Thinking of adding some braids."

"What does she know about *The Gentleman*?"

"Ha," I said. "I'm off the case. Haven't you heard?"

"That's a lie and we both know it," he said. He smiled big and toothy, like he could set a record for cleaning a cob of corn. "You want that money just like all the rest. We are a greedy lot."

"I hope the Winthrop offered you a dental plan."

"Why's that?"

"Keep grinning and find out."

The smile dropped.

I walked away, back toward my car, and spent a minute feeling about the front and rear bumper. I finally found what I was looking for under the left-front wheel well. I pulled off the magnetic tracking device, walked back to Marston's open window, and tossed it inside.

Back at the table, I asked Tracy where she'd stored her brother's things.

"A rental unit," she said. "By the T station."

"Go ahead and drive that way," I said. "Don't go in yet. Circle the block and wait for me to call."

"What's going on," she said. "Who's that man?"

195

"Someone who'd like to cheat both of us," I said.

"Is he dangerous?"

"Only to your sense of smell," I said. "Just drive and I'll shake us both free. I'll meet you there."

29

I sifted through Benny Barboza's personal items for more than two hours. The storage facility was climate-controlled and cool, and the work wasn't very hard, if frustrating. We learned that Crazy Eddie hadn't taken all of Benny's records and CDs. He'd left quite a collection of some oldies but not so goodies: Limp Bizkit, Kid Rock, Insane Clown Posse, Linkin Park, and Massachusetts's shamefully own Godsmack. There were also a lot of kitchen utensils, coffeepots, a waffle maker, and pots and pans and dishes. He kept all four years of his yearbooks from Revere High, programs from Fenway, a jacket that showed he'd lettered in football and track, and a box filled with guns and ammo. Some really nice revolvers and automatics, a lovely Browning nine-millimeter, and several boxes of spare ammo. I also learned he liked to read international thrillers by Robert Ludlum and Tom Clancy.

Tracy said it was his dream to someday visit Europe, drink at a café in Paris, and meet some relatives they had back in Italy.

In all, it was a nice little collection for Benny Barboza that told me a lot about who he'd been. But I found nothing connected to the missing paintings. Tracy wanted to go back through the boxes again. I assured her there was nothing here.

"Keep looking," I said. "You might find something at home. Maybe with your mother's things?"

"I doubt it," she said. "That son of a bitch. If he had it, where the hell did it go?"

"That's the sixty-million-dollar question," I said.

"Is that what that freakin' thing is worth?"

"To some."

"Holy Christ Almighty."

I crossed myself, left Tracy, and drove back to the city. I didn't have the paintings, but at least I had a working theory of who might've stolen them. As to the motive and where they went, I called Murphy. As the originator of the plan, I figured he knew a hell of a lot more than he'd told me. When he didn't pick up, I left a message.

I drove south on Route 1 through Chelsea and over the Mystic River. The rusty barges and big oil containers littered the riverfront. Just as I got to Charlestown, my phone rang with a Miami area code.

"Sam Spade," Epstein said. "How's that Falcon case coming along?"

"Besides learning the cheaper the crook, the gaudier the patter?"

"Yeah," he said. "Besides that."

"I spent two hours in Revere emptying out a storage unit," I said. "I didn't find a thing. It seemed to take even longer putting it all back how we found it."

"The glamorous life you lead."

"Did you guys ever look at a crew in Revere?" I said. "Benny Barboza, Eddie Ciccone, and one Mikey Mike."

"Mikey Mike?"

"I know," I said. "It was the nineties. Like Marky Mark. What can you do?"

"After we spoke, I did pull the files on the robbery," Epstein said. "You know I can't just make photocopies and FedEx them to you."

"But you can confirm or deny certain aspects of the case."

"I can't," Epstein said. "But I will."

"Do any of those names ring any bells?"

"Benny Barboza," he said. "Wasn't he murdered? In that feud with the guys in the North End? Sorry if I can't recall the

199

names. That's a lot of vowels for a simple Jewish boy like me to remember."

"Oy, vey."

"I do know Barboza was a key figure in a big racketeering case," he said. "That kind of went up in smoke when he got whacked. What was left went to the state police."

"I've spoken with the guy who claims he planned the heist," I said. "But he held back a lot of details."

"Devon Murphy."

"You know him?" I said.

"Do I sound like a schnook?" he said. "How could I be the special agent in charge of Boston and not know Devon Murphy?"

"Can I trust what he says?"

"Ha," Epstein said. "You can guarantee he knows a lot more than he's saying. Murphy is always in for Murphy. Maybe you should talk to the Staties who worked those North End killings? Lot of blood and cocaine back then. They might help you get a picture of who was canoodling with whom."

"Whom?" I said. "I'm impressed."

I pulled off by a hydrant, pulled out my notepad, and wrote down the name of a state cop who'd worked the killings. Epstein didn't have a phone number or even know if the guy was still with the Staties. I assured him I could track him down pretty easily.

"For a crime-busting Fed, you're not such a bad guy," I said.

"And for a hardboiled Boston snoop, I might say the same."

"But you won't."

"Get that painting back and we'll talk," he said. "In the meantime, why don't you get a new hobby?"

"I used to whittle wooden figures," I said. "I'd send you a work sample, but they were all incinerated."

"And now?"

"I like catching bad guys."

"Same," Epstein said.

We hung up and I kept on driving over to Cambridge to pick up Pearl. I could toss her some tennis balls while I waited for Devon Murphy to call me back. *Live your life, do your work, then take your hat.*

30

Murphy and I made arrangements to meet at the Ellisville Harbor State Park in Plymouth late that afternoon. I'd never been there, but it sounded like a nice enough spot. Murphy said they were dog-friendly and we could walk and talk at the same time. I conferred with Pearl about the plan and she agreed it sounded like the ideal spot to question a serial thief and liar. The running free on the sand would only be gravy.

"Eddie Ciccone, Benny Barboza, and Mikey Mike Marino," I said. I could recite it like running down a list of important saints.

"Very good," Devon Murphy said. "I'm impressed, Spenser."

"How come you wouldn't tell me straight off?"

"Have you met Crazy Eddie?"

"I've indeed had the displeasure."

"To put it mildly, he's the kind of guy

202

who'd have you kneecapped," he said. "Especially when he's in the joint and impotent to taking action."

"Being impotent against action is the downfall of many a man."

The park had a sprawling rocky beach. Not the kind of beach for the novice, but perfect for wildly adventurous types like Pearl and me. Pearl snuffled at a rotting fish under a tangle of black seaweed. She stood over it, digging at it with her front paws. She looked like a center about to long-snap a football. Far down the rocks, a cluster of shingle-roofed cottages clung to the hill, slightly obscured by a thin fog.

"Nice-looking dog," Murphy said. He was a head shorter than me and had a pronounced limp as he walked, the wind rifling through his thinning white hair. He was scruffy, with white stubble, and was dressed in a black T-shirt, khakis, and running shoes.

"German shorthaired pointer," I said. "Pearl Three."

"Three?" he said. "You've had three dogs with the same name?"

"I had the first Pearl when I was a kid," I said. "The second Pearl came to me from my girlfriend's ex-husband."

"And her name happened to be Pearl?"

"Pearl Two had a very long, silly-sounding

203

official name. We changed it immediately."

"And how long have you had this one?"

"About eight years," I said.

"And when something, you know, God forbid, happens to her?"

"There will be a Pearl Four," I said.

"That's a little nuts," Murphy said. "If you don't mind me saying."

I shrugged. Pearl trotted up, carrying a rotten fish in her mouth. She dropped it at my feet. I thanked her and patted her head and she raced away in a wide, arcing circle, looking for more tasty treats from the sea.

"Speaking of Gino Fish," I said. "How's he fit into this whole plan to rob the Winthrop?"

"At one time, he was involved," he said. "But he didn't have the juice to move the paintings."

"With DeMarco's crew?" I said. "Or later."

"DeMarco's," he said. "After they stole it, they didn't have a goddamn idea of what to do with the stuff. You can't just waltz into an auction and put up an El Greco or Goya. They were hoping for a little piece on the side. And if Gino Fish couldn't arrange it, nobody could."

Devon Murphy limped along at a nice little clip. I realized he wasn't making time for me, he just took me along on his daily walk. His breath was a little labored, and a fine sheen of sweat shone on his broad forehead. His face was ruddy against the white whiskers.

"And then what?" I said.

"You tell me."

"If I could tell you, I wouldn't be down here," I said. "Where did the painting go after the DeMarcos?"

"I can't tell you."

"It's no longer with the DeMarco crew."

"How do you know?"

"A local dealer is trying to put me in touch with the current seller," I said. "With two out of three men dead, I think it's safe to say the painting has moved down the line."

"You're talking about fucking Alan Garner," Murphy said, moving ahead, not looking up at me. "Gino's little boy toy? Watch yourself, buddy. I wouldn't trust that kid with nothing. This is way, way out of his league."

"What if I were to tell you he had the Picasso that got returned?"

"I'd say so fucking what," Murphy said. "That thing was sold off quick. It's small and not so famous."

Somewhere behind us, inland, thunder

made a low, rumbling sound. The rain intensified. Murphy looked up, shook his head, and made a "follow me" gesture with his hand. We walked back to where we'd parked our cars.

"That little sketch was the only thing that DeMarco's crew unloaded," he said. "They got like thirty grand for it. Nothing. I think Gino must've had it warehoused a long time ago. No telling when Garner swiped it from him."

Pearl was back with us now, trotting so close to me that I could easily rest my hand on her head. She was panting hard, tongue hanging loose and free from her jowls. I wished I'd brought a tennis ball. To Pearl, a tennis ball was a close second to a dead fish or duck.

"So who killed Benny Barboza?"

"Come on, man," he said. "Really? What are you trying to do here? Spoil my retirement?"

"Okay," I said. "How about why? Was it for the paintings?"

"Nope," he said.

"You sure?"

"It was all drug business."

"And so who ended up with the painting?"

Murphy stopped, his thin hair blowing

wild now. His Irish face was reddened and wind chapped. He shook his head. "No," he said. "I can't lead you there by the hand. And I'll tell you something: That's somewhere you don't want to go."

"I might disagree."

"If they find out you know, then you'll be dead."

"Others have tried it," I said. "Without much success."

"These guys will succeed," he said. "Try this one on for size. You think I know who has the paintings? Okay. Let's say you're right. Why wouldn't I try and get some of that reward money myself? I mean, you see the kind of car I drive. What a piece of shit. I could use a little cash infusion."

We were close to the parking lot and I unlocked my doors with my key chain. Pearl ran on ahead, soaked from head to claws and patiently waiting for me to let her into the backseat. Before we parted ways, Murphy stared right at me and tilted his head for emphasis.

"If I find out who killed Benny Barboza, would I be getting warm?"

"No," he said. "You'd be so hot, you might just burn your dick off."

"That's pretty warm," I said.

"Damn well better believe it," he said.

31

By the time Pearl and I returned to the Navy Yards, it was late. I poured her some fresh water and chow and set about to cook dinner. The night before, I'd prepped a beef tenderloin from Stillman's Farm with kosher salt and left it in the refrigerator. The tenderloin wouldn't take long. It was meant to be very pink in the center, not more than a hundred and fifty degrees inside. I set the oven to 425° and set out to make the sauce. The meat, rubbed by the hands of the Gods and blessed by holy men, would take care of itself.

I pulled out a large pan and melted a half-stick of butter over medium-low. I added in some chopped shallots with fresh rosemary, cracked pepper, and little cognac. I let everything cook down and added in a little cooking sherry and let the mix simmer. As I worked, I opened up a bottle of Bordeaux and set it aside. Then I cracked open a Sam

Adams to hydrate me while I made a summer salad with mixed greens, pears, walnuts, and goat cheese. Besides the sauce, hydration was key to the cooking.

Pearl had finished scarfing up her dinner and returned to the big leather sofa to rest. She'd had quite a day. I turned on the Sox game and let her watch the sixth inning.

I set the table for one and pulled out the roast. I placed it toward the center of my cooking island to let it rest without fear of Pearl. The sauce was nearly done and I turned down the heat.

I mixed a dressing of olive oil, vinegar, and lemon juice in a coffee mug and then checked on the roast. A few minutes left.

From my kitchen, I could see the sun setting across the moored boats. A large fishing boat was sliding up toward the dock, two men on the bow. One jumped off and the other tossed him the line, tying up for the evening. There was a little bit of wind and the boats rocked softly but strongly tethered to the docks.

I drank some wine. I watched the Sox. The room smelled pleasantly of roast and the sweetness of the sauce.

I ate dinner, did the dishes, and finished the ball game.

After walking Pearl for the evening, I

returned to my kitchen table and poured a third glass of wine. I'd checked out a book from the library on El Greco but over the last few days had little chance to look beyond the cover. As Pearl snuffled and snored, legs sticking straight up at the ceiling, I looked through the big, bold images of Christ, the Virgin Mary, many Saints and noble Spaniards. St. Francis and the stigmata. The view of his beloved Toledo on the hill. I found out he was born in 1541 in Crete and died in 1614 in Spain. In between, he lived and trained in Venice and Rome, in post-Byzantine art and something called mannerism. Being a master detective, I then read that mannerism was about the askew proportions Locke had told me about. Stylized poses and lack of clear perspective.

To understand the lack of clear perspective better, I drank some more wine. Pearl snored as I flipped through the pages.

I read that when El Greco first saw the Sistine Chapel, he wasn't impressed. He told the pope that Michelangelo was a good man but didn't know how to paint. He offered to redo the job himself. Soon El Greco became persona non grata in Rome and was being called a foolish foreigner. He packed his bags for Toledo, Spain, where he developed his own style and technique.

Maybe that's what I needed. A fresh perspective. As Toledo — either Spain or Ohio — was out of the question, I considered some local options. I was studying *Assumption of the Virgin* when my cell phone buzzed.

"Spenser," I said. "Master of off-center perspectives."

"We need to talk."

"Everyone wants to talk to me," I said. "I'm a popular guy."

"It's Garner," he said. "There's something you need to see."

I looked at my watch. It was past midnight.

"Now?" I said.

"This can't wait until morning," he said. "Can we meet at my gallery?"

"It's past midnight," I said. "I'm stuffed with a beef tenderloin and nearly a bottle of red wine. I plan on finishing the bottle. How about a hint?"

"Either you come," he said, "or I'll call that fellow Paul Marston. Nice guy for a Brit. I don't think he'd have an issue rolling out of bed on a moment's notice if it's a chance to see *The Gentleman in Black*."

"Yikes," I said. "Is that what you're offering?"

"I am," he said. "The seller is very interested in coming to terms with the museum. Since you and I have a so-called shared history, and I know you'll do as you say, I'm giving you first dibs."

"That's awfully nice of you," I said. "What's the seller want?"

"No deal yet," he said. "That will have to be orchestrated. But the museum will want proof of life, and I'm here to provide it."

"Tonight?" I said. "As in right now?"

"I thought the private-detective motto was 'We never sleep.' "

"That's the Pinkertons," I said. "I have a different motto."

"And what's that?"

"Coffee before justice."

"Well, then," Garner said. "I'll put on a pot. I'll pour you a mug before we take off."

"I thought the painting was at the gallery?"

"Think of me what you will, Spenser," he said. "But I'm not stupid. We have a nice little drive ahead of us."

"If I'd known we were taking a road trip, I'd have made a mix tape," I said. "Do you like Chet Baker and Gerry Mulligan?"

"Never heard of them," he said. "Hurry up, Spenser. Everyone is nervous about this. Plans change every hour or so."

32

Finding an open parking slot on Newbury Street was much easier at nearly one a.m. I found a spot at the corner of Gloucester and walked across the empty thoroughfare. A light was on in the corner of the ivy-covered building, and I called Garner back to buzz me in.

He greeted me on the stoop with a full coffee mug.

Garner didn't look as if he'd been rousted from his sleep. His longish blond hair was perfectly styled. He had on a pair of skinny black pants, pegged at the bottom with shiny patent leather boots, and some type of lightweight khaki jacket over a designer T-shirt. The T-shirt probably cost more than everything I had on. I was more a Levi's-and-Hanes kind of guy.

"Do you want me to put it in a travel mug?"

"I'll take my chances," I said. "Where are

we going?"

"Ah," he said. He smiled big and held up a finger. "I don't think so."

"You're concerned about the interior of my car," I said. "Or you're driving?"

"I'm driving," he said. "You can leave your vehicle here. You can't know where I'll be taking you."

"I am a trained detective," I said. "I might spot a few things on the way."

"No," he said. "You won't."

He reached into his jacket and pulled out a long strip of black material. I watched him with amazement when he showed the blind-fold.

"Do you plan to shoot a cigarette out of the corner of my mouth?" I said. "Because if not, I'm not wearing it."

"We have strict instructions on how you are to view the work."

"And I have strict instructions on watching my own ass."

"Oh, please," he said. "You'll be completely safe with me."

"I don't know where we are going," I said. "Or who we are meeting. Or how long it'll take us to get to wherever we're going. What could possibly go wrong?"

"Be that as it may."

"I wouldn't let you blindfold me if you

were a French maid wanting to swat me with a feather duster."

"No blindfold."

I drank some coffee. "Not a chance."

"I'll have to speak to my people."

I made an offhand gesture and took a seat by the window. I heard him walk into another room and convey my request. He agreed to a few things and then came back into the room.

"We have a van."

"Good for you."

"It's a large van," he said. "Used to transport paintings. You'll have to sit in the back until we arrive at the location, and again on the way back to the gallery."

"You're making this tough, Alan."

"It will only be you and me."

"So you say."

"I give you my word," he said. "No one will interfere with the viewing of the El Greco. You can keep that gun on your hip. And the one you probably have strapped on your ankle."

"How about the Ka-Bar I often hold in my teeth?"

"Fine," Garner said. He rolled his eyes. "Whatever you like. But we really must be going. We have a limited window here and we don't want anyone to change their mind.

This wasn't easy to set up. Some very, very nervous sellers here."

"How far?" I said.

"A little more than an hour."

I nodded. I finished off half the coffee and set down the mug on a wooden table. Garner picked up the mug and wiped away the slight wetness where it had been.

"We don't have much time," he said. "This is a very rare opportunity. The Winthrop misses out on this and I fear the painting will be gone forever."

"Forever?"

"There are other buyers," he said. "And let's just say they don't reside close to this area code."

Against my better judgment, and about any other sane person's, I crawled into the back of a black Mercedes cargo van. He seemed amused watching me take a seat on a wheel well and look for a place to hold on.

"And I'll need your phone."

"Why?"

"You'd be able to track every turn," he said. "You could follow the van by map."

I hesitatingly handed over my phone and he shut both doors. The car started and we moved off. A divider separated the cargo area from the driver and passenger seats. I felt like I was a prisoner being transported. But unlike a prisoner, I wasn't shackled and I carried two guns, as Garner suspected.

The guns boosted my confidence a great deal.

However, I did not have Hawk, or Z, to follow the van to wherever the hell we were going. I had thought about calling Vinnie, but calling Vinnie to watch my back with Alan Garner would've been a laughable offense. Besides, I didn't want to involve Vinnie unless I absolutely had to. I knew I'd pushed him about as far as I could against competitors in his same line of work. It was bad for business.

I had a light in the back of the van but no windows. I had no phone. About the only thing I could do on the long ride was to count bullets in my gun. So I counted the bullets in my gun. I counted the extra bullets in my pocket. I whistled "They Can't Take That Away from Me." I planned out what I would do if Garner opened the doors to a surprise.

But I had little reason to think Garner would double-cross me or wanted to see me harmed. I wanted to find the painting. Garner wanted money. And the person who held the painting wanted a reward. It was in everyone's best interest that this plan worked out. All one big, happy family.

The ride seemed to last for much longer than an hour, but according to my watch took somewhere right over fifty minutes. My legs ached and my backside was sore. Finally, Garner pulled to a stop and killed the engine.

It was two-ten in the morning.

I had my .38 in hand. If there was a surprise party waiting, I'd take a few with me.

The doors broke open, and bright light flooded into the van. Garner seemed to be alone. He waved for me to get out. We were in some type of big indoor loading bay. I followed Garner up a concrete ramp to two large doors. As he punched in a passcode, I looked around the loading bay. Gray, industrial brick walls. Four large rolling bay doors. One door was open where we entered, but I couldn't see far into the dark. I looked around for any signage that might tell me where I was, but I saw nothing.

I followed Garner into a long, broad hallway to an industrial elevator. The lights above were bright and fluorescent, the floors smooth concrete. A map on a far wall noted directions to different blocks of units. We were in some kind of storage warehouse. But I still didn't see a name or any indication of where we were.

"Quit looking," Garner said. "We could be anywhere."

"I have the tracking skills of a blood-hound."

"Good for you," he said. "Even if you know where we are, the art will be in a different location tomorrow. This is just a viewing area."

I looked at him as the elevator doors pulled open. He turned to the right on the fifth floor of the facility. Given that there were about five hundred thousand similar places outside Boston, we could be absolutely anywhere. It was cold and metallic-smelling. The fluorescent lights buzzed overhead as we walked, turning a few times to arrive at the storage unit.

"I was in a place just like this earlier today," I said. "Never knew I was such a good packer."

Garner didn't answer me. He turned the key in the padlock and pushed up the rolling door. The ceiling was wire mesh, and I could see most of the space in the unit was wide open. There was a folding table set up in the center of the unit. One folding chair and several boxes off to one corner. Garner pulled out a big section of what looked to

219

be poster board with several clamps on each corner.

He set the boards down on the folding table and began to unsnap the clamps, finally pulling the top layer of the boards off and revealing a painting.

The light wasn't the best in the unit, but I recognized the face. It wasn't Benny Ricardo. It was Juan de Silva y Ribera, third marquis of Montemayor and the warden of the Alcazar of Toledo. *The Gentleman in Black.*

"Holy moly," I said.

"Is this what you've been looking for?"

"Indeed."

He carefully turned the painting so I might see El Greco's scrawl on the back. The signature was all Greek to me. "I'll give you some paint chips for the Winthrop to verify," he said. "But my client wants a response within twenty-four hours."

"You still haven't told me what they want."

"Ten million," he said. "No questions asked."

"That won't be easy."

"The good things in life seldom are," he said. "Have you seen enough?"

I looked at the El Greco again. I touched the frayed edges of where it had been cut from the painting. It was very worn and cracked. The eyes of Juan de Silva y Ribera stared right at me from across the centuries.

I nodded and we drove back to Boston.

33

"You had a gun," Locke said. "Why not just turn it on Garner and take the painting?"

"He gave me his word," I said. "And I gave him mine. I've known Garner for a long time and he trusts me. Besides, my loyalty to the Winthrop board has withered a bit in the last few days."

"I heard what they did," he said. "I can't say I'm surprised."

Locke was living out his last weeks on the fifteenth floor of a high-rise apartment in the West End, right around the corner from the Whole Foods. The apartment was spare, with a smattering of corporate furniture and no pictures on the walls. I had the feeling he'd only recently rented it. A nurse had opened the door when I arrived and helped Locke take a seat on a sectional sofa with large plump cushions.

I walked over to the window as he got comfortable. If you looked straight down, you could see a pool and women sunbathing.

"Nice view," Locke said.

"You can see the river, too."

"You can?" Locke said. "I'll be damned."

I turned to look at him. "I've seen the painting, Locke."

His weathered face lit up. He asked his caregiver if she might bring us some whiskey. I wasn't sure if that was ethical or not, or if it even mattered a damn when you were dying. Either way, the woman went to the kitchen and poured out a couple bourbons over ice. We drank from short glasses.

"Was he wonderful?" Locke said. *The Gentleman.*"

"It was odd," I said. "He seemed to look right at me."

"The great ones always do," he said. "Their eyes implore us."

"Maybe," I said. "I think he just wanted out of that crummy storage room."

"Was the painting still in good shape?" he said.

"As far as I could tell," I said. "You could definitely see the edges were frayed where it'd been cut from the frame. But the painting itself, despite some cracking, looked intact."

"And they gave you paint chips?"

223

I patted my shirt pocket, where I kept the small plastic bag.

"Good," he said. "You must turn them over to the museum immediately. And make sure this painting is authentic."

"That's something I wanted to talk to you about," I said. "The Feds said there was some concern the original might not be real?"

Locke took a sip and nodded. "That's true," he said. "But they may not have understood the context. There was an American scholar in the 1950s who claims *The Gentleman in Black* wasn't painted by El Greco but instead by a protégé. He said he'd unearthed paperwork in Madrid that showed the original commission. This was mentioned in some work of scholarship, but neither I nor anyone else at the Winthrop have ever been able to substantiate this. Even if the painting came from El Greco's studio during his lifetime, it's still a singular piece of art."

"I see," I said.

"Have you ever seen *F for Fake*?" he said. "The Welles picture?"

"Not in a long time."

"It brings into question if a work is still important if it's a fraud," he said. "There was one man who painted Picasso as well as

Picasso himself. So well, in fact, that Picasso once verified the forger's work as his own."

"Not my job," I said. "I'm only a facilitator."

"Let the museum and the scholars sort out the lineage," he said. "But you must go immediately to Marjorie Ward Phillips right now and tell her what you've seen."

"She fired me," I said. "If I turn this over, they'll count me out. I don't care for Marj, but I do like money."

"Since you hold the keys, so to speak, you are now in charge."

I shrugged and took a seat in a plump chair across from Locke. I hadn't slept a bit since seeing the painting. All I'd accomplished that morning was going for a short run along the waterfront while I'd waited to hear back from Locke. I made it three miles and then headed straight over. I was still dressed in running shorts and shoes, a navy sweatshirt with the arms and collar cut out.

"Maybe I should change first," I said. "Marj is all about appearances."

"Do you care?"

"Not in the least," I said.

"However, I would recommend you getting some protection."

"I keep a .357 in my desk drawer," I said. "That'd be enough to stop a water buffalo or a person of similar build."

"I was thinking more of a lawyer."

"I know a few."

"Pick the toughest one you know," he said. "And make sure he gets the arrangement in writing."

"I'll make sure she does."

"The Winthrop board tried to fire me several times," he said. "Topper Townsend accused me of padding my expense account even though I always flew coach and stayed at quite modest hotels."

"I don't think Topper could spell *modest.*"

Locke smiled. "Was there any mention of the Goya?"

I shook my head.

"That's a shame," he said. "It's a wonderful piece painted during his dark period. Witches and blood. Skulls and bones. It was a meditation on the occult and of our own mortality."

I nodded. I played with the ball cap in my hands. "How are you doing?"

"I am sitting down and having a cocktail before noon," he said. "It's a fine day. I wish I'd been more aware of them in the past."

"Any words for Marj or Topper?"

"As a veteran investigator and friend of the arts?"

"Sure."

Locke nodded. He had to use both hands to put the glass to his lips. He took a sip and returned the glass to his lap. "Yes," he said. "Don't fuck this up."

34

At four o'clock that afternoon, Rita Fiore took a seat at the edge of my desk and looked around my modest office. I sat in my office chair, fresh and ready for the meet, in khakis, a white linen button-down, and wing tips without socks. As a gift, she'd returned my .40-caliber Smith & Wesson without explanation.

"Just what do you want out of this?" Rita said.

"I want to be paid for my time."

"And the reward?"

"A former employee of Winthrop has a steep medical bill," I said. "His name is Locke and his expenses should be paid in full."

"That's it?" she said. "There's a thin line between nobility and being stupid."

"The reward was never going to be mine," I said. "That money will pay for the return of the painting. It may be more than they can raise."

"Those kind of people?" she said. "I doubt it. They can raise twice that much in one night. One of those fund-raisers with cheese and crackers and smooth jazz."

"Make sure we won't attend."

Rita swung her bare legs back and forth, gently kicking at the side of my desk. "Done."

Twenty minutes later, Topper and Marjorie Ward Phillips wandered inside. Marjorie had on a gray blazer with a white silk top and black pants. Topper looked as if he'd just escaped from a backwoods campsite, with a loose red shirt, khaki cargo shorts, and hiking boots. He had gray socks pulled to his skinny knees. As always, he carried the cane.

"This better be something good, Spenser," Topper said. No hello, no greetings. "I was on a family vacation. Today is my anniversary."

"My condolences to your wife," I said.

Rita snorted. Topper did not smile.

I introduced her as my attorney. Marj and Topper shook hands with Rita and took a seat, and a second later Paul Marston sauntered in. I began to doubt my detection skills. I hadn't smelled him coming. He was suited, well coiffed, and more full of himself than ever. He smirked while standing at attention.

"Nope," I said.

"Excuse me?" Topper said.

"Not him," I said. "This is a private conversation."

"Anything that needs to be said about museum business can be said in front of him," Marj said.

"You're welcome to whisper into his ear later," I said. "In the meantime, he can go sing 'Chim Chim Cher-ee' down on Berkeley Street."

Topper used the silver-topped cane to stand. "If that is all."

"Sit down, Slick," Rita said. "And get rid of Dapper Dan. Unless you don't want to get back your painting."

Topper and Marj exchanged glances. Marj inhaled a deep breath and let it out with a lot of force. Topper's face brightened and proceeded to engage me in some kind of staring contest. I willed my hands not to quiver from fear.

"I don't care for games," Topper said.

I didn't say anything. I looked over at Rita, still sitting on the edge of my desk, and smiled. She didn't show a bit of emotion.

"Paul," Marj said. "Would you mind leaving us alone for a moment?"

"Actually —" Paul said.

"Paul," Marj said, actually being Large Marj now. As she spoke, the windows behind me vibrated a bit.

Marston left but didn't shut the door. We sat looking at each other as I heard him walking down the hall. After a minute, I stood and spotted him down on Berkeley Street. He didn't seem to be singing or dancing. I was in no way disappointed.

"Spenser has seen your painting," Rita said.

Marj lifted her head and wet her lips. Topper leaned onto his cane from where he sat.

"When?" Marj said.

"Last night," I said. "They're ready to make an exchange."

"Which one?"

The Gentleman in Black," I said. "Don't ask me where because I don't know other than it was an hour away. Or it took an hour to get there. But it appears to be intact and in decent shape."

"How on earth would you know?" Topper said. "How would you even know what you saw was genuine?"

"I don't," I said. "But I do have this."

I tossed the paint chips in a Ziploc bag onto the desk. Marj scooped them up, examining them, and then passed them along to Topper. I was pretty sure his circular Harry Potter glasses started to fog from the excitement.

"Good Lord," he said. "Who has it?"

"I'm not really sure," I said.

"How can you not know if they showed you the goddamn painting?" Topper said.

"Why don't you take out the chips and taste them," I said. "You being a man of the arts."

"Ridiculous," he said. "You have to tell us everything you know and everything that happened. You are under a legal obligation."

Rita coughed into her hand.

"Do you have a problem with that?" Topper said.

"In case you don't know, Mr. Spenser was fired," Marj said. "As former contract labor for the Winthrop, we are entitled —"

"Lady," Rita said. "You are entitled to jack shit. Spenser is offering you those pieces as possible verification of the missing painting. If they turn out to be fake, then no one is out anything. But if they do turn out to belong to the El Greco, you and I need to come to some kind of terms."

"I don't believe I've ever heard your name?" Topper said.

"Ever heard of Cone, Oakes?"

"Of course," he said.

"I'm a partner," she said. "Ask your friends. Or at least their wives."

I stood up and stretched. I leaned against the windowsill and crossed my arms.

"They want ten million," I said. "No questions, no Feds, no fuss. They guarantee it."

Being good at harrumphing, he gave it the old college try. It didn't have much weight to it. Rita and I had their full attention. I turned back to look out the window but didn't see Marston.

"We will need current photographs," she said. "And we will need to examine the painting before a dime is turned over."

I shrugged. "I'll let them know."

"But if you think you're going to get any of the reward, think again," Topper said. "You are just a bearer of information, Spenser. It's those who hold the painting who will get the money."

"I didn't figure you'd have it any other way."

Rita reached down and patted Topper's shoulder. She smiled at him the way a pit viper looks at a cornered rat. "You will pay Spenser for all his expenses," she said. "Plus a bonus."

"What kind of bonus?"

"I'm not sure," she said. "But I'll think up a good one."

"All this is very speculative," Topper said. "I will insist that any exchange be handled by our security consultant, Mr. Marston. We appreciate the work here, Spenser, but you weren't asked to be involved. In fact, your involvement complicates matters."

"By helping you get the painting back?" I said. "Sorry to inconvenience you."

Marj shot Topper a look. She nodded with the slow realization that the painting could be close at hand. Looking up at me and no one else, she said, "You will get everything you need."

"Marj," Topper said.

"Oh, shut up, Topper," she said.

"Yeah, Topper," Rita said. "Pipe down."

I smiled.

"This is everything," Marj said. "I hope you know that. Returning the El Greco to its rightful place in the museum means so much to not only patrons of the Winthrop but to the greater art world. Filling that void is immeasurable."

"I'm not doing it for the greater good," I said. "I'm doing it for Locke."

"Oh," Rita said. "We also want all his medical bills paid."

Topper rolled his eyes. "This just gets richer and richer."

All three of us turned to Topper to make

sure he shut his mouth. He tried his best to grimace and sputter. Finally, not being able to handle it, he said, "The board won't be shook down. This isn't some back-alley deal. And we are not your common hoodlums."

"No," I said. "You are hoodlums with funny accents and bony knees. Miss Fiore will make sure the details are put into writing. Then I'll reach out to the broker."

"See," Topper said. "See. He doesn't even know who has the painting. If it exists at all."

"Check out the chips," I said, looking at Marj. "And then call me."

"You and Locke," he said. "The painting and Locke. This doesn't have a thing to do with Locke, and I'll make sure that's a completely separate conversation. His medical issues are none of our concern."

I walked back toward my desk, resting one hand on the edge, standing shoulder to shoulder with Rita. I nodded at Topper. "Why exactly do you carry that cane?"

"If you must know, I have a handicap," he said. "I was badly injured in college playing field hockey."

"Mister," I said. "You don't know what handicapped is if you try and screw Locke."

Rita looked at me, pursed her lips, and grinned. "It's hard to walk with a silver-tipped cane stuck up your ass."

Topper clenched his jaws, muscles flexing in his face. Marj stood up to leave. She placed the plastic bag into her purse and offered her hand. I shook it, and then Rita did. Topper had already gotten up and disappeared down the hall without a word.

After Large Marj left, Rita turned to me and smiled. "Wonderful people," she said.

"Delightful," I said. "Boston's elite."

35

I called Alan Garner on his cell and left a message.

Being one who disliked sitting on his hands, I drove over to the Harbor Health Club to perform a more useful action. I could shower and shave there, and I kept a spare change of clothes in a locker. As I loaded a squat rack, I whistled "Blue Skies" and waved over at Henry, who was training a young couple. He pretended not to know me.

The sun was shining. I'd nearly wrapped up my case. Rita would make sure there was money ahead. As I squatted, I smiled, taking each rep to its proper depth and watching my form in the mirror. I continued to whistle until I spotted Henry's diminutive reflection behind me.

"You finally gone nuts?" he said. "What are you, a freakin' dwarf? Whistling while you work. This is a gym, Spenser. If you're whistling, you're not working hard enough."

"I'm going to pretend you didn't make a joke about little people," I said. "You also look like you could use a hug."

"Try it and I'll knock you flat on your keister," he said. "But I will join you. I've been training people all morning and haven't done crap for myself."

"Train with me and you'll be normal size in no time," I said.

Henry told me to go have sex with myself, only arranged in a more proper Boston syntax.

We did a set of lunges with barbells in each hand. I did a set with double the weight, but Henry's form was impeccable. You could have put a teacup on his head and it wouldn't have spilled. From lunges, we moved on to the incline bench press. Again, Henry used less weight, but his control and execution were nearly effortless. He breathed in and out as if second nature, working the bar off his chest as if was a natural extension. He helped me load the bar and rerack the weights. Not reracking was the cardinal sin in the Harbor Health Club. I saw a guy once walk away from a fully loaded squat rack and attempt to leave the gym. Henry reduced the man to tears.

One also never sat on exercise equipment. You did a set and you wiped it down and cleared the way for someone else. If you didn't know it already, he had a list of the Ten Cimoli Commandments on the wall. It had been hand-painted sometime back in the sixties and not a one had changed. My favorite might have been the first commandment: *Don't be a Putz.*

"You mind me asking why you're in such a great mood?" he said.

"I have solved the unsolvable," I said. "And I'm about to be handsomely paid for my work."

"Well goody-goody for you, Sherlock," he said. "Maybe you can buy a new sweatshirt that hasn't been cut to pieces. You know they have improved workout gear in the last twenty years."

"Not everyone can make satin look so good."

"No shit," he said. "Now get out of the way and let me work."

Henry hopped up and caught the chin-up bar like an orangutan in the wild. He cranked out a set of ten without a bit of strain. I did the same amount of reps but with slightly more strain. Of course, I had an extra hundred pounds on him.

"Hawk called," he said. "Won't be back

239

for another month."

"Does he need anything from us?"

"Does he ever?" he said. "Probably up to his ears in warm bodies and cold caipirinhas. We may never get him back."

We alternated on the chin-up bar for three sets and then turned our attention to some shoulder presses. Henry loved to show off a slight rotation he made on the extension, starting off with his knuckles inward to his shoulders. We worked the shoulders into a triple set with straight bar curls and press-downs with a cable rope.

As we went well past five o'clock, the gym began to swell with young professionals and the gym's afternoon regulars. Being an early-morning guy, I didn't know many of them. As I cooled down on the treadmill, Henry wandered off for his second shift meet and greet.

I watched ESPN as I jogged, catching up with the day's games. The Sox were on the road and on a hot streak. I was sure the day couldn't get any better, until I flipped back to the local news. I spotted Channel 7's Hank Phillippi Ryan working a live shot from a crime scene. I didn't have earphones and could only read the crawl below Hank. There had been a body found somewhere in the Back Bay. Being Boston, a murder wasn't unusual, although the neighborhood was outside the norm. It looked like Hank was doing a standup somewhere on Newbury Street.

I continued to jog, glancing down at the screen. The live shot zoomed in over her shoulder and showed an ivy-covered brick building at the corner of Gloucester and Newbury. Haut de Gamme.

I pressed the emergency stop on the treadmill and caught my breath.

On the screen, a smiling photograph of the victim.

It was Alan Garner.

36

I watched from behind the crime scene tape as Frank Belson emerged from Haut de Gamme. He pulled off some latex gloves and stuck them in the side pocket of his black blazer. He stood on the stoop, talking with a tall woman with blond boy-short hair as he lit the end of a cigar. The woman waved away the smoke as she turned and pointed in my direction.

I waved at the woman, Captain Glass, the new head of Homicide for BPD. She glowered at me and turned her back. Belson walked down the steps and approached the line guarded by several uniform cops. This block of Newbury had been shut down. Lots of flashing blue lights, cop cars, and a gray van from the coroner's office.

"Heard you wanted to see me?" Belson said.

"I've been working with Alan Garner."

"We know," he said. "Spoke to Garner's

assistant. She's pretty busted up, but still with it enough to list you as a suspicious character."

"I'm honored."

"Can you imagine paying fifty grand for a fucking painting?" Belson said, spewing blue smoke from the side of his mouth. "If I had that kind of dough, I'd patch my damn roof before winter. You people in the Back Bay."

"I moved," I said. "Remember?"

"What's your connection to the deceased?" Belson said. He pulled a notebook from inside his coat. He had on a blue shirt under the coat, tie askew as always. No matter how he was dressed, he always looked like an unmade bed.

"I was in the market for a high-end painting," I said. "I thought it would really spruce up my new condo."

"Bullshit," he said. "Garner used to work for Fish, and anything that smells of Gino Fish is rotten. Besides, I spoke to Quirk. He told me you were working with folks at the Winthrop about the missing paintings."

"Are there no secrets in this town?"

"Not many," he said. "You think Garner is tied in with the Winthrop job?"

"You mind if I cross the tape?" I said. "In the spirit of shamus-police cooperation."

He nodded to a black woman in uniform.

She lifted the tape and I stepped under it. I felt like I'd been ushered beyond the velvet rope of an exclusive club. Behind Belson, two men from the coroner's office wheeled out Garner's body. It was zipped up in a black bag. The men wore black and did their job quickly and effectively. After the van's doors were snapped shut, Belson turned to me.

"How'd he die?"

Belson held the cigar in his teeth. "Badly."

"I thought you were going to say blunt-force trauma."

"Nope," he said. "I save that shit for the press. But between me, you, and the call box, he was shot."

"What type of gun?"

"A good one," he said. "He's fucking dead. Now what the hell does a fancy-schmancy guy like Garner have to do with those paintings and Benny Barboza?"

"Ah," I said. "You are up to speed. Sounds like you know everything."

"You can talk to me or Captain Glass," he said. "You talk to me and we can do it right here. You talk to Glass and you'll be up all damn night at headquarters. You'll get worn out. You'll miss dinner. I know how you get when you miss a meal."

I smiled at Belson. We had a long history.

"Garner was the go-between for the Picasso sketch," I said. "It was supposed to be a one-time deal. But he may have known something about the Big Guy."

"The Spanish thing?"

"Yeah," I said. "The big Spanish thing. *The Gentleman in Black.* You did know it was priceless?"

"In my world, everything has a price," he said. We watched the squad cars part and the coroner van drive off slow on Newbury. "Guess Garner knows it now, too."

"Who found him?" I said.

"Boyfriend," he said. "Lee Farrell is inside talking to him now. EMTs gave him some meds to calm down. Guy wouldn't stop screaming, shaking like a freakin' leaf."

"What did he say?"

"Nothing," Belson said. "Farrell doesn't think the guy was involved in Garner's business. I'm sure you'll take a shot at him, too. But if Farrell thinks it's a waste, it's a waste. What I want to know is, who was Garner fronting for?"

"Well," I said. "It wasn't Gino Fish."

"No shit," he said. "C'mon, Spenser. Cooperation isn't a two-way street. Between us, it's the shit street where we both live."

"I don't know where Garner got the sketch," I said. "And I don't know who, or

245

if, he was working with someone else."

"Okay," Belson said. "What the hell do you know?"

"I know that you know, that I'll go where you go."

"Christ." Belson tilted his head back to look at the sky. He pulled the cigar from his mouth and exhaled a big blue cloud. It was very pretty in the glow of streetlamps. Several onlookers had gathered along Gloucester. The television news crew had set up tripods and lights. A spokesperson was talking to a gaggle of them.

"You want to talk to Glass?" Belson said. "Because if you're holding out anything, it's gonna ricochet like a balloon loaded with dog shit all over yours truly."

"Lovely image," I said, pointing at his pen tapping on an empty notebook page. Belson nodded. As I spoke, he began to scribble. He smoked and looked me in the eye as he wrote. Belson was a man of true talent. I ran down all the events from the meet with Large Marj in the Common, on to the Four Seasons bag check, and then our conversation at the gallery where we stood.

"What did he tell you about the Big Guy?"

"That he could arrange a deal for the museum," I said.

"You think he was bluffing?"

"I think he had the inside track on some-thing."

"What?"

I shrugged.

"He couldn't have been lying to you," Belson said. "Garner being such a fine upstanding dealer on Newbury Street. I will forget that he used to shack up with one of the biggest goddamn crooks this city has ever known."

"So jaded, Frank," I said. "How'd you get that way?"

I watched as Captain Glass spoke to a couple plainclothes cops and made her way over to us. Her hair was wet, slicked back to her skull, as if she'd just taken a shower before getting to the scene. She placed her hands on her hips and looked me up and down. She had on no makeup, her face looking freshly scrubbed.

"What's he have to say for himself?" Glass said.

"For a middle-aged snoop, I'm in pretty damn good shape," I said. "Just the other day I maxed out with more than three hundred and fifty on the bench press. I am a terrific cook and an above-average dancer."

"Get Spenser's head examined," Glass said. "If he's just seen what we'd seen, he

247

wouldn't be so goddamn glib."

"He's seen it," Belson said. "Lots of times."

"I told Frank what I know," I said. "I came across Garner while looking into the Winthrop heist."

"Gee," she said. "Maybe it's unrelated. Especially in such a high-crime neighborhood. Where were you earlier this afternoon?"

"Doing squats with Henry Cimoli at the Harbor Health Club," I said.

"Headquarters," Glass said. "No free rides, not on something like this. We'll take you there. Right now, I have to go feed the fucking vultures."

She nodded toward the gaggle of news reporters gathered at the street corner. She smoothed down the slight wrinkles in her pinstriped jacket and trousers, her tan silk shirt open at the collar, showing just a thin silver chain.

"Garner told Spenser he could make a deal for that big Spanish painting," Belson said.

"Where is it?"

"East is east," I said. "And west is west. And never the twain shall meet."

"Shit." Glass gave me a hard look and

then shook her head. "I guess we'll just have to see about that."

37

I was so taken aback by Captain Glass's tongue-lashing the night before, I got up at six a.m. and drove straight to Mystic, Connecticut. I was set to meet with the two retired Staties who'd worked the Benny Barboza homicide and its larger implications with organized crime. Will Zimmer and I had agreed to meet at the Mystic train station coffee shop. He said his old partner Rich Roebuck, who lived in nearby New London, might join us.

Like most cops I knew, Zimmer was early. He was seated inside the small wood-frame station that, besides selling tickets, sold coffee, T-shirts, and coffee mugs. He was an average-sized guy with close-cropped white hair and a stubbly white beard, wearing faded blue jeans and one of those ventilated fishing shirts. He had a deep tan and a lot of lines in his face.

We shook hands and sat in a private-looking grouping overlooking the loading platform.

"Benny Barboza," Zimmer said. "Now, that brings back memories of the old Hit Parade."

"Epstein said you guys took over the investigation."

"Well," he said. "*Took over* may be too strong a word. We'd been investigating Jimmy Morelli and his crew for a long while. Everyone knew who did it. We just tried to bring it into a larger case involving the war between Jimmy and the Old Man."

"How far did you guys get?"

"Rich should be here in a second," Zimmer said. "He stayed on a few years after me. But he'll tell you the one big disappointment in our careers was not locking down that crew. The Barboza hit was nasty business. It was a personal FU to the Old Man, who really loved Benny. I think he loved Barboza more than his own kid."

"I know Jackie DeMarco," I said. "Can you blame his old man?"

"What a cheeseball," he said. "Jackie was a kid when we were watching his father. He was on some kind of baseball scholarship up in Blackburn. I gotta admit, the kid had a hell of an arm."

"He washed out after a year," I said. "And

then took over the family business."

"Running tow trucks?"

"Yep," I said. "Also got involved with some crooked judges a little while back. He was funding some private prisons for teens."

"Nice family," Zimmer said.

"Salt of the earth."

"Did you ever think the hit was about more than just cocaine?"

"Nope," Zimmer said. "What else was there? I can't quite put into words, Spenser, how much cocaine we were talking. They trucked it up from Florida. They had a hell of a network."

"Jackie still does business down in Tampa, St. Pete," I said.

"So did Jimmy Morelli," he said. "He had a nice house out on Davis Islands. We were down there a lot working with FDLE, trying to shut down his middleman. Had some luck there, but not so much. I can't go too much into the past, but I'll say that the De-Marcos wouldn't have cried a river of tears if their competition got shut down."

"Did Barboza talk with you?"

Zimmer looked at me and smiled. He picked up a thick coffee mug stamped with the Amtrak logo and smiled. "Let me get you a cup of joe," he said. "I think I see Rich pulling up."

I stayed put as Zimmer headed over to the counter. Another man, this guy a little rounder than Zimmer, walked inside and nodded at him. He was bald and red-faced, with a white Vandyke beard. Zimmer pointed at me and the man moved in my direction. Rich Roebuck had on khakis and a white T-shirt under a short-sleeved blue shirt worn like a loose jacket. Despite the loose jacket, I could tell he still carried a gun.

"Spenser?"

I nodded. We shook hands. We talked for a bit, until Zimmer joined us with fresh coffee and a muffin for his old partner. We discussed our mutual pals, Captain Healy and Brian Lundquist. As Roebuck ate, I developed a case of muffin envy.

"You mind us asking why you're looking into a twenty-year-old homicide?" Zimmer said. He handed me my coffee. "Not that we mind. It's just few people beyond the family gave a crap for Benny the Blade. He wasn't exactly a beloved member of society."

"I'm not interested in the murder," I said. "Merely how it might connect to the theft at the Winthrop Museum. Two paintings and a Picasso sketch were taken about a year before he died."

Zimmer nodded. Roebuck remained impassive.

"Sure, I remember that," Zimmer said. "It was a big deal. But they got the paintings back, right? Last week, some big dog-and-pony show in the Common?"

"Only the sketch," I said. "I'm still looking for the paintings."

"And you think Benny the Blade might've socked one away?" Roebuck said.

"Maybe," I said. "Maybe not. I can assure you it wasn't kept in his family storage unit in Revere. But I did find some pristine copies of Limp Bizkit's greatest hits. I was hoping you two had heard something about it."

"Drugs," Zimmer said. "Lots of coke and broads. The only thing artsy these guys did was the weekend matinee at the Purple Banana."

"Did you ever speak with Eddie Ciccone?"

Roebuck lifted his eyes. He exchanged a glance with Zimmer. He'd yet to touch his coffee. At the counter, my corn muffins looked forlorn. I'd wait until I'd earned a reward to get one. Or maybe one or two for the road home.

Zimmer nodded approval at Roebuck.

"We concentrated pretty much exclusively on Jimmy Morelli and his brother, JoJo," Roebuck said. "They ran the North End and were the stronger of the crews. I'd like to think the work we did helped shut down their show. Jimmy Morelli retired. JoJo Morelli got cancer and kicked the bucket."

"Did you ever hear talk about them and the heist?"

Zimmer smiled. He sipped some coffee and pulled out some silver sunglasses from one of the many pockets on his fishing shirt. The shirt was such an intense aqua color that it hurt my eyes. He cleaned the lenses and set them on the table.

"I don't think these guys gave two shits about art when an empire was at stake," Zimmer said. "But for argument's sake. If they'd have had some big-time painting from the Winthrop, we would have heard something about it."

"I'm pretty sure Barboza helped Eddie and Mikey Mike Marino steal it."

"Doesn't mean he kept it," Roebuck said.

"I know," I said. "But I wondered if you found sound kind of connection to the art during your investigation. Even if Benny was killed in the drug war."

"Wasn't there some kind of big reward on those things?" Zimmer said. "A few million?"

"Five," I said.

"Rich and I are retired," he said. "And

living off state retirement. If either of us had heard a whisper about our guys involved with that heist, we'd be on it like a super-model and a ham sandwich."

"What did you guys find at the crime scene?" I said.

"Benny Barboza in the trunk," Zimmer said. "The car was clean. Didn't find any prints. He was shot with a .45. All of it close work. The stabbing happened while he was still alive. We figured whoever killed him was trying to get some information. Never found the murder weapons. Never found the crime scene. No witnesses. No infor-mants. No confessions."

"And it was all pretty much chalked up to a war with the Morellis?"

"We expected a lot more blood," Zimmer said. "We had a wiretap on Morelli's house and there was talk about the killing. They talked about waiting for retaliation from the Old Man. But nothing good enough to make a case."

Roebuck nodded, leaned back into his seat, and finally took a sip of his coffee. I wondered if this might be a moment to grab a muffin.

"Did you read the report?" Roebuck said. "The homicide file from BPD?"

I nodded.

"Did you notice anything missing in it?"

"Besides a lack of basic grammar?"

The cops didn't laugh, but they were still smiling. Roebuck leaned forward and pinched off some blueberry muffin. As he chewed, he looked over his shoulder at the young woman working the counter. In a low voice, he said, "They cut off Barboza's nuts," he said. "The guy who did it gave them to Morelli as a gift on Columbus Day."

"Who was the killer?"

Zimmer shrugged. Roebuck stroked his gray goatee.

"Doesn't matter much now," I said. "We're just a bunch of ex-cops talking about an old case."

Roebuck looked at me, nodding, still stroking his goatee. "JoJo Morelli," he said. "Did it himself. Someone probably snatched Barboza off the street and took him to JoJo. But JoJo did the dirty work. Nobody fucked with that guy and got away with it."

"And I can't talk to JoJo."

"Not without a Ouija board," Zimmer said. The men laughed.

"Lot of bad luck with these paintings," I said. "Two guys in the crew are dead and third guy is in jail."

"You think Jackie might have some answers for you?" Roebuck said.

"Jackie and I aren't the best of pals," I said. "We have a complicated history."

"Twenty years is a long time," Zimmer said. "But I'd watch your step with these guys. Jackie DeMarco may be half the man of his old man. But their memories run long. Trust us on one thing, nobody likes no one kicking up some old dirt. Especially off the dead."

"Consider me forewarned."

Roebuck finished the muffin. I was envious. He looked at me, crumbs still strewn on his Vandyke.

"I heard about you," he said. "Know what you do and have done. This doesn't scare you a bit."

"Not really."

"What'd you do to Jackie, if you don't mind me asking?" Zimmer said.

"I embarrassed him a time or two," I said. "And a friend of mine might've shot and killed one of his guys."

"Bad blood," Roebuck said.

"It ain't good," I said.

"You never know how these things shake out," Roebuck said. "Jackie might be a true and authentic art lover. Probably has that painting hanging in his garage in Southie right now."

"Right alongside this year's Hooters

calendar," Zimmer said. "You got someone to watch your back?"

"Yep."

"Is he any good?" Roebuck said.

"One of the top three in Boston," I said. "Present company included."

"Pretty cocky," Zimmer said, smiling. "Hope it pays off for you."

I shook the men's hands, bought two corn muffins, and drove back to Boston. I ate only one and saved one for later. It was all I deserved.

38

I parked in the garage under Post Office Square and walked a few blocks over to the address on Milk Street where Dominic J. Nuccio, attorney at law, kept an office. Although Nuccio never came through with his mysterious client, I figured he might know a thing or two about the death of Alan Garner and perhaps offer a line of communication with Jackie DeMarco. I'd found numerous clips in *The Globe* about Nuccio representing both father and son over the years. Amazing how the Internet had simplified my sleuthing. If only Sam Spade could've used Google.

"Hey," Nuccio said. "You can't just walk in here. I've got an appointment with a client."

I walked in anyway and took a seat. Nuccio sat behind a large desk piled high with files and papers. He had a small white box stamped *Mike's* open and a pastry in hand.

The room was dark, dim light showed from half-closed blinds, and a desk lamp gave off a soft yellow glow.

"Is your client a cannoli?"

"Can a man just get a coffee break?" he said. "Jesus. Where's my secretary?"

"Taken with my good looks and charm."

"If she just let you barge in here —"

"No," I said. "I insisted."

It looked like it had been a rough day in court. His suit was rumpled and his curly gray toupee looked askew. The secretary showed at the door, out of breath and apologizing. Nuccio held up a hand and sent her away.

"What do you want, Spenser?"

"I'm still waiting to hear about your mystery man."

"Well," he said. "He's thinking it over. When I know, you'll know. If you could just shut the door on the way out."

"Or I could just go talk to Jackie myself," I said. "Although the last time I did that, it didn't go so well."

"Jackie who?"

"Give me a break, Nuccio," I said. "You've only been to court for Jackie DeMarco since he was breaking windows in the North End. And by the way, I like Modern better. You don't have to wait so long waving dollar bills around to get help."

"I've been going to Mike's since I was a kid," he said. "And so what if I've represented Jackie DeMarco? I represented his father, too. It's all in my book."

"I know, *Boston, the Mob, and Me,*" I said. "I saw it for ninety-nine cents on Amazon. You really should hire a better graphic designer. The font you used is an embarrassment."

Nuccio leaned back in his chair. It was black leather with a very high back, making him seem much smaller than he actually was. Although I was pretty sure the idea was to make him look larger, more grand. He drummed his fingers on his table, absently reaching with his free hand and adjusting his hair.

"Alan Garner is dead," I said.

"Never heard of him."

"You read *The Globe*?"

"Sure."

"Front-page Metro," I said. "Ever heard of Gino Fish?"

"Sure," he said. "Mr. Fish was a client."

"Garner was his right-hand man," I said. "Just like you, he promised the return of *The Gentleman* for a price. But unlike you, he knew where to get it and even showed it to me before someone shot him. Being a veteran sleuth, I'm thinking your visit and Garner's offer to broker might be related."

"Even if it was, ever heard of attorney-client privilege?"

"Can we please cut the cannoli?" I said. "Does Jackie still have the painting or not?"

"I never said Mr. DeMarco has the painting."

"You said your client could put his hands on it."

"But I never said my client was Mr. DeMarco," he said. "And if I had said it was Mr. DeMarco, I did not state he had the piece in his possession, only that my client could get his hands on it in a goodwill gesture to the museum and the city of Boston."

"And for the five million reward."

Nuccio made an offhand gesture and smiled.

I crossed my legs and looked at Nuccio across his desk. It was hard to see him, as the papers and files had been stacked so high. I had to crook my neck to the side in order to keep eye contact. He pushed away the box from Mike's and crossed his arms over his chest.

"Can we please get to it?" I said. "I know DeMarco has been on your speed dial for years. You dedicated your book to his late father and dedicated chapters to their family history. I also know that twenty years ago, Crazy Eddie Ciccone enticed a young and naïve security guard named Chad Hartman to open the back door to the Winthrop Museum with promises of a night of pleasure from a girl named Charity. Eddie and Benny Barboza tied up Hartman and another guard. They stole a Picasso sketch, a Goya, and a priceless El Greco. Mikey Mike Marino was the wheelman. It's widely known that that the three amigos were in the DeMarco crew. Two of the men are dead and one isn't talking. So it brings up the question, does DeMarco still have the painting? Did he already sell it? Or did Benny Barboza or Mikey Mike Marino bury it so deep no one recalls where they put it?"

Nuccio stroked one of his wild eyebrows as he listened. When I finished, he stood up and adjusted the blinds in his darkened office. Little dust motes spun around in the slatted light. He took a breath and paced a bit, trying to figure something out or doing a bit of courtroom posturing. The walls were lined with pictures of Nuccio and many of his famous clients. Several of them I recognized from their mug shots.

"Who is this Garner person?" he said.

"He brokered the deal on the Picasso

sketch," I said. "He offered the museum a deal for the return of the El Greco. But before the plan could be put in motion, someone shot him."

"That has nothing to do with nothing."

"It has something to do with something," I said.

"But not my client."

"Of course not."

"You don't believe me?" Nuccio said, moving back behind his big padded leather chair. He placed his forearms on top of the chair and widened his eyes. He had probably had more hair in his bushy eyebrows than natural hair on his head.

"You won't even admit your client is De-Marco," I said.

"This matter is all very complicated," he said. "Delicate, too."

"Jackie DeMarco is many things," I said. "But not delicate."

Nuccio grinned just a little. He continued to study me as he stood behind the chair. He swallowed and nodded as if agreeing with himself.

"I can't promise a painting," he said. "But maybe I can help you sort out some of this crapola you've been swimming through."

"Are you tossing me a life preserver, Dominic?" I said. "Gee, thanks."

265

"Sink or swim out there, baby," he said. "And I can't confirm or deny any of the story you told me."

"But you know a guy who knows a guy."

Nuccio walked around the chair and sat back on his leather throne. He reached down and took a bite of the cannoli, stuffed with chocolate and powdered with a lot of sugar. He chewed for a long time, savoring his treat, and then swallowed.

"Did you tell the cops about me coming to your office?" Nuccio said.

"Nope."

"That's good."

"But if DeMarco was working with Alan Garner, it won't be long until they'll be knocking on his door."

Nuccio reached for a napkin and wiped his mouth. He drank a little coffee and pointed at me with a long, bony finger. "I'll get you a meet with Jackie," he said. "But if you screw him or screw me, you're on your own."

"Wow," I said. "You're too good to me."

"He calls the time and the place," Nuccio said. "That's not up for debate. No way. No how."

"I'm so excited. I just don't know what to wear."

"Oh, and Jackie doesn't like you," he said.

"But I guess you know that."

"No offense taken." I shrugged. "The feeling is mutual."

39

"When did they stop making the El Dorado?" I said.

We were both sitting in Vinnie's car, that year's Cadillac CT6 sedan. It was black, with a dark tan interior. The car was steeped in that rich new-car smell.

"They haven't made the El Do for fifteen years," he said. "Christ. Where you been?"

"Fleetwood?" I said.

"They haven't made Fleetwoods in twenty," he said. "Next thing you know, you're going to ask me about the Edsel. Trust me, that didn't work out."

In a realm all its own," I said.

"Sunroof, Bose stereo, V-6 turbo," he said. "Top-grade leather. Galvano chrome accents."

"What's Galvano chrome?"

"I'm not sure," Vinnie said. "But it's nice stuff. Full-grain aniline-dyed leather. That means it's thick and strong, not like that cheap crap they put on Chinese sofas."

I felt around the dash and examined the deluxe accents, and the futuristic GPS and odometer.

"It suits you," I said.

"And that old boat of a car suits you, Spenser," he said. "Where'd you pick that up? Some Army-Navy store?"

"Quincy."

Vinnie nodded. We'd just pulled up in front of Jackie DeMarco's impound lot in Southie. The last time I'd been there with Hawk, a few bullets had flown. Vinnie had a few questions about Alan Garner and believed his presence might calm future altercations. I wasn't so sure. But happy to have the company.

"Remember that time Joe Broz wanted me to kill you?"

"Which time?"

"When you humiliated his son out in the woods," he said. "You should have put down that mutt right there and then."

"Joe and I worked it out," I said. "But his son tried for me anyway."

"And you shot him in the fucking kneecap," he said. "Let me make a clear distinction here. Jackie ain't Gerry Broz."

"He's not Al Capone, either," I said. "Or Albert Schweitzer."

We watched the impound lot, waiting for Jackie's call. When Jackie was close, they'd open the gates and let us in. Jackie would grant me an audience from his hubcap throne. As Vinnie shifted in his seat, I noted the edge of the automatic in his shoulder holster.

"Sorry about Alan," I said.

"Me, too," Vinnie said. "He was just a kid when he came on with Gino. I don't think he had a freakin' clue about the life. He was smart, interested in all that artsy-fartsy stuff. He knew antiques, paintings and shit. Liked to dress nice, wear fancy clothes. I think he dug working for a powerful guy."

"Was he as close to Gino as I've heard?"

"Alan grew up in Lawrence," Vinnie said. "Family didn't have a lot of money. Father was a plumber, a mean, lousy drunk. Kicked him out when he heard he was gay. You know the story. Alan came to Boston, led the big party life that was all fucking and dancing. He grew to appreciate the finer things. You know? Gino was able to make that happen. Alan always had a sporty little car, nice place to live in the South End, didn't have to worry for money."

"He didn't live with Gino."

"Nope," Vinnie said. "He didn't want anything to happen to the kid. Gino knew his private life put his public one in jeopardy. In case you don't know, most wise guys aren't exactly socially progressive."

"Many made the mistake Gino was weak because he was gay."

"But never twice."

"Just how did you go from Broz to Fish?"

Vinnie shrugged, turned down the music on the radio. *The Greatest Hits of Eddie Fisher.* He kept his eyes trained on the expansive lot of DeMarco towing. There were hundreds of cars in the lot and only three construction trailers parked in the center. I recalled the last time I'd been there, Hawk out of sight and taking out one of DeMarco's men.

"Joe was retiring," he said. "It was either become some kind of personal assistant or go to work for Gerry."

"I can't imagine you taking orders from Gerry Broz."

"Me and you both," he said. "Joe understood me going with Fish. I don't think Joe approved of Fish's lifestyle and stuff, but he did respect the way Fish ran his business. He knew the man's word was good and he did what he promised."

"How old were you when you started working for Joe?"

"Seventeen," he said. "Right out of high

271

school. College wasn't exactly an option."

"And working for someone like the De-Marcos or the Morelli brothers wasn't an option, either?"

"Sure," he said. "I knew those guys. But your mom being Sicilian won't get you too far. I never would be running things. I'd never had the respect for my Irish side."

"Funny how things like that work," I said.

"Hilarious."

"What do you think Joe and Gino would make of Jackie DeMarco?"

"They wouldn't trust him," he said. "De-Marco is a new animal. He's a reckless, stupid hothead. His word doesn't mean jack. Half the time he's talking straight out of his ass."

"Great," I said. "This should be a productive conversation."

My cell phone rang.

I answered it and told the caller our location. The gates to the tow truck company rolled open and Vinnie drove his Cadillac on into the yard. We parked up close to the trailers, nose pointing back toward the gate. Vinnie unlocked the doors and reached for the handle.

"Here we go."

"Yep," Vinnie said.

40

"You're a lucky man, Spenser," Jackie De-Marco said. "You know that, right? Considering the shit show that happened right here the last time. For me to allow you to drive on in here and have a civil conversation is kind of miraculous."

"I prayed long and hard for it, Jackie," I said. "I feel so fortunate."

"Always with the smart mouth," he said. "You gotten older, Spenser, but always with the same fucking smart mouth."

I showed my palms in a modest gesture. Vinnie stood at my side. He had not said a word since walking into the construction trailer set in the center of the hundreds of impounded cars. He had on a slim gray linen suit and a starched dress shirt with a black tie. A crisp white show hankie in the pocket and silver cuff links. His salt-and-pepper hair was cut with precision.

Jackie DeMarco had on one of those

bright blue oversized dress shirts that the salespeople promised were slimming if worn untucked. Jackie needed his money back. He was even more bloated in the middle and in the face than he was when I saw him last. His black hair was long and shaggy around his ears and face.

We all sat in a little grouping of mismatched furniture: a couch, a big leather recliner, and a couple folding chairs. He'd decorated the walls with a poster of Tom Brady and a few *Playboy* centerfolds. One particular work of art showed a nude woman bent over the open hood of a Ferrari.

"Let's cut the shit," DeMarco said. "I'm sure Nuccio told you that I want in."

"Want in to what?"

"That missing painting," He said. "The El Greeko. Whattaya think? It's mine."

"El Greeko?" I said. "You continue to amaze me, Jackie."

Vinnie was standing. We exchanged a look, and Vinnie covered his smiling mouth with a hand. Two more men were in the room with us. I didn't recognize either of them. They were big and dumb shooters that tried to look tough but had given Vinnie Morris a wide berth when he'd strolled into the trailer.

"So where is it?" DeMarco said. "You find

that fucking thing and I better get my cut. That's nobody's shit but mine. It belongs to me."

"Actually," I said. "It belongs to the Winthrop Museum. But continuing on your course of logic, please do let us know why you consider it your property."

"Didn't Nuccio tell you?"

"Nuccio wouldn't even say he worked for you," I said.

"He said you know the crew who stole it."

"I do."

"So it's fucking mine," DeMarco said.

"Possession is nine-tenths of the law," I said. "But you don't have it."

DeMarco let out a long breath and took a seat in a folding chair across from me. He set his elbows on his knees and looked up at me. "Ain't none of this legal," he said. "But right is right."

"Only when it's wrong."

"Christ," he said. "You are such a fucking ass ache. If you think you're gonna fucking la-dee-da around the city, scoop up that painting, and make some dough, go ahead. But you better spend it real quick."

Vinnie shook his head. He lifted his chin at DeMarco. "This is a waste of time," Vinnie said. "This asshole doesn't know where it is."

"Asshole?" he said. "Better watch it, Morris. My crew took it. That means it belongs to me."

The two big guys at the edge of the trailer turned their attention toward us. One of them brushed his right hand at his jacket. Jackie lifted his eyes at them and shook his head.

"Two guys in your dad's crew are dead," I said. "And one has become a license-plate artiste in Walpole. Nobody seems to know what happened to the art other than the Picasso sketch ended up with a dealer named Alan Garner."

"That was from a long time back," he said. "Before I took over. They unloaded that piece right after the job. That was chicken-shit stuff."

"Did you kill Garner?" Vinnie said.

"Fuck no," he said. "That's not my style."

"Let's hope not."

"Is that a threat, Vinnie?" DeMarco said.

Vinnie eyed him coldly and nodded. De-Marco tried to look tough and cool. But I saw his face flush as he swallowed. He turned his small black eyes back on me. I was offended he found me less threatening.

"Benny Barboza pulled that heist for my father," he said. "He didn't care nothing about the art, but he knew a big piece like

276

that might get my old man out of prison. That's why they did it. It was all done for love and respect."

"Sounds like a *Lifetime* movie," I said. "I'm tearing up just thinking of it."

"Only my old man didn't want to use the ace in the hole," he said. "He wanted Benny to keep the piece hidden until everything cooled down. He pissed off the Feds, and they'd lean on him even harder. He wanted to do his time with no trouble. My old man was like that. Smart, always thinking ahead."

I tilted my head and studied his chubby, tanned face and small, mean eyes.

"Whattaya looking at?"

"Searching for the family resemblance."

"Benny hid it away," he said. "And then he got fucking whacked."

"By whom?"

He lifted his eyes up at Vinnie and stared for a short moment. He then looked back at me and said, "The Morelli brothers."

"I heard that was over coke."

"Maybe," he said. "I don't know if anyone knows anymore. But they wanted Benny down to hurt my father. They were close. Benny was family."

"And the paintings?"

"Whattaya think, ace?" he said. "The Morellis jacked the painting. Spoils of war and all that horse shit."

"Then why come to me?" I said. "If you know who has the paintings."

"Because Jimmy Morelli and my old man made peace before my dad died," he said. "I can't go into the North End and rough up an old fuck like Morelli. Besides, Morelli says he doesn't have it. He says that's all on his no-good brother."

"Okay," I said. "Then we talk to his brother."

"His brother died last year," he said. "The fucking big C. But I know for a fucking fact that fat bastard hung that El Greeko on his wall at his summer place up in Maine. I know people who seen it. You want to find it, go talk to his bigmouthed, big-titted wife, Angela, and find out what gives."

"Wait," I said. I held up my hand. "Are you trying to hire me, Jackie?"

"I'm saying that I'm offering you some very exclusive fucking information, Spenser," he said. "And if you're as goddamn smart as you think you are, you'll follow up on it and make us all some money."

"Working for both a respected museum and a disreputable hood might be construed as unethical."

"Fuck ethics," he said. "I'll give you twenty percent of the five mil. How's that sound?"

I looked back at Vinnie. He shrugged. Vinnie was a practical man.

"Why don't you just do it yourself?" I said. "If you're so sure."

"She won't talk to me," he said. "And I don't want to get my good name mixed up with all this shit. If you didn't look around this place, I got a huge professional operation down here."

"Doesn't want the Chamber of Commerce to get mad," I said.

"All those bastards who get their cars towed might get pissed," Vinnie said.

"Why are you just now interested in this?" I said.

"The reward wasn't as big."

"If Angela Morelli can get the painting," I said. "We may have to cut up the pie even more."

"Do what needs to be done."

"How sure are you, Jackie?" Vinnie said. "That the Morellis got the paintings?"

"Hunnard and ten fucking percent."

"That much," I said.

"Okay," Jackie said. "Got it now? You unnerstand the complexity of the situation?"

"A Mafia musical chairs," I said.

Jackie nodded. I stood up. Nobody shook hands and Vinnie and I both walked from the trailer. The two big guys gave me a hard look as I passed. Vinnie moved past them as if invisible.

As we crossed the lot, Vinnie turned to me and smiled. "I thought you said the museum said there would never be a reward for you?"

"True," I said. "But what Jackie doesn't know can't hurt him."

"He's never known much."

"Let's hope he's right about this one thing."

41

It was Susan's turn to cook, so we had reservations at Harvest. She'd arranged for a corner table near the open kitchen, and as the waiters walked past with loaded trays, I eyed my options. Susan read the summer selections while I decided on a hamburger. A burger and cold beer at Harvest were tough to beat. Of course, a burger and beer anywhere were seldom disappointing.

Susan set down her menu and removed her reading glasses. She chose the Scottish salmon, with another vodka gimlet. We ordered and I told her about the events of the last two days.

"Mafia musical chairs," she said. "I like that."

"It's taken a while to untangle the knot."

"If it were simple, the Winthrop would've figured it out years ago."

"Or if they'd let BPD handle the case," I said. "And not let the Feds try and make it a fancier show than it really was. Lots of international travel on the taxpayer tab."

"Didn't you punch out Jackie DeMarco last time you saw him?"

"Nope," I said. "Just a shot in his kidneys to get his attention."

"And he still was willing to talk to you?"

"Money," I said. "The international language."

"I thought that was love."

I shrugged. The waitress brought me a fresh beer and Susan a gimlet. Speakers played some classic Coltrane overhead. The restaurant was dim and quiet, warm yellow light spreading across the open space. Dark polished wood and stainless steel.

"Love is a smoke raised with the fume of sighs," I said.

"My," she said. "A big heart and a big neck."

"Don't all good Jewish girls get what they want?"

"But of course," she said. "I asked for a man with a forty-eight-inch chest who could quote the Bard."

I raised my beer. We touched glasses. Susan spotted her friend Judith Marvin Webb across the room and offered a demure wave.

"I'm glad Vinnie joined you today," she

said. "That gives me some comfort."

"He pretty much insisted," I said. "Alan Garner was a friend, and he feels like he owes Gino to see it through."

"Quite a complicated code of ethics."

"Vinnie's a dying breed."

"And Hawk."

"Of course."

"And you," she said. "And Z."

"We are trying to pass it on to the next generation," I said. "You used to be able to rely on someone's word. Hoods have to live by a certain code, too, or they won't be hoods for long. Their word is pretty much all they have."

"So Jackie now expects to be compensated?"

"I'll let Jackie take it up with the Winthrop."

"Won't that violate your code?"

"No," I said. "Unless he gives me something solid. The reward is up to the Winthrop. I'm just a hired hand, ma'am."

"Like *Shane*?"

"Only taller."

"So tomorrow you'll drive over to Bedford and ask the missus of the late Morelli brother to hand over the painting."

"That's the plan," I said. "What could go wrong?"

"I'm sure she'll just take it down from her wall and hand it over," she said. "I mean, with your charm and charisma."

"I could charm the pants off a snake."

Susan drank a little of the gimlet. Her large eyes peered over the rim of the glass. Under the table, she patted my knee. She looked dubious but smiled.

As she did so, I looked toward the bar and spotted the profile of a familiar face. Only this time he had on a Sox ball cap that didn't quite go with the suit. He leaned over a tall beer and furtively turned to stare at our table. Men often turned to stare at Susan. But this guy was looking right at me. It was Paul Marston.

"Excuse me for a moment," I said.

"Someone you know?"

"Unfortunately."

I walked over to the bar and tapped Marston's shoulder. He turned around with a feigned look of surprise.

"Just getting a bite," Marston said. "Nice place. Has it been here long?"

He smiled widely and swiveled his stool to face me. The cologne cut right through the pleasant smell of tonight's seasonal specials. "Sorry to hear about your contact," he said. "Best laid plans and all that sort of rubbish."

"And now, with a lack of anything better to do, you're back to watching me?"

"The board remains unconvinced you actually saw *The Gentleman in Black,*" he said. "The paint chips have proved to be inconclusive, I'm sorry to say."

I shrugged. "You should try and curl the bill of the hat," I said. "You look ridiculous."

"Oh, yeah?" he said. "Thanks. Who's the lovely lady you're with?"

"Someone who doesn't like interruptions," I said.

"Introduce me."

"Nope," I said. "If you think I'm tough, just wait."

Marston smiled up at me, looking very silly in the Sox cap. He wore it far back on his head like a child, with his hair loose over his forehead. "Where are we headed tomorrow?"

"Garner's dead," I said. "I guess it's all over."

"Is that why you met with Mr. DeMarco today?" he said. "How did that go, by the way?"

"Why don't you ask him yourself?" I said. "You guys will get along famously. You could talk fashion. You're into hats. He's into the untucked look."

"I offered DeMarco a solid deal with full

backing of the Winthrop."

"Good for you."

"They don't need you anymore, Spenser," he said, smirking. "We have everything you do."

I reached for the bill of his cap and tugged it down over his eyes, and told him that he looked much better. I returned to my seat with Susan.

"Who is that annoying man?" Susan said.

"My rival on the case."

"You have no rival."

"Exactly."

42

The next morning, I drove to Bedford and a planned community built around the old Huckins Farm. Angela Morelli lived in a pleasant, respectable two-story house that backed up to a horse pasture. The house was painted a flat gray with white trim, flanked by a two-car garage and a lot of new landscaping. The trees were short, tied to stakes, and surrounded by fresh red mulch and a neatly clipped lawn. If the wife of the late JoJo Morelli was looking for respectability, this seemed to be the right address.

I parked in her driveway and knocked on her front door.

A woman in a sleeveless black silk top and fancy jeans opened the front door. She was blond and barefooted, much younger than I expected, and very well made up for ten in the morning. Her makeup looked so perfect it had to be airbrushed. Her nails had been painted a bright blue and her blond hair bleached nearly to the roots. Being an expert in the field, I noted she was tanned, toned, and surgically enhanced.

"Mr. Spenser?" she said.

I nodded. She invited me in. The home was pleasant and uncluttered but decorated very much like a furniture showroom, with impersonal art and extra-large furniture groupings. Big frilly pillows, brass lamps, and tasseled rugs. She invited me to join her outside and we walked through the kitchen to a flagstone patio. She'd already set out a coffeepot and two cups onto a wrought-iron table.

The pasture was the centerpiece of the development, with houses and condos ringed around it. Several horses huddled together by a water trough, only one with the decency to acknowledge our presence before continuing to drink.

"Like I said on the phone, I don't really know what to tell you," Angela said. "JoJo did for JoJo, and I didn't ask a lot of questions. I didn't really know his whole story until after he died, with the criminal accusations and all that kind of stuff. You know he got cancer a few years ago? Died last year. Kept on thinking he was gonna beat it until the end."

"I'm very sorry."

She shrugged. "I knew what I was getting into with an older man," she said. "Some nice old ladies at Saint Leonard's set us up. They told me the Morellis were good people and that JoJo was a real gentleman."

"Was he?"

"To me and his family, he was a prince," she said. "To all others, he was a prick."

"Are you still in contact with your brother-in-law?"

"Jimmy Morelli is a prick to everyone," she said. "Even family. Just what is it you want to know, Mr. Spenser? Because I can't get all into the family business. That could get my tit into the ringer."

"Did your husband ever mention the robbery at the Winthrop Museum?" I said. "A Picasso sketch was taken. Two priceless paintings?"

She didn't seem to be listening as she continued to watch the horses playing in the field. It had been a while since I'd been around such large animals. My Western instincts were heightened. I wondered if she'd be impressed if I lassoed one and rode about the pasture bareback like when the Lone Ranger met Silver. Maybe that'd get her talking.

"There were two big paintings?" she said.

I nodded. She shook her head, reaching

289

to the center of the table and several apples set in a wooden bowl. She grabbed for one and toyed with it in her hands, rolling it back and forth.

"I'm sorry," she said. "I only know about one."

I thought it highly unprofessional to perform a spit take. I restrained myself.

"JoJo and I had this big one for a while," she said. "The scary-looking Spanish guy with the serious black eyes. Yeah, we had it. We hung it up at our place in Maine. He really loved that thing. He didn't allow us to show it to everybody. It was a real special thing, like when he broke out the old Fabian records and the sambuca."

"Did you know it was stolen?"

Angela laughed. She pulled together the silk top over her chest, where buttons couldn't be buttoned.

"Of course," she said. "With those two brothers, not a lot wasn't. But I didn't know what it was, the connection to the museum, until I saw it in the papers a few years ago. When I asked JoJo about it, he told me to shut my freakin' mouth and never mention it again. And being a good Italian wife, I didn't."

The top buttons on her blouse were unbuttoned and offered a view of a lot of the enhanced cleavage. It was like trying to not stare into the sun.

"Are you really a private eye?" she said, still playing with the apple in her hands. "Or just a crook?"

I reached into my pocket and showed her my license.

"Is that really real?"

"Yep," I said. "I traded ten box tops for it. Lucky Charms."

She smiled and set her bare feet to the ground. "So I can trust you?" she said. "As a real professional."

"Absolutely."

She touched her finger to her lips as if considering, and then patted my knee. I tried not to whinny and trot around the open field. "And you work for the museum?"

"Sort of."

"What does 'sort of' mean?" she said.

"Right now I'm independent," I said. "But if you help me recover the painting, it will go straight back to the Winthrop. You'll be a hero."

"And the reward?" she said.

"You'd get your fair share," I said. "Although only one man has been able to produce the painting so far."

"Would he fight us for the money?"

"No," I said. "He's dead. I was hoping you might explain what happened."

"Jesus," she said. "Everyone gets dead with that painting. Did you know that? That's why I wasn't sad to see it leave. JoJo said the painting was bad luck. He said the guy before him died, too."

I placed the coffee cup back on the table. A brown horse had wandered up to the fence, staring at us as we spoke. I sincerely hoped he didn't get involved with the Morelli brothers. The Mob and horses shared a bad history.

"The police believe your late husband killed the previous owner."

"Huh," Angela Morelli said, patting my knee again. She got up from the table and wandered up to the fence line. She offered a horse the apple in the palm of her hand. The horse took it.

The sun was shining, a little steam rising off the edges of the pasture. The horse had finished the apple and was nudging her for more. I wondered if she might tell me more about her late husband's business and the missing painting if I did the same. I followed her to the fence.

"JoJo was a violent man," she said. "He was raised that way, same as Jimmy. They did a lot of bad things. I know that."

"Did he ever tell you how he got the painting?"

"No."

"Do you know where it went?"

We stood under a large sprawling elm. She walked up to me and placed a hand on my arm. She was a good deal shorter than me and had to crane her neck upward to look into my eyes. "I don't know you," she said. "Or if I can even trust you."

"Bonded and insured," I said. "I also can perform one-armed push-ups and whistle while I work."

"Is that a fact?"

"Don't I look trustworthy?"

"You look like a violent man, too."

"Not at all." I shrugged. "I'm a real pussycat."

She smiled and took her hand off my arm. She walked back to the small patio and took a seat. I joined her and didn't say a word, waiting for her to talk.

"Are you married?" she said.

"Pretty much," I said.

"A shame," she said. "All the good ones are either taken or dead. I loved JoJo. He took care of me and made sure I was taken care of after he was gone. I just want to make sure none of this comes back on his memory."

The sun slanted off the deck and across half of Angela Morelli's face. She again brushed her bangs and looked right at me, squinting and pursing her lips.

"I only want to find the painting," I said. "The Morellis' other business is separate."

"When JoJo got sick, he gave it to his brother for safekeeping," she said. "He believed he was gonna beat everything and we would get it back. After he died, I asked Jimmy about it and he pretended like he didn't know what I was talking about. Jimmy. What an asshole."

"You think he still has it?"

"I was with JoJo up in Maine when he handed it over," she said. "To one of Jimmy's flunkies, Ray Russo. I drove with JoJo over to a Howard Johnson somewhere in Portland. JoJo had wrapped up the painting with packing blankets and duct tape. Ray had some kind of moving van. I watched him move it from the back of our Tahoe and into the van. I saw the whole thing. JoJo came back inside and ate a plate of fried clams and acted like it never happened."

"And the painting went to his brother?" I said.

"Where else would it go?" she said. "JoJo and Jimmy. Thick as thieves."

"You think you might offer me an intro to

Jimmy?"

"After all the things he said to me at the funeral?" she said. "I'd rather eat glass than talk to that prick. Besides, he won't talk about the painting."

"Why not?"

"He's scared of it," she said. "Thinks there's too much blood on it."

"He may be right."

43

I drove back downtown to my office and worked through lunch on a detailed expense report for the Winthrop. Whether or not I found the painting, I expected to be paid. If the board didn't agree, they could take it up with Rita Fiore. I knew several pit bulls with less tenacity.

I had just closed the books and printed out the current invoice when Frank Belson and Captain Glass knocked on my door. I let them in and offered them a seat.

"With what I have to say, I'd rather stand," Glass said.

"My client chairs are very comfy," I said. "Ask Frank."

Belson wore a pained expression but took a seat anyway. He was disheveled as always, smelling strongly of cigars. Glass was in her ever-present pantsuit, black with a green blouse, and no-nonsense black shoes. She leaned against my file cabinet as I returned to my desk.

"I'm disappointed in you, Spenser," she said.

"My girlfriend is a therapist," I said. "She'll help me deal with your disapproval."

Frank leaned forward and pinched the bridge of his nose. I set my feet up on the edge of my desk.

"You lied to us," she said. "I can understand you lying to me. But lying to Lieutenant Belson? Haven't you two been friends for a long time?"

"Okay," I said. "I touched up my hair. I thought it made me look younger."

"You didn't tell us Alan Garner showed you the painting," she said. "You told us about the incident in the Common, seeing him on surveillance and all that, but nothing about your midnight ride to Winchester."

"Damn," I said. "I didn't know it was Winchester. How did you know it was Winchester? I am genuinely impressed."

"Don't worry about it," Belson said. "We were straight with you and we expected you to be straight with us."

"I have a certain obligation to my clients."

"That's bullshit," Glass said. "Who do you think told us about your adventure with Garner? He showed you *The Gentleman in*

Black and gave you paint chips to prove it was authentic."

"I heard they didn't check out," I said. "So all of this doesn't matter much."

Glass shoved my shoes off the table. "It matters a great deal to us," she said. "It shows us that you were holding something back. You used to be a cop until you went into whatever business it is you do."

"That business that I do well."

I thought I saw Belson smile. It flickered on his face for a moment but then quickly disappeared. Glass moved back to the file cabinet and leaned against it with her shoulder. She let out a long sigh. Belson straightened up and rubbed the stubble along his jaw. "Why didn't you tell us?"

"I needed to see how it played out," I said.

"With Garner dead?" Glass said. "How the hell was that supposed to work?"

"If it was known he had the painting, then the crazies would have really come out," I said. "Do you broadcast all you know about an investigation?"

Glass swallowed, eyes narrowing. She pointed a very long finger in my direction. "You don't think this was a grand omission?" she said. "I've worked murders for junk that isn't worth fifty bucks. How much is this goddamn painting worth?"

298

"Somewhere in the neighborhood of sixty to seventy million," I said. "If it were taken to a legitimate auction."

"And the fact that our victim had possession of this painting within twenty-four hours of his murder doesn't mean something to you?" she said. "I thought you were a real hotshot."

I set my elbows on the desk and stared at her. "My ego bruises easily," I said. "Please be delicate."

"We've been chasing our tails, Spenser," Belson said. "For fuck's sake. It took us most of the day to find out where Garner had taken you."

"Just for the hell of it, how did you find out?"

Belson opened his mouth. But before he could answer, Glass said, "That's none of your business," she said. "We have our job and you have yours. Maybe if I peed standing up, you and I could exchange information at the urinal."

"Sure," I said. "That's how Frank and I met. We've done it so long, he doesn't even splash on my foot anymore."

"Who said the paint chips didn't check out?" Glass said.

I lifted my eyebrows. "Perhaps I was misinformed."

"They checked out," Belson said. "Same type of painting. Same era and some other kind of scientific shit."

"What you saw was legit," Glass said. "Besides his boyfriend, you were the last person to see Alan Garner alive. And when you did, he just happened to show you a priceless painting. I'd say that makes you a pretty good suspect."

"Really?" I said. "You think I killed Garner and took the painting? Why didn't I just go ahead and kill him when he showed it to me?"

"Hell of a motive, Spenser," Belson said. He grinned just a bit.

"Best one we have," Glass said.

"Then arrest me," I said.

"Not yet," Glass said. "Just what were you doing with Jackie DeMarco yesterday at his place in Southie?"

I shook my head. I was really beginning to hate my lack of privacy these days. First Paul Marston and then Boston Police Homicide. I wondered if they'd been charting my bowel movements as well.

"We're old friends," I said. "We shared a pizza. Had some laughs."

"You killed one of his guys two years ago," Belson said. "He must've gotten all that straight with his priest. Forgiveness being

300

his thing and all."

Glass walked up toward me and took a seat beside Belson. She crossed her legs and turned her chin to the side as her eyes wandered over me. I smiled back at her.

"Did Garner represent DeMarco in this?" Glass said.

"I can't say," I said.

"Christ," Belson said.

"Did DeMarco's old man steal the painting?" Glass said. "And all these years later, he's wanting to cash in?"

"I can't say."

"Damn it, Spenser," Belson said. "What the fuck can you say?"

"Pound for pound, Willie Pep may have been the best boxer in history," I said. "And note for note, Ella Fitzgerald could outsing Caruso. And between you and me, I don't think the Pats have a chance in hell of going back to the Super Bowl."

"It's like that," Glass said. "Right?"

"Jackie DeMarco isn't involved," I said. "Although he'd really like to be."

"Bullshit," Glass said. "You also went to go see Eddie Ciccone at Walpole last week. Ciccone was a known B-and-E man about the time of the Winthrop job and used to run with the DeMarcos."

"If I knew where to find that painting, it

301

would be back on the second floor of the Winthrop," I said.

"Arrest him," Glass said.

"Captain," he said. "Come on."

"Frank?" Glass said. "This isn't a test. It's a fucking order. When you got a dog that acts up, you slap him on the nose."

"Arf," I said. I stood up and reached for my ball cap on the hat tree. "And what's the charge?"

Belson shook his head and held my door open wide. "I'm really not sure."

"Obstruction," she said. "And for continually raising my blood pressure and pissing me off."

"Is that one new on the books?" I said.

Belson nodded, reaching into his jacket for a half-finished cigar. He plucked it into the side of his mouth as he watched me lock up.

"Can you hit the lights and siren on the way to headquarters?" I said, whispering to Belson as we moved down the steps.

"Only if it makes you happy," Belson said.

44

The sit-down with Belson and Glass was both long and unproductive.

When Belson dropped me back at my office, I found Vinnie Morris waiting for me. He was parked outside the Restoration Hardware in the old Museum of Natural History and flicked his lights as Belson drove off. It was dusk and the downtown streets glowed with a soft, purplish light.

I walked across Berkeley and leaned through his open passenger window. The sidewalks still radiated heat from the hot day.

"You in trouble?" he said.

"Cops wanted some crimestopper tips."

"You give 'em any?"

"Just one," I said. "Follow the money."

"Get in," Vinnie said.

"Where we going?" I said.

"To follow the money."

We drove over to the North End, where

Vinnie parked in front of the Daily Catch on Hanover. Jimmy Morelli's smoke shop was a block over, on Prince Street. A wooden sign shaped like a cigar reading *Amore* hung outside. Vinnie walked in the front door and down into a basement. As we entered, the swell of smoke hovered at eye level. A lean old guy and two hefty men sat in a semicircle of leather recliners, watching ESPN. The two big guys fumbled to their feet when they saw Vinnie.

Vinnie held up the flat of his hand. He opened his jacket to show his empty holster. The hefty men, one in a red tracksuit and the other in a baggy Ortiz jersey, turned to the old, slim guy. He had gray hair, a hangdog face, and a droopy gray mustache. Cigar in hand, he waved them back to their places and lifted his eyes to us.

"Vinnie," he said. "Been a long time."

"Jimmy," Vinnie said.

"Didn't know you liked cigars," he said.

"I don't," Vinnie said. "They smell like dog turds to me. We came to talk."

Jimmy Morelli looked at me like I was a veal cutlet. I wasn't sure whether to look tough or curtsy to an old Mafia boss. I decided to simply nod. Morelli placed a fat cigar back in his mouth.

"Alone," Vinnie said.

Morelli snapped his fingers and Shamu and Free Willy got up to leave. Shamu wore his authentic Sox jersey loose over a wife-beater. Even with the loose material, I noted the bulge on his right hip.

Jimmy kept staring at me, puffing on the big cigar. He finally broke into a smile. "I know you," he said. "You're fucking Spenser. Right?"

Being such an eloquent bastard, I nodded again.

"You killed Frank Doerr, back in the day."

I shrugged. "Frank and I disagreed on a few things."

"Fucking Frankie Doerr," he said. "What a piece of shit. You killing him made my life a lot easier. Come on, sit down. You smoke, Spenser?"

"I used to," I said. "Gave it up for Lent."

"Lent's over," he said.

He had me there. Morelli got up, walked to a side table, and handed me a cigar. I accepted it. *When in the North End . . .*

Jimmy handed me a cutter and a lighter. I don't think I'd had a cigar since I'd first started out in the business. I used to smoke when I had my office over in the Combat Zone. My windows hadn't been painted shut yet.

"Sorry to hear about Broz," Morelli said,

looking to Vinnie. "And now Gino. Not a lot of us left."

I took a seat in the leather grouping. I lit the cigar and took a puff. The basement shop was dim, decorated with a lot of framed prints of the old country and Cuba. The Coliseum at sunset, grapes ripening on the vine, virginal women rolling cigars on their thighs.

"A friend of mine was killed last week," Vinnie said. "Alan Garner. He worked for Gino for a long time."

"Sorry to hear it."

"He promised Spenser here that he knew the whereabouts of some of the loot from the Winthrop Museum."

Jimmy Morelli's slow, good-time smile faded behind a plume of smoke. His eyes were black and hooded. He reached to wipe a bit of tobacco off his tongue.

"We were hoping you might know something about it," Vinnie said.

"About the guy getting killed?" Morelli said. "In case you ain't heard, I'm retired. I've been out of the life for a long while. My wife and I just got back from one of those Perillo tours. Floated down the fucking river, drank Barolo, and talked about the beauty of life. That life I used to lead is over a long time, my friend."

"What about the painting?" I said.

"Painting?" Morelli said. He shrugged.

I drew on the cigar and crossed my legs. Me and good-time Jimmy Morelli, pals. *The Gentleman in Black?*" I said.

"Never heard of him."

"Your sister-in-law said JoJo handed it over when he got sick," I said. "She said it was a big hit over sambuca and cigars at their beach house in Maine."

Morelli opened his mouth and then closed it. As he searched for a decent answer, he plugged the cigar into his mouth and took a long draw. He lifted a hand and waved away the smoke.

"I don't know nothing about that."

"Jimmy," Vinnie said. "This is important. We wouldn't be here otherwise. It got a friend killed. It also ain't no small nothing. Whoever finds it gets five mil."

"Oh, yeah?" Morelli said.

"That ain't just cheese and crackers."

"Sure, sure," Morelli said. "Okay, okay."

"Will you help?" Vinnie said.

"Why should I?"

"How about old times' sake?"

"Let's say I might have some knowledge of a painting like that," Morelli said. "If I try to explain a pretty complex situation, I might find my ass hurting talking to the

Feds in Government Center. I'm too old for that shit, Vinnie. I like to take it easy. I get along with everyone. Everyone gets along with me."

"No trouble with the Feds," I said. "Statute of limitations has run out. The museum just wants the painting back. No questions asked."

"So you say," Morelli said.

"I do," I said. "And everyone else involved."

"But now you got some queer friend of Gino's dead and bunch of schnauzer tits running around Boston making trouble," Morelli said. "Come on. I got money. I don't need the aggravation."

"Did you ever have it?" I said.

Jimmy Morelli smiled at me. He tilted his head, more smoke spewed from his mouth. "Maybe."

"Help me help you," I said. "I get paid. You get paid. The museum gets back a masterpiece and all of Boston is singing 'Sapore di Sale.' "

"Great song," Morelli said. He hummed a few bars. He had a smooth weathered voice that resounded off the brick walls.

I nodded. Vinnie nodded. We were making some fine progress down in the North End basement. Morelli slapped at his thigh and stood up again. It looked as if he hadn't stood in a while, his knees growing stiff. He walked over to a small bar along the wall and poured himself a whiskey out of a cut-glass decanter.

"You boys want anything?"

"Only answers," I said.

"I wish I could help you help me," he said. "But that painting is long gone. And to be honest with you, it was nothing but a lot of ass ache when we had it."

I purposely did not mention the circumstances of how it came into the hands of the Morelli brothers. I didn't think laying the blame of the murder of Benny Barboza would grease the situation along. He reached into an ice bucket and added two cubes to his whiskey and returned to his chair. He groaned like an old dog as he settled back in.

"You know what *sfortuna* means, Spenser?"

"Not exactly," I said. "But it doesn't sound good."

"*The Gentleman in Black* is *sfortuna,*" he said. "Bad fucking luck. It was bad luck to museum, bad luck to the man who stole it, and bad luck to my late brother. I don't want any of that stuff. Like I said, I don't need that kind of aggravation."

Something went cold in me. I had the feeling that Morelli was about to tell me that he'd destroyed El Greco's work painted more than five hundred years ago.

Morelli grunted and shook his head. "That's Ray Russo's trouble now," he said. "The goddamn rat fucker."

I looked to Vinnie. Something shifted his eyes. He took a deep breath, sitting there cool and still in the big recliner, smoke around him.

"Can we talk to Ray?" Vinnie said.

"If you talk to Famous Ray, I'd like to talk to Famous Ray," he said. "He turned on some good people. His own people. He buddied up with the Feds and cut a deal. What he did coulda got me sent down to Atlanta for the rest of my fucking life. Can you imagine that? My own cousin, our mothers being sisters and all."

"You don't know where he went?"

"Witness protection, Vinnie," he said. "It's like that. Damn rat fucker. He has that big ugly painting, probably hanging in some shitty garage out in Scottsdale or Tucson. Probably looks at it when he takes out his riding lawnmower and gives me and everyone he ever knew the big FO."

I looked to Vinnie. "Fantastic."

"I don't know where he went," Morelli

said. "And I gotta make peace with what he done. But if I were looking for that old painting, I'd go see that crook Devon Murphy. Ever heard of him?"

Vinnie looked to me.

I nodded. "Indeed I have."

"Him and Famous Ray cooked up some scheme to sell it to a fucking sheik of Araby or sumshit," he said. "Famous Ray wouldn't quit running his mouth about it, said we'd split the dough right down the middle. I told him no, thanks. I didn't want to touch that thing. They want to deal with the old *Gentleman in Black,* then that luck was on them."

"Quite generous," I said.

"Yeah?" he said. "I think so, too. And then what does Famous Ray do but turn right around and stick it in my backside. I got no love lost for him."

"You might say he's dead to you," I said.

"I might," Morelli said. "But I won't. I think he and that Irish prick Murphy unloaded that fucking thing together."

"It's still in Boston," I said.

"Spenser's seen it," Vinnie said.

"No shit?" he said. "Better ask Murphy about it then, because you sure as shit ain't getting to Ray Russo. He sticks his skinny little fucking neck out of whatever hole he's in and he'll get it chopped off."

We shook hands and Vinnie and I walked up to Prince Street. The air smelled fresh and clean. I stubbed out the cigar and we headed back to his Cadillac.

"How was it?" Vinnie said.

"As terrible as I remember."

"Devon Murphy?"

"Yep."

45

The next morning, Vinnie and I drove south to Plymouth. I'd picked him up at the bowling alley at dawn and brought along donuts and a thermos full of coffee. Sometimes my thoughtfulness astounded even me. The morning light was harsh over the highway and I reached for my sunglasses on the dash.

"Murphy's in Plymouth?" Vinnie said. "Christ. What is he, a fucking pilgrim?"

"He'l fear not what men say," I said. "He'l labor night and day."

"Sometimes I think you got your own language, Spenser," he said. "Talking to yourself like that."

"Hazard of the job," I said. "Surveillance and tail jobs can make you a little crazy."

"A little?"

I shrugged. I opened the box of donuts on the center console as we drove. The Land Cruiser was big, plenty of room for two toughs and their donuts. Vinnie grabbed a basic glazed as we curved south on Route 3. It was a bright, beautiful day as we drove onto Main Street, the downtown a gathering of red-brick storefronts and old white churches. There were plenty of pubs and antique stores. Most of them had cute little names like the Driftwood Public House, Pilgrim's Progress, and the Captain's Den. We parked by the old post office and walked across the street to a gathering of storefronts by the town square. The First Parish church of Plymouth dominated the square. In its shadow, a woman dressed in pilgrim garb handed out tour fliers to tourists. I'd had the bread at Plimoth Plantation. It was very good.

We walked down the slope of Market Street and into a large brick building. A hand-painted sign on a plate-glass window announced *Smith & James Antique Appraisers and Auctions.*

"Does Murphy know we're coming?" Vinnie said.

"Nope," I said. "But this is where his landlady said we'll find him."

"Terrific."

The inside of Smith & James was expansive and voluminous with furniture, toys, paintings, sculptures, and leather-bound books. At the entryway stood four old horses from a merry-go-round and a full-size captain's wheel. Glass cases held coins, silverware, and handwritten letters from another age. Vinnie walked ahead of me, picking up an old duck decoy, studying the price tag on the bottom.

"Hundred bucks?" he said. "For this? You got to be kidding me."

"That's where bidding starts," I said. "It only goes up from there."

"For a fucking duck?"

There were model ships, old maps, and one section devoted completely to movie memorabilia. A framed half-sheet from *Bad Day at Black Rock* caught my eye when I spotted Devon Murphy staring at a far wall. He had on a light blue guayabera, his white hair loose and scattered as always, with some black reading glasses down on his nose. He held a pen and notebook in hand, jotting down prices of several racks of vases in a tall shelf.

"You've been holding out on me, Devon," I said.

He turned to look at me. Murphy pulled off his glasses, holding them with his pad of paper.

"Whattya want, Spenser?" he said. "I got an auction in thirty minutes. I told you everything. You got everything."

"Except for Famous Ray," I said.

He pushed up the glasses on top of his head. He twisted his jaw a bit as he watched to see if I was serious.

"JoJo Morelli got the paintings as the spoils of war," I said. "When he got sick, he placed them in the hands of his brother's right-hand man. You and Famous Ray were going to cash in big with some money people in the Middle East."

"Bullshit," Murphy said. "All bullshit. Sell the painting to some rich sheik? Where did you get all this crap, Spenser? I mean, really."

Vinnie walked up to us. He reached up onto the shelf and pulled out the piece Murphy had been admiring. He turned it over, searched for the price, and whistled.

"Lotta money for a vase," Vinnie said.

"It's not a vase," Murphy said. "It's a nineteenth-century Japanese chamber pot from the Edo period."

"Whattya do with it?" Vinnie said.

"Same thing Devon's been doing on us," I said.

"Come on," Murphy said. "You better get your money back from whoever sold you that lie. I never worked with Famous Ray. I barely even knew the guy. You think I'd do business with those animals? Use your head.

What fucking idiot said that? I'll punch him right in the mouth."

Vinnie set the pot back on the shelf. "Jimmy Morelli," he said. "But I'd think twice before calling him an idiot."

"Or punching him in the mouth," I said.

"That, too," Vinnie said, lifting the lid on the pot and staring inside. "Oh, I get it. You shit in it."

"You could have just told me that Famous Ray ended up with *The Gentleman in Black*," I said. "It really would've cut down my travel expenses."

"I don't know nothing about Famous Ray," Murphy said. "Or the Morellis. I've been real patient with you. If you'll both excuse me, I need to get these items arranged. They're opening the doors to real customers soon. This is how I make a living."

"All this stuff is yours?" Vinnie said.

Murphy looked at him.

"So if one of these were to break?" Vinnie said. "You'd be swimming in Shit Creek?"

Murphy's mouth stayed open. He shook his head as Vinnie lifted up a small vase that looked older than Methuselah's grandmother.

"That's part of a matched set," Murphy said. "From the Edo period."

Vinnie tossed it up in the air and caught it with one hand. I stepped back and he tossed it to me. I caught it with two hands.

"You fucking monkeys," Murphy said. "You want me to call the cops? I'll call the cops. I'll do it."

"Tell me where to find Famous Ray," I said.

"I don't even know the guy."

I pitched the vase to Vinnie. He pretended to bobble it like a tight end with a tricky pass. But Vinnie was a shooter. He had great hands. I noticed the vase was very light and covered with a gold patina as it flew in the air.

"That's from the 1850s," he said. "During Okugawa Shogunate's reign. I have it on loan from a real wealthy family."

"I bet, Murphy," Vinnie said. "In other words, you swiped it."

"It's worth nearly ten thousand bucks."

"And I'll crack it like a chicken egg if you don't tell Spenser where to find that painting."

"From Benny Barboza to JoJo Morelli to Famous Ray," I said. "And now El Greco stops here. Where is it, Murphy?"

Devon Murphy looked at us both. His face was very red and I noted a little sweat popping out on his wide forehead. He

318

wasn't buying it. He lifted up his chin and told us to go fuck ourselves.

Vinnie shook his head and tossed me back the vase.

"Go long," I said, gripping it in my right hand.

Vinnie smiled and ran down the aisle of the antiques warehouse. I pulled back my right arm, pumping it like Steve Grogan used to do.

"Okay," Murphy said. "Okay. Jesus Christ. Okay. Give it back. Just give the damn thing back."

"Where?" I said.

Murphy reached into his pocket and pulled out a little handkerchief. He wiped his brow and smoothed down his wild, thin white hair. He closed his eyes and pinched his nose. Vinnie walked back from his pass route.

"We couldn't unload it," he said. "Something like that? A fucking El Greco? It's too damn hot. The buyer backed out."

"And Famous Ray?" I said.

"You'll never find him," he said. "Jimmy Morelli's been searching for him. He wants him dead and Ray knows it. Last time I saw Ray, he had the painting. But I don't know what he did with it. I got no idea. That's it. All right? Can you just give me back the vase and leave me alone?"

A few antiques shoppers had turned to stare. But they just as quickly went back to picking through stacks of antiques.

"Don't lie to me," I said.

"That's it," Murphy said. "That's all I got. Are we done here?"

I tossed the vase up in the air, but before I could catch it, Murphy snatched it, turned his back, and walked far away.

"Touchy guy," Vinnie said.

"Says that's all he knows."

"Bullshit."

"Probably," I said.

"And now?"

"How far can a guy named Famous Ray go underground?" I said.

"With Jimmy Morelli putting out a hit?" Vinnie said. "Deep."

46

We drove back to Cambridge. I dropped off Vinnie and picked up Pearl.

Susan didn't even see me, as she was in session. I walked upstairs, rescued Pearl from an afternoon of boredom, and took her back to the Navy Yard. As I worked out the latest details, we took a walk and played with the tennis ball at the small park by the USS *Constitution*.

It was well past seven by the time Epstein called me back. Pearl and I had taken a little jaunt by the marina, and I stopped off at a park bench overlooking the fishing boats. Pearl was tired, content with lying down in the grass and chewing on a tennis ball.

"You and my secretary are now on a first-name basis," Epstein said.

"I'm never on a first-name basis," I said. "Last name only."

"Like Fabian."

"Fabian was Fabian's first name," I said.

"Last name Forte."

"How do you remember all this shit?" Epstein said.

"It's a gift," I said.

There was a long pause on the line between Boston and Miami. In the old days, it would make a nice steady hum. Now the silence was crisp and electric. I heard the squeaking of an office chair and Epstein gently sigh. Pearl shuffled the tennis ball into one side of her mouth. She looked like a Major Leaguer chawing a big plug of tobacco.

"You got my message," I said.

"Ray Russo," he said.

"Know him?" I said.

"Famous Ray?" Epstein said. "Yeah, I know him. You do realize I was special agent in charge of Boston for several years? We tend to know about guys like Famous Ray."

"I need to speak to him."

"He's what we call incommunicado."

"So nice for him," I said.

"As I'm sure you already know, he turned witness against a few old wise guys in Massachusetts and Rhode Island," he said. "Ray was a big help to us. He came through like he promised, said what he'd told us on the stand. He did his duty and started a brand-new life."

"Can you get a message to him?"

Again the silence, the squeaking of the office chair down in Miami. A hum down in his throat and then a long groan. I pulled the wet tennis ball from Pearl's mouth. She sat at attention, head up high, staring at the ball.

"I take it that's a no."

"That's a maybe," he said. "I can see if I can pass him a message. Is this still about that damn painting or you onto some new cockamamie case?"

"Same old cockamamie case," I said. "It seems that Famous Ray didn't leave Boston empty-handed."

"How solid is your information?"

"Straight from the godfather's mouth."

"Don't tell me you talked to —"

"I did."

"Jesus Christ," Epstein said. "You think maybe Jimmy Morelli told you the painting ended up with Famous Ray so you'd lead him right to where X marks the fucking spot?"

"No," I said. "He said he's made peace with his enemies. He enjoys a nice cigar, drinking Barolo. Did you know he took one of those Perillo tours to the Old Country?"

"If I had to take a river cruise with a bunch of white hairs, I'd have to shoot myself."

"I've followed the El Greco from the heist," I said. "It went from DeMarco's crew, into a hiding spot with Benny Barboza, and then into the hands of the Morelli brothers after Barboza's demise."

"And how the hell did Famous Ray end up with it?"

"As you know, Ray was Jimmy Morelli's right-hand man," I said. "Jimmy didn't want to touch it. Says it's bad luck, only it sounded much scarier in Italian. Famous Ray tried to fence it with a local crook named Devon Murphy. Murphy says they didn't have any takers and Famous Ray skipped town with it when he got into cahoots with you guys."

"I can't lead you to Ray Russo," Epstein said. "You're a solid guy. I trust you. But putting you in direct contact with a man with a price on his head violates a few rules."

"But you could get him the message?"

"The message being 'Where's the fucking painting?' " Epstein said.

"Exactly."

"He won't say."

"I figured," I said.

"And we can't pressure him," he said. "Our witnesses get our protection, do their thing, and then we start them off in a brand-new life. As far as most people are concerned, Ray Russo doesn't exist anymore. The names of witnesses, particularly Mob witnesses, are a highly guarded secret within the Bureau."

"I understand," I said.

"But you still want me to slip him a message?"

"Yep."

"Can you promise me that anything you learn would be between you and Famous Ray?" he said. "You can't share a word, a hint, with Jimmy Morelli or any of his pets."

"I do solemnly swear."

"The Winthrop job," Epstein said. "I can't say I'm surprised it would circle back to Ray. He's a real fast talker. I can ask the local office to send out one of Ray's handlers, make an inquiry about the painting."

"You know where to find me," I said.

"Unfortunately," Epstein said. And hung up.

I stood up from the bench and Pearl trotted at my side. A detective's best friend.

47

Early the next morning, Marjorie Ward Phillips invited me to breakfast at the Taj hotel. That I'd just worked out and happened to like the Taj perhaps played in my acceptance. I also wanted to see where the Winthrop stood if I recovered the painting, that being a long shot now that the last man standing had been given a new name and identity. We had a better chance of locating Jimmy Hoffa or D. B. Cooper.

"You've been treated rather poorly, Spenser," she said, before we'd even been able to order. "I want to make things right with us."

"Breakfast is a start."

"Please," she said. "Is it too early for a drink?"

I looked at my watch. It was ten o'clock.

"Not from where I'm sitting," I said.

We sat in the back of the café by a plateglass window facing Newbury Street. She ordered us two Bloody Marys. I was surprised to have heard from her and even more surprised by her friendly demeanor. Her attitude and body language couldn't have been more different from that on her visit to my office with Topper and Marston. She looked tired, drained of her posturing.

"We were so close," she said. "Damn it."

"I heard the paint chips checked out."

"You can never be completely certain," she said. "But yes."

"Although your man Marston told me different."

"He's not my man," she said. "That's Topper's hire and his problem. Right now he wants us to give part of the reward to some local hoodlum who claims he can steal the paintings back for us."

"Jackie DeMarco."

"Yes," she said. "How did you know?"

"I know Jackie," I said. "And he can't get the painting back for you. He had nothing to do with Alan Garner and doesn't know who has the painting now."

She studied my face. "But you do?"

I didn't answer. The waitress brought over two Bloody Marys. I looked forward to replenishing my vitamins. Henry had taken me through a long and somewhat arduous workout. I drank some and studied the menu.

"Can you get it?"

I shrugged.

"The reward is still in play."

"I'm getting tired of hearing about the reward," I said. "The museum has seemed to operate more with a stick than a carrot."

"That's Topper," she said. "Not me."

"It has been both."

Marj pursed her mouth, nodded. Her grayish-blue eyes trained on me as I downed a healthy portion of the Bloody Mary.

"Is it your feelings?" she said. "Or your professional pride?"

"It's more of an insult on my intelligence," I said. "I want your word that Locke will be taken care of."

"He isn't well, you know?"

I nodded. The waitress sauntered up and I ordered two poached eggs over hash. I'd been getting the same thing since the Taj had been the Ritz. Now I had heard it was going to be called something else, but I'd still order the same.

"What do you know beyond what Mr. Marston has told us?"

"Everything," I said.

"About the whereabouts of the Goya and the El Greco?"

"I'm close to the El Greco."

"How close?"

"I know who ended up with the piece," I said. "Now I have to find them."

"And from your reputation, I know you are very good at finding things."

"If I do, I'm sure they will expect a reward."

"Naturally."

"And Locke," I said. "I want the exact terms as outlined by Miss Fiore."

"I know she's your attorney," she said. "But she's quite an unpleasant woman."

"Only to those who are unpleasant to her."

Marj stirred her drink, eyeing me. "This whole business with the board and Topper has really worn me down," she said. "I'm afraid that if I don't reclaim at least one of the paintings, they will fire me before I'm due to retire."

"The board not showing commitment to their word?" I said. "I'm shocked."

"I don't blame you," she said. "Now where has the person gone? When can you talk to them about terms to return *The Gentleman*? First those goddamn letters and then the cloak-and-dagger with Mr. Garner and then now this. I don't really think my nerves can handle much more of this business."

"Drink up," I said, raising my glass.

Across Newbury Street, I watched a gray

sedan pull to the curb, a man inside looking in the direction of the café. He wore a baseball cap and mirrored sunglasses. It was hard to see his face. If I excused myself from Marj, I might sneak up on him and get his new license plate. But he'd probably see me and drive off before I could cross the street. I continued to wait to see if he got out from behind the wheel.

"Spenser?" Marj said.

I nodded. My Bloody Mary was gone. My strength halfway returned.

"You are not all you appear."

"Down deep, I'm really a Native American princess."

"When I first met you, I thought you were a thuggish brute," she said. "Just another thick-necked detective who thought art was nothing but a lot of nonsense."

"And then you heard me sing."

"Sadly, no," she said. "That wasn't it. I see how much you care about Locke, and finding what's been stolen because you do what you've promised. You understand the meaning and value of this art."

"Gee, thanks," I said. "I also don't scratch the furniture and am completely housebroken."

"It's more than that," she said. "So many so-called men I meet are either like Topper with disdain for anything that isn't gilded or grilling out sausages on game day."

"I happen to be an aficionado of fine sausage."

"Oh, shut up," she said. "I'm trying to say you actually understand why art matters beyond just monetary value."

Our food arrived. Large Marj and I barely spoke as we ate. As she reached down to cut into her eggs, she actually smiled at me. Over her shoulder, I watched the silver sedan pull away from the curb and drive away from Newbury toward Arlington. I watched it go.

"Is there something the matter?" Marj said.

"Not sure," I said.

She stared at me, fork in midair, as if she didn't understand me.

"I guess it's all a matter of perspective," I said.

48

As the former head of the BPD burglary squad, I was betting dinero to donuts that Bobby Wright might know something about an old fence like Ray Russo. I called ahead to Wright's security company, and again he agreed to meet with me outside the Quincy Market.

It was late afternoon, nearly four o'clock, by the time I made it through the early traffic. Wright waited for me in the rotunda this time, leaning against a standing table and checking his iPhone. He had on jeans and a red golf shirt with the insignia of his company on the pocket. His lean black face lit up with a smile when he saw me.

We shook hands and walked into the Market, searching for a decent cup of coffee. The Market was still crowded and we had to weave ourselves through the tourists and office workers.

"You found that old painting yet?" Wright said.

"Getting close."

"Don't say that," Wright said. "Not until you've got the goods in hand."

"I am curious about a guy named Ray Russo."

Wright laughed. "Damn," he said. "Famous Ray is mixed up in all this shit? Should've known."

"I heard besides driving Jimmy Morelli, he also was a fence."

"Big-time fence," Wright said. "Not a lot that Famous Ray didn't sell out back of his shop in the North End. For a long time he stole restaurant equipment. He'd double deal, back and forth, slick as goose shit. He'd sell some new place all kinds of kitchen equipment and then two weeks later steal it back. He'd do the same to the next guy. And so on and so on."

"I have it on solid authority that Ray ended up with the paintings from the Winthrop."

"Ha," Wright said. "That is a true fix, isn't it? With Ray turning evidence for the Feds and then performing a disappearing act."

"It definitely complicates matters."

We walked over to the Starbucks counter and ordered two coffees. After we doctored our coffee with our preferred additives, we continued back into the Market. It had grown hot outside, and the Market, while crowded, was nice and cool.

"Any chance of you working with the Feds?" he said. "I'm sure they'd jump on taking the credit for someone else's detective work."

"Working on it," I said. "But if Ray is settled into his new life and new identity, do you think he'd step forward for something like this?"

"Famous Ray may be not so famous now," he said. "But he sure as hell will pay attention to any of that reward money."

I nodded and drank some coffee. A woman walked past, holding a young girl in her arms and yelling at a young boy who'd dashed ahead to the cookie counter. He had his face pressed flat against the glass as his mother snatched him by the shirt. The smell of the warm cookies had proved too much.

"I don't hold up much hope for the Feds," I said. "I'd need to find someone outside the Morelli family who Ray trusted."

"Someone who might know where he's gone?"

"Exactly."

Wright stopped cold and took a sip of coffee. He brushed off a little foam from his thin mustache and nodded in thought. "You talked to Fat Freddy yet?"

"Fat Freddy?" I said.

"Sure," he said. "Con man, bookie. Feds know him. He's probably the son of a bitch who roped Famous Ray into turning away from the family. Even if you don't get shit from him, you should meet the guy. Last I heard he was keeping the book somewhere on Revere Beach. If anyone knows what happened to Famous Ray, it'd be Fat Freddy. Shouldn't be hard to find. Freddy kind of stands out."

Wright held his hands out from his stomach to demonstrate Freddy's incredible girth. He told me a few details on what he knew about him and where I might find him.

"If Freddy is the conduit to Ray Russo, why doesn't Jimmy Morelli shake him down?"

"Because I know something Jimmy Morelli doesn't know," Wright said. "Morelli actually thinks he can trust Fat Freddy. I, on the other hand, based on years of detective work, know Fat Freddy's true nature. And where he places his true allegiance."

"Money."

"Loves that money," Wright said. "And Famous Ray, too. I guess ol' Ray picked the right time to skip town. You're the second guy wanting to know about him this year."

"Don't tell me the other was British and smelled like Louis the sixteenth," I said.

"Nope," Wright said. "It was a state cop working an old homicide."

"The Benny Barboza murder?"

"Yep," he said. "That's it. The guy was retired but said he liked to work his cold case file in his spare time. I thought that was pretty crazy. The last thing I wanted to do after I left the department was work a bunch of old cases. Especially if I wasn't being paid for it."

"Was the guy's name Zimmer?"

"Yep," he said. "That's him. Had another dude with him. Sears?"

"Roebuck," I said.

Wright laughed and we descended the stairs out of the Market and back into the early-evening heat. "Come to think of it, they asked me a few questions about the Winthrop job, too."

"They thought Famous Ray might be connected to the paintings?"

"I can't recall if they connected the job with Ray or Barboza," he said. "But there was definitely talk about the Winthrop heist. They thought I might have heard something before I left the job."

"That's funny."

"How's that?"

"I met those guys a few days ago," I said. "They acted surprised Barboza might've been connected to the theft and pretty much dismissed it."

"Either they got bad memories," Wright said. "Or they're yanking your chain, Spenser."

"My chain's been yanked plenty on this case," I said. "It's getting a bit sore."

"Can't even trust a cop," he said.

"I don't like it," I said.

"Watch your back, man," Wright said. "Too much money riding on finding that lost art."

"You think I can reason with Fat Freddy?"

"No one ever has," he said. "But give it your best shot and let me know how it goes."

49

That night, Vinnie and I parked across from a dilapidated one-story cracker box on Ocean Avenue in Revere. The pinkish paint was molting and chain-link fence wrapping the diminutive property sagging off the posts. The house had been built high off a concrete block foundation that served as a small basement. There were two entryways, one under the front stairs and one at the top of the stairs. All along the step railing, someone had hung wet T-shirts and swim trunks. Two pairs of the swim trunks looked as if they might fit an Indian elephant.

"Fat Freddy won't talk to you."

"So I heard," I said. "But I can be very persuasive."

"Not in the way that a guy like Fat Freddy needs," Vinnie said. "He's used to people trying to get tough. The guy spent most of his life shaking down people who owed the Morellis money and then keeping the book when he got too fat."

"So he hasn't always been Fat Freddy?"

"No," Vinnie said. "He's always been fucking fat. It's just now he's too fucking fat to leave this shithole. He's not a good guy. He's done some very bad things."

"I'm shocked."

"No," Vinnie said. "Really bad things. He's into teen girls. That's why he likes to be this close to the beach, so he can sit his fat ass in a deck chair and watch all young girls in their bikinis. He's a real sicko. I heard he once exposed himself to a nun. Who does shit like that?"

It was also obvious Freddy wasn't one for yardwork. The little grass he had spread out high and ragged. Several trash cans were left overflowing at the curb right under a *No Parking/Tow Zone* sign. A lone chair sat in the middle of a backyard cluttered with old a/c units, broken bicycles, and a rusty propane grill. There was a worn path between the lone chair and the back door. Only the storm door was closed and you could see into the kitchen.

"I made some calls," Vinnie said. "Your cop is right. If anyone knows how to find Famous Ray, it's Fat Freddy."

"The cop I know said Jimmy Morelli doesn't believe Freddy would hold back."

"That's true," Vinnie said. "Fat Freddy is Jimmy's little fat fucking cannoli. He's always been his blind side. Just look how Freddy's best buddy turned on the family. Jimmy shoulda seen it coming."

"They should've put on a vaudeville act," I said. "Fat Freddy and Famous Ray. They'd have really pulled 'em in."

"Oh, the Morellis had an act," Vinnie said. "Not much singing and dancing. Just a lot of bleeding and screaming."

I looked into the side mirror and down the long stretch of Ocean Avenue. I turned back and looked at the house and the street beyond.

"No one followed us," Vinnie said. "Give me a little credit."

"I have two sets of people following me," I said. "That I know."

"On the same team?" Vinnie said.

"Nope," I said. "One is very good. And one is very bad."

"The bad one is the British guy?" he said. "The one who's been riding your coattails."

"Yep," I said. "He followed me and Susan last night to Harvest."

"No shit," he said. "You don't follow a guy when he's on a freakin' date. That's just bad form. What'd you have?"

"The burger," I said.

"Yeah?" Vinnie said. "They make a great burger."

Vinnie had parked in an unlit patch of the street. We waited in the car as three kids on bicycles passed us, looking into the car but all uninterested. Vinnie pulled out his gun, checked the magazine, and slipped it back under his coat. It was a nice coat, light blue linen, worn over a pink gingham shirt. Vinnie's eyes stayed on the back door of the house.

"You wait here," he said.

"I prefer to do my own heavy lifting."

"Nope," he said. "I need to find out who killed Alan. And you need to find your freakin' painting."

"Agreed."

"But there are places you won't go," he said. "And many things you won't do. I don't have that problem. Me and Fat Freddy speak the same language. He'll lie to you all day long, like a freakin' rug, Spenser. With me, he'll know he can't."

I nodded.

"I need you here," he said. "You see any of Fat Freddy's guys trying to go in, you stop them and have a chat."

"While you try and reason with Freddy's better nature."

"Sure," Vinnie said. "Reason with him.

341

Exactly."

I didn't like it but agreed. We tapped fists like two wrestlers in a tag team.

Vinnie opened the driver's door and crossed the street. I watched him push open a broken gate and walk through the yard to the back storm door. The windows were open and I could hear the sounds of Revere, the hum of air conditioners, a broken muffler on a passing car, and kids yelling at each other from down the block. I could also smell the ocean and feel the warm wind off the water. It was all very pleasant until Vinnie got down to work.

From inside Freddy's place, I heard some yelling. And then I heard some crashing. The light flickered about from inside the glass storm door. I heard the high-pitched sound of a man screaming and then furniture breaking.

I watched the street. No one noticed. No one passed.

I tapped out the rhythm of "Ain't That a Kick in the Head" on the passenger door. More crashing sounds came from inside the small house. But less screaming. The arguing seemed to have subsided. After a few more minutes, Vinnie walked out of the back door, combing through his salt-and-pepper hair with his fingers and straightening his jacket.

I watched him walk across Ocean Avenue and climb back behind the wheel of the Cadillac. His light blue linen jacket now had a few fine flecks of blood.

"I know a good dry cleaner," I said.

"Never works," he said. "I just got this jacket, too. Fit me like a glove."

"Very nice."

"Fat Freddy," he said, cranking the ignition. "Tried to argue me about it."

"How long did that last?"

"Not long," Vinnie said. "Hard to argue when you can barely stand up."

Vinnie knocked the car in drive and we made a squealing U-turn in front of the house.

"Swears he doesn't know who killed Alan Garner," he said. "But Famous Ray is in Memphis."

"Him and Elvis," I said. "You got Ray's new name?"

"Don't insult me, Spenser," he said. "Not after my coat got ruined."

"We'll send the bill to the Winthrop," I said.

50

"Memphis?" Susan said.

"I've worked cases in South Carolina and Georgia, twice," I said. "I feel this is a natural progression to conquer the South."

"I think you look for excuses," she said. "You like the food too much."

"Biscuits and barbecue never killed anyone."

"It's probably killed a lot," Susan said. "Go easy down there, Big Daddy."

"Should I pack my seersucker suit?"

"You hate seersucker," she said. "In fact, you loathe it."

"I was so excited about the trip that I nearly forgot."

I was at Susan's place, standing in her kitchen and making the most of the odd assortment she kept in her refrigerator. As Susan had been juicing a lot, I found just enough to cobble together an authentic Cobb salad. She didn't have any chicory greens, but she did have parsley, watercress, and romaine. I was also pleasantly surprised to find two boiled eggs and some sliced turkey fresh from Whole Foods. I vigorously chopped the greens and turkey while Susan made us drinks.

"I can't imagine starting my life over again," she said. "Did this Ray Russo have a family?"

"He was twice divorced," I said. "One grown son. But they were estranged and hadn't spoken in years."

"Hence the reason to speak to his hefty pal."

"I didn't speak to him," I said. "Vinnie facilitated the information."

"I'm sure he did," she said. "And will Vinnie be traveling with you to Memphis to help facilitate even more from Mr. Russo?"

"Never mess with a hot streak," I said. "I don't even plan on changing my underwear."

"You might want to rethink that plan if you wish to get lucky."

"I prefer to think luck is based on skill," I said.

She handed me a vodka martini. You couldn't eat a Cobb salad without one. It was a law in California. I had taught Susan a trick I'd learned from my pal Drew at

Legal. Keep your vodka in the freezer and bury your vermouth in your backyard.

"Be prepared for Russo to shut you out completely," Susan said. "He may actually think of himself as a whole new person."

"And that whole new person may be still scared shitless of Jimmy Morelli," I said. "Guys in the North End have been known to hold a grudge."

"Why do you think he went against them?"

"Excellent question," I said. "From all accounts, Famous Ray was a known and trusted member of the family."

I set down the martini and started to make the French dressing. It was an old recipe of an inexact mixture of red wine vinegar, lemon juice, olive oil, Worcestershire sauce, coarse mustard, and salt and pepper. I never wrote it down, but somehow it always tasted the same.

"I should bottle and sell this sauce," I said.

"You and Paul Newman."

"Why not?" I said. "We both have the same piercing blue eyes."

"But a very different nose," she said.

"It only adds to my rugged good looks."

I set aside the dressing and drank half the martini. As the last piece of the salad puzzle, I heated a black skillet for the bacon as I cut up a tomato. I then removed the seeds and chopped it into tiny pieces. All the ingredients to the salad sat in pretty piles on the chopping block.

"Do you know much about Ray Russo's new life in Memphis?" Susan said. "Let me guess. He's an Elvis impersonator."

"Sadly no," I said. "Even better."

"A pizza chef?"

"Let's not stereotype."

"A thief with ties to organized crime?"

"Not anymore," I said. "It looks as if he's found God."

"Like your con man down in Georgia?"

"Nope," I said. "I think it's authentic. Or at least he believes he's authentic. Famous Ray Russo is now an ordained minister at an interdenominational church off Elvis Presley Boulevard."

"Aha," Susan said. "I knew there was an Elvis connection."

"Haven't you heard?" I said. "He's everywhere."

I removed the bacon from the pan and slipped the pieces onto the block. I chopped the pieces and set them aside with the crumbles of blue cheese. I arranged the chopped greens, tomatoes, eggs, cheese, bacon, and avocado in neat sections in two wooden bowls. I reached into the freezer and retrieved the vodka.

"Careful, big fella," Susan said. "What time's your flight?"

"Six," I said. "Layover in Atlanta. We'll be there by ten."

Susan snatched the bottle from my hand. She reached into the refrigerator and grabbed me a beer. "You'll thank me in the morning."

"How about I thank you more after dinner?"

"What did you have in mind?"

" 'Love Me Tender'?"

"How about 'All Shook Up'?" she said, taking a sip of martini. She looked both innocent and devilish at the same time, as only Susan could do.

"Even better," I said, leaning over the counter and kissing her hard.

51

Within an hour of touching down in Memphis, Vinnie and I had a rental and were cruising down Elvis Presley Boulevard. According to Fat Freddy, Ray was now a pastor at the Light Keeper Church only a few miles from Graceland. I said it was time to shake, rattle, and roll. I couldn't help myself. It was my first time in the city.

"What's his new name?" Vinnie said.

"The Reverend Theo Doménikos."

"Famous Ray Russo a Greek?" he said. "Jesus Christ. Now I heard everything."

"Not just a Greek," I said. "*The Greek.* El Greco was Doménikos Theotokópoulos."

"So he does have the painting?" Vinnie said.

"Or at least he was very inspired."

"I known Ray for a long time," he said. "It's best I go up to him first. He trusts me. He won't run."

"He won't think you were sent by Jimmy

Morelli?"

"Never," Vinnie said. "Ray might not like me. But he'd never think I'd throw in with Jimmy Morelli. Or do his dirty fucking laundry."

There wasn't much glitz on Elvis Presley Boulevard. In fact, it reminded me a hell of a lot of Route 1 cutting though Saugus. We passed a lot of used-car dealers, cheap hotels, pawnshops, and fast food franchises. Someone had spray-painted the words *Superman a Dam Fool* on the side of a condemned restaurant.

"Why the hell would Elvis live here?" Vinnie said.

"Probably didn't look like this in the fifties," I said. "Lots of room to drive his pink Cadillacs."

"I like Elvis," Vinnie said. "My sister and I used to go see all his movies at the Suffolk Drive-in. She loved Elvis. Couldn't go a day without talking about how good-looking he was. I was impressed with the women. He made this one picture, I can't recall the name, with Nancy Sinatra. He was a race car driver or something. I thought that was pretty cool. I liked Nancy about as much as my older sister loved Elvis."

"You can get her a souvenir."

"She has one of those clocks with Elvis

swinging his hips," he said. "Maybe I can get her a snow globe or something."

"Memphis is your oyster."

"I don't think Ray's gonna know what happened to Alan," Vinnie said. "I think that whole thing was a fake out."

"All I know is that I saw it," I said. "And the Winthrop confirmed the paint chips. So whatever Ray had is now with someone else."

"Whoever killed Alan."

"Yep," I said. "Looks that way."

We spotted Elvis's old house on the left and the museum complex across the street. Two miles down the road, I turned onto Gateway Drive and drove for a mile until I saw the small white church on the right. The sign outside read *NEED A LIFEGUARD? OURS WALKS ON WATER. Light Keeper Church, Theo Doménikos, Pastor.* The building was white brick and slope-roofed, with two skinny stained-glass windows facing the street.

"Toto, we're not in Revere Beach anymore," I said.

"Theo Doménikos," Vinnie said. "Living down the street from Elvis. You almost got to hand it to Famous Ray."

"Almost."

I parked in the empty parking lot and we

351

both got out and stretched in the hot morning sun. It had been a warm summer in Boston, but nothing like this. I felt like I was walking into the steam shower at the Harbor Health Club. The air conditioner had barely had time to dry the sweat on my T-shirt.

As we turned the corner, we saw a man high on motorized scaffolding touching up a sun-faded portrait of Jesus, hands outstretched in a peaceful gesture. The man turned to us as we walked up close, paintbrush in hand. He was a short Hispanic man in white coveralls and a white hat, both splattered in blue paint.

"We're looking for Pastor Doménikos," I said.

"He no here," the man said.

"Do you know when he'll be back?"

The man shook his head and went back to touching up Jesus's outstretched right hand. Vinnie had walked ahead of me, reaching the front door of the church. He pulled off a flier and handed it to me. It looked like there was a potluck supper later that evening. Half of the bill was in English and the other in Spanish.

"Multicultural," I said.

"An Italian posing as a Greek, posing as a minister who speaks Spanish," Vinnie said.

"Not a bad cover."

"Let's check in to our hotel," I said. "Maybe get something to eat before we check out the other addresses I've found."

"Anything to eat down here besides grits?"

"Vinnie, you wouldn't know a grit if you saw one."

"It's just fucking polenta," he said. "Don't try and fool me."

He had me there. We got into the car and headed back the same way along Elvis Presley Boulevard.

"Small church," Vinnie said. "Supper for the poor, reaching out to Mexicans, and all that. I don't see Famous Ray's angle."

"Maybe he's not working an angle," I said.

"Famous Ray?" Vinnie said. "He's been working schemes since he was born. He may change his town, his looks, and his name, but deep down he's the same. I know a thousand guys like Ray, and as much as they want to be somebody else, nothing's ever gonna change. You know how many guys I know would give their left nut to go straight? But if being a crook is in your DNA, nothing's gonna change. He's got something cooking down here. Probably donations. If it were me, that's what I'd do."

"You're a cynical man, Vinnie Morris."

"And you ain't, Spenser?" Vinnie said.

"Come on. I know you. You know me. Let's eat. I can deal with Ray's bullshit better on a full stomach."

52

Vinnie and I found a place called The Bar-B-Q Shop on Madison Avenue. We drank cold Ghost River on draught and ate ribs. The ribs were lean and well done with a dry rub. Both of us polished off an entire rack each. The clean bones lay on a plate in between us.

"Not bad," Vinnie said. "We don't have shit like this in Boston."

"Nope," I said. "Good shit is hard to find."

"I wonder if Ray misses a good Italian meal?" Vinnie said. "Maybe we should've tempted him with some stuff from Salumeria Italiana."

"With every good answer, we feed him a stuffed olive."

"And with every wrong one, he gets a knuckle sandwich."

The first address I'd found wasn't good. A man named Doménikos had lived there a few years ago, but a neighbor told me he was in his eighties and had been put in a nursing home. The second address was in midtown Memphis off Rembert Street. The street was lined with small houses and crooked mailboxes. Famous Ray had taken up residence in a small white house up a sloping drive. The house looked to have been built in the forties, with few improvements since. A mailbox hung by the front door overflowed with bills and fliers, some of them addressed to Doménikos, others to someone named A. Lisle.

I knocked on a few doors. "Father" Doménikos had lived there earlier in the year but moved out a few months ago. No one knew where he'd gone.

We decided to check in to the Peabody Hotel and rest for a couple hours. I lay on the bed and flipped through the news and ESPN, checking the games. At five, I showered and changed into fresh clothes and met Vinnie in the lobby. He had on a rust paisley sport coat over a wide-collared white shirt, black trousers, and polished black shoes. His hair was slicked back and had on a pair of gold 1970s Elvis glasses.

"Elvis has entered the building," I said.

He jacked his thumb at the shop by the elevators. "Lansky Brothers," he said. "They made all his clothes. I figured what the hell."

"You'll look right at home where we're going."

"Sure," Vinnie said. "Right. Exactly what I was thinking."

Twenty minutes later, we were back on Elvis Presley Boulevard. Vinnie drove this time, windows cracked to let out the floral fragrance sprayed in the rental.

"At the church, he'll be insulated," I said. "We need to talk to him alone."

"Rental's got a big trunk."

"Maybe a more subtle effort."

"Hold him up by his ankles and shake out the truth," Vinnie said.

"Perhaps I should be the one who talks with him."

Vinnie nodded and we turned onto Winchester, following the road back to the Light Keeper Church. The lot was filled with pickup trucks and battered cars. White lights had been strung from landscaping posts on the front lawn. Several tables laid out with red-and-white checked tablecloths with families milling about. Mostly black members, but many Hispanics, too.

Vinnie parked down the street. He turned off the ignition, looked to me, and shrugged.

"He ain't gonna talk."

"I should be the one to ask."

Vinnie nodded. He offered his fist. I

bumped it and he tagged me in.

I got out and walked back down the street to the church. I had seen pictures, mostly mug shots, of Ray Russo. I knew his general build, the shape of his face. I couldn't be sure he wouldn't run when he saw me. But I'd worn a new pair of Asics and was confident he wouldn't get far.

As I passed the tables, families speaking in Spanish and English, I admired the food laid out. Barbecue, tamales, fried chicken, and beans. Hot homemade tortillas and some kind of dish that looked like fried fish heads. I saw the same man who had been painting the mural of Christ on the side of the church.

He was dressed in a blue Memphis Grizzlies shirt that hung to his knees. The front read *Grit & Grind.* When he saw me, he nodded. He simply pointed to the front of the church. I nodded back and mounted the steps. The front doors were wide open, the sanctuary dimly lit. The pews looked to be old and mismatched, the carpet a threadworn red. At the altar, I saw a man kneeling before a large cross.

We were alone.

There was the sound of laughter and music outside.

When I walked up on him, the man

turned. He was gaunt and gray-bearded, dressed in black jeans and a black dress shirt. He looked more like a hippie than a Mob guy. But there was no mistaking Famous Ray.

"Not here," he said. "I knew you were coming. Take me where you want. I'm tired of running."

53

"I didn't come to kill you."

Famous Ray got off his knees and turned back to me. His eyes had dark circles under them. He looked to have lost fifty pounds since the time of his last mug shot. He wore a large gold cross around his neck. Lean, wiry, and somewhat haggard, he had the appearance of a portrait from long ago.

"Who are you?"

"My name's Spenser," I said. "I'm a private investigator."

As he looked at me, his dark eyes darted from me to the back of the church, and then to the side doors.

"What do you want?"

"The Gentleman in Black."

He nodded and swallowed, running a lean hand over his face.

"Did Jimmy send you?"

"I work for the Winthrop Museum."

"You got some kind of ID?" he said.

He hadn't lost his East Boston accent. I opened my wallet and showed him the credentials given to me by the Commonwealth of Massachusetts.

"You're the guy who killed Frank Doerr?"

"I guess that will be my epitaph," I said.

He let out a breath and sat down on the steps to the altar, the carpet even more worn and threadbare here. A PA system had been set up under the large cross, lots of wires and speakers showing. Famous Ray looked tired, resting his elbows on his knees.

"Sorry you came all this way," he said. "I don't have it."

"You're going to have to give me more than that."

"And if I don't?"

"I'll drop Jimmy Morelli a postcard," I said. "He is looking for you."

"How'd you find me?"

"Does it matter?"

A side door opened and the short Hispanic painter walked into the sanctuary carrying a shotgun. He kept the gun aimed at me but his eyes up at Pastor Doménikos.

Russo/Doménikos shook his head and said something rapid in Spanish. The man's eyes were on me but didn't move. He looked like a little fireplug, sure-footed and rooted to the ground. It didn't look like he was going anywhere. Again, Ray spoke to him in Spanish. This time the tone was harsh. The short man lowered his shotgun and headed back out the side door.

"That's Miguel," he said. "He's a good friend."

"Looks like you have a nice life here."

"Better than I ever hoped to deserve," he said. "The Feds gave me a few options of where I could go. I'd never been to Memphis. I always liked Elvis."

"And the church façade?"

"It's real," he said. "I don't have to work. I don't have to do anything. I didn't want to do this. I had to do this."

"Some might say it's a calling."

"It's hard to understand," he said. "It was hard for me to understand. But I knew things were different."

He smiled as he spoke, a calm expression on his face. He'd shaved his beard thin across his jawline, narrowly connecting with his mustache along his chin. His dark eyes took me in, seeming very much at home inside the tiny brick church.

"I don't want to cause you any trouble," I said. "I was hired to find the painting."

"It's long gone."

"Where?"

"Can I ask how you knew I had it?"

362

"Friend of the family."

"Jimmy Morelli," he said. "He still wants his cut."

"As do a few others in Boston."

"Jackie DeMarco?"

I shrugged. He smoothed down the thin mustache with the back of his hand.

"Do you believe in fate, Mr. Spenser?"

"I attended the final game of the 2004 World Series," I said. "Yes, I do."

"Divine intervention?" Ray said. "That God has a purpose for us all?"

"Pastor Doménikos," I said. "That discussion would take much more time than you and I have."

He smiled. He liked me referring to him by his new name. I could smell the corn and meat cooking on the grill outside. Tejano music began to play.

"I'm glad you were able to start over," I said. "You and I both know you've done some rotten things in your life. Not many people have that kind of opportunity."

He nodded.

"I have a friend who's been searching for these paintings for almost twenty years," I said. "He's very ill. I promised I'd find them for him."

"Not for the money."

"Nope."

"I may be a man of God," he said. "But I am still suspicious."

"Did you sell them?" I said. "You and Devon Murphy?"

He shook his head. "We tried," he said. "The Goya was in really bad shape. The guys in DeMarco's crew weren't careful and made a rough time of it. But *The Gentleman* was pristine. Nearly perfect. You should have seen it."

"I have," I said.

"Where?"

I told him about my trip with Alan Garner. He said he didn't know Garner but didn't disagree that what I saw was authentic.

"It changes you," he said. "Some people don't get it. Jimmy used to call it bad luck. It wasn't bad luck for me. It helped me put things in perspective, thinking about all those eyes on it over the years. You realize everything you do in life isn't worth squat. My place in the world. That stuff I done? None of it would matter in fifty years, let alone four hundred."

"Did you leave it with Murphy?"

"This is my new life, Spenser," he said. "I don't want to walk backward."

"If you've thrown away your old life," I said, "what does it matter anymore? It may not matter to you. But it matters a hell of a

364

lot to the museum and to my friend."

"How sick is he?"

"As sick as you get."

"Cancer?"

I nodded.

"My mother died of cancer," he said. "It's not pretty to watch. Your body turns on you."

"I won't tell the cops we talked."

Russo/Doménikos smiled and stood from the steps. He smiled at me some more, finding some warmth and comfort in something I didn't see. He placed his right hand on my shoulder and looked at me with old black eyes. "The cops know."

I didn't answer.

"After I made a deal with the Feds, two state cops tracked me down here," he said. "They wanted the painting. They said if I talked, they wouldn't tell Jimmy where to find me."

"I'm sure for the greater good of the art world."

"I told them where I'd stashed it in Boston," he said. "I didn't need any trouble. I'd already bought this building, started this church, and began my new life."

"A lot to lose."

"Do you know these men?"

"Indeed I do, Pastor."

54

When we arrived in Boston the next afternoon, Frank Belson was waiting for me at baggage claim.

"Moonlighting for Uber?" I said.

Vinnie looked up from the baggage carousel, gold Elvis glasses pushed high on his head. He met eyes with Belson and reached for his hanging bag. He snatched the handle and walked in the opposite direction.

"You and Morris?" he said. "That's a dream team."

"I think I just lost my ride."

"You're in luck," he said. "I offer one-way transportation to headquarters. I'll even take the fucking scenic route through Southie."

"To what do I owe this honor?"

"A British dandy named Paul Marston got three in the head last night," he said. "Figured you might know something about it."

"As you already know, I was in Memphis."

"I understand you didn't like him."

"Couldn't stand him."

"He was sitting outside your place in the Navy Yard when he got shot."

I shrugged. I eyed the carousel for my bag. I'd brought Pearl back an official Elvis hound-dog collar. I couldn't wait to give it to her.

"He worked for the Winthrop," I said. "Talk to them. He'd been tailing me."

"I guess he knew you were out of town," Belson said. "A jogger spotted the body in some shitty old Land Cruiser parked by the pier."

"Gunmetal gray like mine?"

"Yep, because it was your freakin' car."

"Messy?"

"No," Belson said. "Nice and neat. Three bullets in the back of a man's head looks like Martha Stewart's kitchen."

"Shit."

"Come on," he said. "You won't get that truck back for a while. Glass wants to have a chance. After that, I can take you to Susan's."

"How did you know I wanted to go to Susan's?"

Belson didn't answer. I spotted my bag on the carousel, grabbed it, and followed him to the elevator and up to the parking garage. As soon as he paid the toll and hit the highway, he punched up the cigarette lighter and set fire to a nub of a cigar.

"Funny how every bastard who comes to Boston gets to be a Sox fan," he said.

I let down my window to get some fresh air. After Jimmy Morelli's shop, I'd had enough of cigar smoke.

"Marston had on a Sox cap," I said.

"He's a lot leaner," he said. "But about your same height."

"Someone mistook him for me."

"Damn, Spenser," he said. "Who said you've lost a step?"

"Muddling through my car at night," I said. "Someone could've easily made the mistake."

"Good thing you were gyrating those hips down south," he said. "Or me and Quirk might be forced to say something nice about you to the papers."

"You old softie."

"Glass is another story," Belson said. "She'd give the press a solid 'No comment.' "

"Jackie DeMarco?" I said.

"Who better," he said, driving with one hand, ashing the cigar outside the window with the other. "Maybe you and Susan

368

should take a little vacation until we sort out this shit sandwich you served up."

"I got a little sorting to do on my own."

"You find the painting?"

I didn't answer. Belson shook his head and groaned. He picked up his cell and muttered a few affirmatives into the phone before tossing it onto the seat between us. The unmarked car was this year's model, but the interior looked a decade old. In the flickering afternoon light, Belson's five-o'clock shadow had reached six.

"Can you tell me why Jackie wants you dead?" he said. "Again?"

"He thinks I have the painting."

"But you don't."

"Nope."

"And you won't tell us who does."

"Not until I'm absolutely sure," I said. "And I've gotten it safe and sound back to the Winthrop."

"Son of a bitch," he said. "I'm trying to run a little interference for you because I know that even though you often walk through shit, you come out smelling like Chanel Number Five."

"Ah, Frank."

"Don't 'Ah, Frank' me," he said. "Your buddy Topper Townsend and his fuddy-duddy silver cane have been rattling a lot of desks at headquarters. He firmly believed you'd killed Marston until we proved to him that you were out of town. Even now, he wants to see travel receipts, video of you in your hotel. That guy talks to all of us like we carry his fucking water. I can't stand him."

"We agree on some things."

"Hell," he said. "We agree on most things. But this crap has gotten too hot. Let's sit down, let me know what you know, and let us handle it from here. Okay, ace?"

"How long have we known each other?"

Frank puffed on his cigar and took the off-ramp to Roxbury.

"Long enough."

"And do you expect me to agree?"

"No fucking way," he said. "But I told Glass I'd try. Now you'll have the extreme pleasure of spending some time with her. And let me warn you, she ain't serving you no hot coffee and donuts. It's not that kind of shit anymore."

"Canapés?"

"Christ Almighty."

55

It was nearly midnight, and I was lying on Susan's sofa with my head in her lap. After traveling all day and spending some quality time with Captain Glass, it took only a double of Blanton's and two aspirins to soothe my aching head. We had on the television. Pearl snuffled and snoozed at Susan's feet while Ben Mankiewicz introduced *Beat the Devil* on TCM.

"Sounds like your kind of movie."

"I've seen it," I said. "Bogart loses in the end."

"He always loses in the end."

"Me and Bogie," I said, getting to my feet, and walked back to Susan's kitchen. Pearl obediently followed while I poured a fresh drink.

When I got back to the sofa, Susan sat upright and settled into the far corner. She had a shrink look on her face, although it was difficult to take her seriously with her hair up in a bun and a mud mask on her face.

"You look like a shrink."

"I am a shrink."

"And you look concerned."

"I am concerned."

"I'm not," I said. "I have the matter firmly in my grasp."

"Um-hmm," she said. "By *firmly,* you mean that you have to wrestle a priceless work of art from two state cops with questionable morals."

"Ex–state cops," I said. "And their morals aren't questionable. They're deplorable."

"Why not just tell Belson and Glass?" she said. "Or your friend Epstein."

"And let them have all the fun?"

"A man was murdered because someone thought he was you."

"True," I said. "But if the shooter thinks I look like Paul Marston, they're not very good."

"I hate to say it," she said. "But your ego might someday be your undoing."

"What's done can't be undone."

"What the hell does that mean?" Susan said.

"I'm not really sure," I said. "Let me finish this drink and I'll let you know."

On TV, Bogart was tooling about the

Amalfi Coast with Jennifer Jones. They looked like they were having a hell of a time. I took another swig and stretched out my feet. My bag remained unopened at the top of Susan's staircase.

I had just about grown comfortable when my cell skittered across the coffee table. Pearl pricked her ears at the sound. I looked down at the screen and recognized the number. Against my better judgment, I answered.

"Where the hell have you been?" Devon Murphy said.

"Down where the catfish are jumping and the cotton is high."

"I called your office a dozen times," he said. "I stopped by twice. Met your secretary. The broad with the blue hair?"

"She's not my secretary," I said. "And like I said, I've been gone."

"But you're back now?"

I looked to Susan and she lifted one eyebrow. Sensing a shift in the balance of power, Pearl hopped up between us and rested her head in Susan's lap. Traitor.

"Indeed I am."

"We need to talk," he said. "Can you meet me at the auction house?"

"How about noon?"

"How about now?"

"It's midnight."

"I got a fucking watch," Murphy said.

"I can't tonight."

"You want *The Gentleman in Black*?" he said. "Or not."

"You told me you didn't know where to find it."

There was a long pause. Pearl turned on her back and pressed her hind legs into my thigh. She made a deep groan and shuffled in Susan's lap.

"Okay," Murphy said. "I may have lied a little."

"That's lying a lot."

"Oh, well," Murphy said. "You know how it goes."

"Why should I trust you now?"

" 'Cause I've been the swingman to that big old painting since the Morelli Brothers stole it."

"I heard."

"Did you find Famous Ray?"

"Was Alan Garner fronting for you and your silent partners?" I said.

He didn't answer. I heard crunching sounds, like he was working over some hard candy in his molars. I waited for him for about twenty seconds, until he asked if I was still there.

"It's late," I said. "Call me tomorrow at

my office."

"The seller wants to move tonight," he said. "Either you're in right now or I go to someone else."

"Craigslist?"

"Better than that," Murphy said. "You've seen the painting. The way that man's eyes look at you, trying to read your freakin' mind. Like you're just a passerby, a speck of time that few will recall."

"I'll have to make some calls to the museum."

"Don't make me wait," he said. "These guys don't wait for no one."

I hung up and Susan put on a pot of coffee for me. After I showered and changed, I called Vinnie and told him to bring some backup.

56

It was two a.m. when I got to Plymouth in Susan's car. Vinnie and two guys in his crew followed me in his Cadillac. As I got close to the town square, Vinnie flicked his high beams but kept driving down Main Street. I parked on the square by the old church and walked around to the unlocked side entrance Murphy had told me about. It was dark and cavernous inside Smith & James Antique Appraisers and Auctions. Only a few hanging lamps burning down the center of the warehouse.

I pulled the .38 from under my jacket and called out to Murphy.

"Spenser," he said. "Hey. Back here."

I kept on walking past a display of vintage tabletop radios, old board games, and samurai swords. Murphy stood by a large worktable, shifting through parts of an old suit of armor. He held the helmet in his hands. It looked about as authentic as a

Mexican cheeseburger.

"Sixteenth century," he said. "I got it at an auction in London. If you look closely, you can see the sword damage on the codpiece."

"I forgot mine," I said. "Should I be concerned?"

He didn't answer. I looked down at the armor and up at Murphy, his face covered in shadow while he worked.

"Where's the painting?"

"Oh," he said. "It's not here. What the hell are you thinking? This ain't amateur hour. We got rules and plans to follow."

My gun hung loose at my side. I searched around the cavernous space for any movement or sounds. It was still and electric, only the gentle buzz of the lamps overhead.

"I'll take you to *The Gentleman*," Murphy said.

"In Mystic."

He stopped fumbling with the suit, carefully placing the helmet onto the worktable. I noticed several drops of blood on the table, another one tapping onto the wood. He leaned forward in the sliver of light to look at the blood on his fingers. He'd been beaten so badly his eyes were merely slits, large welts and bruises across his cheeks, with a busted lip.

"I tripped and fell."

"Zimmer and Roebuck?"

He shook his head, trying to smile, but stopping short with the sliced lip. "You found Famous Ray?"

I nodded.

"Where was he?"

"Does it matter?"

"Nope," Murphy said. "Not at all. The piece has bounced around like a fucking Ping-Pong ball in twenty years but somehow keeps on coming back to me."

"Jimmy Morelli says it's bad luck," I said. "Looks like he was right."

"Those cops didn't do this," he said. "They found the piece as some kind of game in their retirement. It was either solve this old case or do fucking tai chi in the park. They knew they were smarter than those fancy-ass Feds, realizing the art had never left Boston."

"And to the victor —"

Murphy reached for an old rag and cleaned the blood off his face. He winced as he did so, holding on to the edge of the worktable for stability. With slow movement and a lot of pain, he inched forward toward me as if he wanted to tell me a secret.

"Did you speak to the museum?"

"Of course," I said, lying through my bicuspids.

"And they've agreed to the full reward?"

"If you can produce the painting Alan Garner showed me last week."

"Alan Garner didn't know crap about *The Gentleman,*" he said. "Or any of the stolen art. We just needed his contacts at the fancy-ass gallery on Newbury Street. He swore to us that he could not only move the painting but arrange for the transport overseas."

"And when he didn't?"

"He should've been more like Fish," he said. "Good to his word."

"Did you kill him?"

Murphy coughed out a laugh, placing a fist to his mouth. I looked down at the foot of the armor, half expecting to see a MADE IN CHINA stamp.

"He didn't make a deal with me," he said. "Now are you ready to make the deal? Or not? They wouldn't work with a guy like me, with the record I got. After all the fiddle-farting around you've been doing since taking the job, I figured you were ready to finish the job."

"You and I meet Zimmer and Roebuck," I said. "I see the painting. And then I transfer the money."

"Yep."

"And what else?"

379

"There's nothing else," he said. "I'm paid. You're paid. Those two old cops and the museum make an agreement. It's as easy as making a BLT."

"Why didn't you just arrange this when we first met?"

"Like I said, I was the swingman," I said. "Now, with other parties involved, time is of the fucking essence."

"Those cops didn't beat you," I said.

Murphy closed his eyes. His face looked like two-week-old hamburger meat. Whoever had worked him over had probably worn a ring, slicing lots of deep cuts and scrapes.

"I'm sorry, Spenser."

The big overhead lights cut on in quick succession down the rows and rows of antiques. Murphy pushed both hands on the table to keep himself on his feet. Somewhere a door swung open and I heard shoes clattering on the linoleum floor. I raised the gun at Murphy.

"What'd you do?"

"Didn't have no other option."

Down the long aisle, Jackie DeMarco walked toward us. He had a baseball bat in his right hand and four guys marching behind him. He had on a black muscle shirt and long workout shorts. He looked like he'd just walked away from batting practice. As he got closer, he smacked a few Tiffany lamps toward center field. Colored pieces of glass flew in all directions.

I noted he wasn't wearing a codpiece and would be an easy shot.

"Our driver is here," Jackie said. "Don't be a hard-on, Spenser. Let's go."

"Where we headed, Jackie?" I said.

"Mystic," he said. "You play nice and I'll buy you a fucking pizza."

"I make the deal with the museum," I said. "And then you steal the painting."

"Nope," he said. "I take back the fucking painting. That painting has always been mine."

"Actually, it originally belonged to the Diego de Castilla," I said. "Since then, it's passed through hundreds of hands and owners. The lineage is quite fascinating, if you could read."

"Well, it's fucking mine," he said. "And those crooked cops will trust you. You make the deal, get the fucking painting, and we'll take care of the rest."

"Gee," I said. "You're a true tactician. I make the deal and you'll take care of the rest. Meaning you'll probably kill me and the cops."

Jackie shrugged. I had to hand it to him.

He had big traps, probably spent a lot of time in the gym doing shrugs in the mirror. The four guys behind him stood close by. One of them, a short, stocky guy, picked up an old toy airplane and studied its wings.

"I don't want to step on your lines," I said. "I believe this is when you tell me this is an offer I can't refuse."

"Don't even fucking try," Jackie said.

"You could just shoot me here."

"But then I wouldn't get what was owed to me."

"It would be a shame to disappoint you."

"You got it."

I looked to Murphy, wiping the blood out of his eyes. I shook my head with my own disappointment. Somewhere out there, Vinnie and his duo were waiting. I'd told them to hold off unless they heard shots and to follow me wherever Murphy had arranged. Now we'd just have a caravan. Nothing like a little confusion to make an exchange work for the better.

"Can I ask what's in this for me?" I said. "Besides a pizza."

"You don't fuck up and I'll let you'll live," Jackie said.

"Jackie," I said, sliding my gun back into my belt. No one made a move to take it from me. "You really are too good to me."

57

Two of DeMarco's guys rode with me to Mystic, one in the passenger seat and one directly behind me to make sure I followed directions. The guy beside me was short and thick, built like a life-sized garden gnome. I didn't get a good look at the guy behind me, but in the rearview he had an unpleasant face with a big honker and a deep scar across his right eyebrow. He gave me directions as I drove.

About halfway there, I had enough and looked at the guy in the backseat. "You know, my phone has Siri."

"But Siri won't shoot you in the head for taking a wrong turn," the guy said.

"They told Murphy I was to come alone."

"You go in alone," he said. "You drop us at the gates."

"A hint of where we're headed?"

"A place called Elm Grove," the guy beside me said. "It's a fucking cemetery."

"Ominous," I said.

"Opens up at six," he said. "You drive straight down the road. When the road doubles back to the gate, the guys will meet you there. They said there's a spot overlooking the river."

"Lovely."

"Don't worry," he said. "We'll be watching you."

"I feel so much safer," I said. "If the dirty cops miss, you'll try and finish the job."

"Try?" the man beside me said.

"All the dipshits try," I said. "It's a Boston tradition."

I looked into the rearview again. The ugly guy smiled. The big gnome beside me started to laugh. We all laughed together in merriment as we headed into danger. I started to recite the Saint Crispin's Day speech but figured they'd heard it all before.

I turned off the interstate and followed a state highway for a mile or so. At a large sign that read *Elm Grove Cemetery*, the man behind my neck told me to make a right turn.

"You're good," I said. "Maybe better than Siri."

"Shut the fuck up," he said. "And pull over there by Jackie."

I drove through the ornate iron gates and

followed DeMarco's big black SUV where it had pulled over by a large statue. I got out with my newfound friends. Jackie and his other pal got out, too.

Jackie stretched and yawned. It was dawn, and the morning light was a dark purple, with lots of shadows around the marble headstones. I looked up at the marble figures on the pedestals. It was a woman cradling her young son, a book held open in her lap. The figures were so lifelike, I almost expected them to peer down at us.

Jackie didn't notice anything around him. He might've been in a Sam's Club parking lot in Dorchester. He lit a cigarette and pointed out the Mystic River on the far side of the cemetery.

"Follow the road until it doubles back," he said. "Park your car by that big open spot at the river."

"Your associates have been over this."

"Well, I'm fucking going over it again," he said. "Don't try and get away. Don't try and get smart. And don't fuck this thing up."

"Wait," I said. "Do you have a piece of paper and a pen?"

"Shut up, Spenser," he said. "We're gonna move the cars, but we'll be around. These two cops will be here in an hour."

"They're probably already here."

385

"Nope," he said. "I got a guy watching the entrance. It didn't open until six."

I nodded. Jackie was perhaps a bigger moron than I'd figured.

"Either way," I said. "There's no chance they'll bring the painting."

"No shit, Nostradamus," he said. "Just keep 'em talking about the reward and how the transfer works and all that crapola. And me and the boys will catch 'em with their pants down."

"So to speak," I said. "I really hope they wear pants."

"This is a nice, quiet place," DeMarco said. "It'll work as good as any other. There's one landscaping guy who rides around in a truck. We'll keep him occupied until we get what we want. Stick to the plan and nobody gets shot."

"Then why'd you take a run at me the other night?"

"Because I didn't."

"At the Navy Yard," I said. "Somebody shot a guy who very loosely resembled me. He was pilfering through my truck."

"Then what do you care if he's dead?"

"I care because it was supposed to be me."

Jackie tossed down his cigarette onto the gravel road and rubbed it out under his jogging shoe. "Don't I know what you look like?"

I nodded.

"And if I wanted you dead, don't you think I could get the job done?"

"Sorry I doubted you," I said. "But I had to ask."

"I'm good at what I do, Spenser," he said. "How about you just shut your big fucking mouth and see how this all works out. The day ain't over yet."

"Only that day dawns to which we are awake."

"Are you fucking awake?"

"Barely," I said. "It's been a long night and I haven't had much coffee. Long night for you, too. You had to beat up an old man."

"Don't get in a huff over Murphy," De-Marco said. "You can't trust that Irish prick for nothing. Only way to know he's telling the truth is to hold a lit cigarette to his nuts."

Out of the corner of my eye, I spotted two figures darting between marble monuments. One had on a baseball cap and silver sunglasses. The other carried a rifle. It wasn't Vinnie Morris or his crew from the bowling alley.

"So I'm just a sitting duck," I said. "I'd hoped to play a more vital role."

"Your role is to draw them in and then get the fuck out of here."

"Not very creative."

"You don't have to be creative," he said. "When you're lucky."

"Luck is the residue of hard work and design," I said. "Both of which you are in short supply of."

"What do you know about fucking design?"

I opened my palm and kept looking over his shoulder. I watched the two men continue around a mausoleum and disappear into the cemetery. A few seconds later, they ran to another large monument. I didn't change my gaze over Jackie's shoulder. His three guys stood together, bunched up and speaking among themselves. All their eyes were on me, completely unaware of the two old cops sneaking up through the cemetery.

"You've got about as much subtlety as a rhino in a pastry shop."

"Just don't get in our way," he said. "Unnerstand? Hey. Hey. Are you fucking listening to me?"

"Shut up for a second."

"What did you say to me?" he said. "Have you lost your goddamn mind, Spenser, talking to me like that? Do you know what I'll fucking do to you?"

"I said, shut your damn mouth, Jackie."

I spotted the glint off a rifle scope as De-Marco took a swipe at me. He leaned far and hard into the punch and nearly lost his feet. As I stepped back, a shot rang out in the cemetery and his men scattered.

Jackie was down on his knees, holding his hands to his thick, bleeding neck.

I dropped to the grass and rolled behind a headstone. There was a lot of screaming and yelling, men giving directions as DeMarco seemed to be in a great deal of pain.

And it had started off to be such a lovely day.

58

As I hid behind a gravestone and fed more
bullets into my revolver, I hoped Vinnie and
his crew hadn't decided to stop off for Egg
McMuffins. All the shooting and yelling had
turned lovely Elm Grove into somewhere
west of Tombstone. Jackie was shot, bleeding, and squirming behind a large pedestal.
He'd taken off his black tank top and
wrapped it around his neck to stop the
bleeding. His large white stomach hung over
his shorts, reminding me of a beached whale
I'd once seen on the Cape. The blood
covered his chest and arms as he pressed
the shirt to his neck with his right hand and
fired with his left.

The shorter and rounder of the ex-cops,
Roebuck, had a rifle set atop a marble crypt.
The crypt had been built into the rolling
hill and provided some excellent cover for a
guy with a rifle. In all the shooting, Jackie
and one of his crew, my chatty navigator,

had been shot. Sadly, DeMarco looked like he'd recover. But for the ride home, I knew I'd need to rely on Siri.

I was about a football field and a half from where Roebuck had set up shop. Zimmer had maneuvered over to a position closer to the highway. Between them, they held us at the apex of a V. They could take shots at us all day long, or until the cops arrived. But they couldn't get out of the cemetery without passing Jackie's SUV and Susan's car.

I had no idea what kind of shape De-Marco and his boys had left Murphy in. But if he could have contacted the ex-cops, they'd know this wasn't my call and what to expect. Since I was there as a conduit with the Winthrop, I sincerely hoped they wanted to level the playing field and work an exchange. But as it had probably been them who had killed Marston thinking he was me, I didn't much care if they got out alive. All I needed was someone to lay down some good shots from behind.

I'd hoped these guys didn't plan ambushes like Branch Rickey planned ballgames. Roebuck continued to shoot in our direction, and some chipped marble rained down on my head. I returned fire.

As I ducked back behind the headstone, I

391

heard the quick *pop-pop-pop* of an automatic pistol. Vinnie and his pals had joined the party.

It was down to two of DeMarco's shooters. DeMarco yelled and emptied the magazine of his Glock. He fumbled for a spare magazine in his cargo shorts. He was bloody and drained of color. He couldn't have hit the broadside of a tow truck.

"Motherfuckers," DeMarco said. "Lousy motherfuckers."

It was quiet for a moment. The grass was thick and green where I lay. The headstone was for *Antoinette M., only daughter of Erastus J. and Mercy C. Williams.* She'd died in 1858 at only sixteen. Right now, she was saving my ass. I touched the headstone and inched forward, squeezing off two shots at Zimmer.

He returned fire as the big gnome from my car duck-walked up to me. He had a fat stainless-steel Taurus in his hand. With two of his guys down, he looked at me wild-eyed for directions. I yelled for him to get down. As he opened his mouth to say something, a bullet caught him in his head and jacked him onto his back in the grass.

Ex-cops: 2. DeMarco: 0.

Jackie's last guy had joined him under the large statue. He pressed Jackie's tank top onto his boss's neck, Jackie's face completely white now, as he muttered and cursed, not making much sense. Spit flew from his lips, pointing at me, as if the ambush had been all my fault. If I hadn't insulted him, he'd be dead by now. *Gratitude.*

Another shot from the rifle whizzed past the monument.

Then a rapid succession of three shots. The cemetery was still. Either Vinnie, probably Vinnie, or one of his crew had taken out Roebuck and his hunting rifle. Now Zimmer was somewhere back from the road, making his way to where DeMarco and his man huddled under the statue of the woman reading with her son. I wondered if anyone had read to Jackie as a kid. Probably not.

From where I lay between two old headstones and over the rolling hills, I could barely make out the Mystic River. Zimmer and Roebuck would've hiked in from the road, probably parked at the seaport and followed the shore to the cemetery wall. With his partner out, Zimmer would have to follow the same path to escape. But he'd have to pass through us first. Everything was very still and quiet. Wind cut in off the river and rattled the branches of a plum tree in full bloom, flowers fluttering to the ground.

I heard footsteps on the gravel and turned to see Zimmer edging around DeMarco's SUV with a shotgun. Jackie's boy reached for his gun as Zimmer leveled the shotgun at them both.

I shot Zimmer in the chest. He dropped hard and fast.

I walked over to where Zimmer lay. He had on a sensible pair of khakis and a black windbreaker over a T-shirt. His mirrored sunglasses lay cracked and broken off his head, a very ugly wound opening up on his chest.

I swallowed and let out a long breath, looking down at him.

Over the rolling hills, I saw Vinnie Morris wave from atop the mausoleum where Roebuck had set up shop. He waved his arm toward me, to let me know all was well. From back toward the entrance, two of Vinnie's guys walked toward me. One was the fat guy from the bowling alley, now carrying a sawed-off shotgun. His normal Hawaiian shirt had been replaced with an XXL black T-shirt.

"Motherfucker," DeMarco said to me, in a whisper.

"You're welcome."

His guy looked about eighteen, thin-faced and lean, in a white T-shirt streaked with Jackie's blood. His hands shook in front of him.

"Get it together," I said. "I'll help you get Jackie into the car."

"He's hurt," he said. "It looks bad."

"Probably," I said. "But he won't want to stick around here."

We both picked up DeMarco and walked him to the SUV, placing him into the backseat, with him still calling me unpleasant names. I took that to be a good sign.

I walked with Vinnie's guy across the cemetery to the rolling hills where several mausoleums had been built into the earth, each of them with a locked gate before the door. Vinnie had taken a knee on the hill, standing over Roebuck. He said Roebuck was alive.

I scrambled up the hill. Roebuck was on his back. The front of his gray shirt was now mostly bright red. Vinnie had made no effort to administer medical help.

"He's fucking gone," Vinnie said. "And we need to go, too."

"Hold on," I said.

I knelt beside the rotund old cop. The black baseball cap had been knocked on the ground and his bald head shone with sweat.

"Where's the painting?" I said.

Roebuck just stared at me, his bright blue eyes staring right up at me as if he was about to speak. His lips moved, but he made no sound except hard, raspy breaths.

"Jesus," Vinnie said. "Let's get the fuck out of here."

As I stood back up, I noticed a silvery glint in the man's hand. I pried up his cold, chubby fingers and found a single key. Roebuck closed his eyes and then opened them. Along the gravel road doubling back to the entrance, Vinnie's other guy pulled the car around. Vinnie was already halfway to the Cadillac.

"Where is it?" I said.

"Right here," Roebuck said. "Down below."

I took the bloody key and scrambled down to the narrow gravel path lined with mausoleums. Vinnie was yelling for me as I slipped the key into the lock and found it turned with a hard snick. I opened the gate and stepped inside the cold, airless room. It was much cooler under the earth than it was outside, and the air had a sweet, earthy smell. The morning light cut in from the doorway and spilled on the many names written into a marble wall. Only one of the crypts was open, a slot wide enough to fit a casket.

I didn't have a flashlight and couldn't see as I reached inside. I felt the cylindrical shape of a tube. I pulled it out and ran for the door. Somewhere in the distance, I head sirens. I ran to Vinnie's Cadillac. The tube was as long as a rolled-up rug and had to lay between the front seats, extending all the way to the back.

Vinnie drove with me in the passenger seat and his two guys in the back, to where I'd parked Susan's car.

"You think that's it?" Vinnie said. "The fucking painting."

"I hope so," I said. "Be a shame if it was a poster of Donnie Osmond."

"Fucking guys," Vinnie said. "What was DeMarco thinking?"

"What he always does," I said. "Nothing."

"His guys dead?"

"Two of 'em," I said. "Other drove him out."

"How's he?"

"He'll make it."

"What a shame."

I got out and we switched the big tube to Susan's car. I looked in my rearview for flashing lights the whole way back to Boston.

59

"Well done, Spenser," Marjorie Phillips Ward said.

"The incident in Mystic has been a great embarrassment to the Winthrop," Topper said. "I think that should go on record before dispensing with any accolades to Mr. Spenser."

"It could have been far worse."

"Three men dead," he said. "Including a former police officer. Two others were known members of organized crime."

"Next time I'll ask questions first and shoot later," I said. "But you would have never seen the painting again."

All three of us were seated across from each other in the Winthrop's boardroom. Marj was dressed in black, with a green flowered scarf wrapped around her thick neck. Topper wore some kind of gray fringed poncho over a plaid shirt, his silver hair combed loose down his back.

"So much blood," Marjorie said. "So much violence. I understand why the policemen were there. I have heard Mr. Roebuck's hospital confession. But who were those two criminals? What did they have to do with the painting?"

"They belonged to the same group that stole the painting twenty years ago," I said. "They believed they were entitled to the reward. I've explained it all to the police on multiple occasions."

"Well," Marjorie said. "They won't see a nickel of it."

Topper turned his round black glasses toward me. "Locke is dead," he said. "I'm sure you've heard."

"I was with him."

Topper cleared his throat. He rested his hand on the edge of the boardroom desk, pursing his lips, staring at me.

"So he knew you'd recovered *The Gentleman*?" Marjorie said.

I nodded.

"Did it give him much comfort?" she said.

"As much as it could," I said. "It was a very long night."

She told me she was very sorry. Topper remained silent. He tapped at the screen of his cell phone, momentarily glancing up with boredom.

"His medical expenses will be paid," she said.

I nodded.

"And all of yours as well," she said. "But I would like to speak to you in private about the matter of the reward."

I smiled. I leaned back in my seat and shifted my gaze to Topper and Marj.

"The matter isn't as straightforward as you might expect," Topper said. "It has yet to have a full inspection by our curators. And we have many legal issues to work out regarding the safe return."

"I figured," I said. "You're not exactly a straightforward guy."

"I don't have time for such nonsense," Topper said. "I have a meeting in less than an hour. The press will need to be notified, events explained, and the news of *The Gentleman*'s return celebrated. Give him the check for his expenses and send Spenser on his way. I would rather not have him involved. And he is not to speak to the press."

I looked down at the cane in his hand. He noted my gaze on the silver handle, met my eyes, and then turned away.

Marjorie stood up and we walked out of the boardroom and the Winthrop offices and into the gallery. It was just after-hours and the lights shone on plants in the plaza and into the large hallways to the galleries. We bypassed the Red Room, where *The Gentleman* once hung, and rounded the marble staircase into the central garden and then down into the basement. She pushed through a series of metal doors with a security passkey until we entered a large space filled with racks loaded with paintings and sculptures. In the center of the room, *The Gentleman in Black* stood on a large easel, back in its gold frame. Paintbrushes and a magnifying headset sat on a nearby workbench.

She stood back to admire it, as we had when it had just been an empty gold frame. I had my hands in my pockets, waiting for her to tell me why my time hadn't been worth the reward. I had never expected it, but I would have never refused it.

Marjorie reached over to turn some carefully placed lights onto the painting. And there he was, again, dignified and inquisitive in the stiff black cloak and frilly white shirt. The dark eyes stared down at Large Marj and me as he had to King Philip on down to Constance Winthrop. I felt a little satisfaction for a moment. But it passed. I didn't have the same feeling I'd had at the warehouse with Alan Garner. Something was off.

"This isn't the painting I saw."

Marj gave a thin, sad smile. "And how can you be so sure?"

"The eyes," I said. "They lack life."

She wet her lips and crooked her head to examine *The Gentleman.* She turned to me and stared with a thin, forced smile and a small bit of new appreciation.

"Interesting," Marj said. She turned and waddled toward the door. She straightened the silk scarf around her neck. "Your check is at the front desk, Spenser. Please turn out the lights and turn in your ID badge on your way out."

60

"You got to be shitting me," Vinnie Morris said.

"I shit you not."

"The painting is a fake and that fat broad doesn't even care."

"Haven't you seen the news?" I said. "The art world is overjoyed. Marjorie Ward Phillips has been hailed as a hero before her retirement. Topper Townsend is planning a Spanish fiesta with all the tapas and sangria you can stomach."

Vinnie and I stood across from each other at his bar atop the bowling alley. He hadn't opened up for the night, and it was only us. Racks of clean glasses, cut-up limes and lemons, and fresh bottles of booze waited within Vinnie's grasp.

"How far did you track Devon Murphy?" he said.

"Two days after Mystic, he boarded a plane for London," I said. "From London, he flew into King Khalid International Airport in Riyadh."

"Where the fuck is that?"

"Saudi Arabia."

"Jesus Christ," Vinnie said. "That little leprechaun tricked us all. DeMarco, those ex-cops. Even Alan Garner."

"I doubt he tricked Alan Garner."

"You think he killed him?" Vinnie said. "Because Garner knew he'd switched the painting?"

"Indeed I do."

Vinnie nodded. He reached under the bar and pulled out a bottle of twenty-three-year-old Pappy Van Winkle. He uncorked the bottle and poured us both a healthy measure.

"Where'd you get this?" I said.

"Fell off a truck," Vinnie said.

I drank some of the bourbon. It tasted much better than Fighting Cock or Old Crow.

"Heard anything about DeMarco?" I said.

"Yeah," Vinnie said. "He's convalescing down in Tampa. He claims he wasn't even close to Mystic when that shit show went down. He told the cops that his two guys must've been working on a side job."

"Stand-up guy."

"Not many left."

We clicked glasses.

"I got something for you," he said. Vinnie reached into his pocket and dumped a handful of tickets out onto the bar. "Your reward. Free passes for bowling. I thought maybe you and Susan needed a night out or something. I know she gets tired of fancy restaurants and cocktails every other night."

"What about shoes?" I said.

"Shoe rental is extra," Vinnie said. "Let me see what I can do."

"Susan will be thrilled."

He placed the bottle between us and turned on several neon signs against the wall. He flipped some knobs, and the speakers hummed to life as the CDs started to shuffle. He topped off the bourbon.

"You know, I don't give a flying fuck about that painting," he said. "It's Murphy that bothers me. The guy tricks us, kills Alan, and then sells off that art for a million bucks."

"Many, many millions."

"I liked Alan," Vinnie said, rolling the whiskey around in the glass. "He always treated me nice. He didn't deserve what he got."

"Murphy has to fly back sometime," I said.

"I think you and me should be waiting on him when he gets back," Vinnie said. "Ask him a few questions."

"Yep," I said. "Might let Belson know, too."

The music cut on and began to play over the speakers. Vinnie tapped out a rhythm with the horns. Tony Bennett reached for the tree of life and picked him a plum. Vinnie hummed along with the music, staring out onto the expressway.

" 'The Best Is Yet to Come'?" I said.

Vinnie nodded. "You better believe it."

ACKNOWLEDGMENTS

Special thanks to Stephen Kurkjian for his outstanding book on the Gardner heist, *Master Thieves.* The book is by far the best on the subject and highly recommended. Also, thanks to Myles Connor, master art thief, for his time and patience in teaching me the tricks of the trade.

ABOUT THE AUTHOR

Ace Atkins is the author of over twenty books, including six Quinn Colson novels, the first two of which, *The Ranger* and *The Lost Ones*, were nominated for the Edgar Award for Best Novel (he also has a third Edgar nomination for his short story "Last Fair Deal Gone Down"). In addition, he is the author of several *New York Times*–bestselling novels in the continuation of Robert B. Parker's Spenser series. Before turning to fiction, Atkins was a correspondent for *The St. Petersburg Times*, a crime reporter for *The Tampa Tribune*, and, in college, played defensive end for the undefeated Auburn University football team (for which he was featured on the cover of *Sports Illustrated*). He lives in Oxford, Mississippi.